Contents

"Love is a force more formidable than any other. It is invisible—it cannot be seen or measured, yet it is powerful enough to transform you in a moment, and offer you more joy than any material possession could."

~Barbara de Angelis

Love Bites

Write More Publications
New Adult
Paranormal Romance Anthology

Featured Authors:

Elaine White
Kim Stevens
Theresa Oliver
Dana Piazzi
Stephanie Parke
Vanessa Hancock
Ashlea Burns
Susan Burdorf
Becca Boucher
Monica Blanton

Write More Publications
Kissimmee, FL

Copyright © 2014 Write More Publications

First Edition

Published by Write More Publications

All rights reserved. The reproduction of this work in whole or in part in any form by any electronic, mechanical, or other means, now known or hereafter invented, including xerography, photocopying and recording, or in any information storage or retrieval system, is forbidden without permission of Write More Publications, www.writemorepublications.com

Reprinting excerpts for reviews is permitted.

First Write More Publications Printing 2014

All the characters in this book are fictitious. Any resemblance to actual persons, living or dead, is purely coincidental. All work is from the imagination of the author.

All rights reserved.

ISBN-13: 978-0692022252
ISBN-10: 0692022252

A record of the Library of Congress serial number can be acquired from the publisher.

Manufactured in the United States of America

Broken Dreams
The Belesone Pack—Prequel
By: Elaine White

Chapter 1

Milo went over the paperwork one more time. He double checked every signature, every misspelling, and every order that it held. He was done … finally. He glanced at the clock, frustrated. It was two in the morning and he had school tomorrow. He sighed, switched off the lamps, and sat in the dark, letting his natural defenses grow.

Milo was the Alpha of a hundred strong wolf-shifter pack. He would never classify them as werewolves for the simple fact that werewolf legends and stories never seemed to adequately portray the shifter life. He was writing to another pack that night, and he hadn't been able to turn in until it was completed. Pack business always came first, even before homework. Tonight, he still had some math homework that needed to be finished, but he was too tired to complete it before going to bed. Math wasn't his subject at the best of times, but it was a necessary tool for a leader to learn and utilize. He would have to ask his teacher for more time tomorrow.

The good thing was that his teacher was another shifter. They all lived in the same community and it helped when things got difficult. If he had to, he could just use his Alpha status—as leader and protector of his pack—to explain away certain things … like homework. No one questioned the Alpha.

Milo's eyes adjusted quickly to the darkness, and he made his way over to the door and out into the hallway of his house. He should have been heading to bed, but the usual nagging feeling drew him outside again. This time it wasn't just his wolf that wanted to run free; it was his very soul. His true mate—the one person that his heart was meant to beat for, the one soul that made his complete—was out there somewhere. Close. Finally close. Milo had no idea how long he had felt her within his heart, how long he had been able to tell whenever she was close by, but it felt like it had always been that way.

True mates were the only kind of happiness a shifter was destined for. No wolf-shifter, old or young, no matter from what pack, was ever meant to be with anyone other than their true mate. For that reason, Milo had never even kissed a girl before, even though he was nineteen. No holding hands, no kissing, no hugging, no attraction. It was all saved for his true mate, meant only for her. Whoever this mystery girl was that he was drawn to, Milo Belesone had been created just for her. And the very thought that she was close by sent his heart racing and his spine tingling with apprehension.

What if he found her tonight? What if she loved him back? What if she didn't love him? What if she wouldn't accept him? What if they kissed? What if they didn't?

His mind was in utter turmoil. For years he had felt that connection between them, but no matter how close she felt at times, he still hadn't found her. Sometimes, the connection completely disappeared for days or weeks, which wasn't normal. He knew that mates just didn't disappear from one another's lives. Yes, his mate was out there, he knew it with every fiber of his being, but for some reason, he kept losing her. It was as if she was able to consciously cut off their connection whenever she wanted and it felt so much like rejection that Milo grieved for her often.

A true mate should never refuse the one that they were made for, but the laws of free will meant that they could. Milo had felt enough heartache in his lifetime to know what would happen if his mate rejected him. It would be unbearable.

He rushed downstairs and out the front door of the Alpha house—the biggest in the village—careful not to disturb anyone. The guards at the door didn't so much as blink as he raced past them and out into the forest. He often went for late-night runs. It was the only way to ease the tension and the pressure of being the Alpha ... the only way to grieve in peace.

Milo barely got halfway to his destination when the grief began to overwhelm him. The connection had disappeared again. He fell to his knees, not breathing hard, not panting or out of breath, but from the sheer struggle to keep his emotions in check. An Alpha should never be rejected by his mate. He felt worthless, useless, and stupid, unworthy of his title and the respect that it gave him in the pack.

Now, he needed his extra senses more than ever. He allowed himself to walk the remainder of the way toward his chosen spot. Milo stepped through the trees and into the clearing, returning to the place where he felt most connected to his mate, and began undressing. He would need his clothes intact for returning home in the morning, but for now, he needed his wolf. He needed to feel everything, to sense everything, to see everything just in case she was near. He laid his clothes on a nearby boulder and allowed his body to shift and contort into a large wolf. He was the biggest of his pack as Alpha, and it felt good to feel his strong muscles forming, to have firm, sure footed paws leading him into the middle of the meadow.

It was the most beautiful place that he had ever seen. Milo walked his wolf body into the very center of the meadow and lay down, then placed his head on his front paws. The grief overwhelmed him now, as always. She wasn't here. She had never been here. Somewhere inside, he continued to hope that the beauty of the area and his strong scent that he left behind there would draw her to the meadow, but it never did. The beauty was lost to him yet again. The blues and yellows and greens of the wild, overgrown grass with its weeds and flowers created a multitude of scents and wonder for the wolf to watch. The bees were busy, the birds were chirping away and it was a safe haven amongst a village of people.

Comfort and sadness suddenly swept over him. He needed this place … now, more than ever before. Milo knew that he was very lucky that he had been given time, since he had been made Alpha so young—at just seventeen—by his father's illness and his grandfather's death. He had time to train, learn and to step up to his position, time to drop out of school for his last two years and focus on being Alpha. However, he had gone back to school as soon as he was ready, repeating his lost years to show the others in the pack how important education was. He was their leader, and he had to set a good example, but he had also been granted a rare privilege: he had been given more time to find his true mate than any other Alpha.

Most Alphas were supposed to be united to their true mate by the end of their eighteenth birthday, when they officially became a man. Eighteen was the age when their true mate bond really developed into something that made it possible for two true mates to find each other. All they had to do was to pass each other, look into each other's faces and they knew. It was instinctual, and the wolves inside of them helped along the way.

Milo had a good sense of his true mate even before that—almost like a radar—to tell him when she was close and when he was most likely to find her in their lands, but he had never found her. He began to wonder if he ever would.

This continual feeling her presence and then losing her again was making him insane, making him worry for her safety. What had happened to break their connection? Milo let out a sigh that, in his wolf body became a small huff. He was running out of time to find her. His twentieth birthday was fast approaching and he wasn't sure that he would be allowed to continue searching for her once it passed. No Alpha had ever ruled his pack this long without a mate.

True mates made Alpha's stronger, faster, more resilient wolves. True mates made them complete. And how could Milo forget the most important factor of being an Alpha—to produce an heir. He certainly couldn't do that alone, but he also knew that he couldn't do that with anyone other than his true mate. He had to find her soon … before the Elder Council got ideas of finding him another girl.

It could only happen to an Alpha. Only Alpha's were ever allowed to take a mate that wasn't their true mate. The only exception was when a true mate died and the other was left alone. Then, they were allowed to take another to their hearts, but Milo wasn't sure that he could even do that. How could he be with a girl that wasn't his true mate? To kiss her and love her and give her an heir? His every sense screamed at him how wrong it was, but he had no choice. He had less than fifteen days until his birthday. If he hadn't found his true mate by then, he knew that he would be forced to do the unthinkable. His choice was simple: find his true mate or step down as Alpha.

***

Leo was worried when he woke up and didn't find Milo in his room. He looked in the study and in the kitchen, but there was no sign of him.

"When did you last see the Alpha?" Leo questioned the guards at the door.

"He went out last night and he hasn't returned," he said. "Is everything all right?"

This was the last straw. Leo nodded, taking a deep breath. "It will be."

Leo left the house and headed over to the one place that he knew Milo would go. Just as he expected, he found the large wolf lying on the grass, his eyes wide open, staring into space. "Alpha, it's morning. We're going to be late for school," he said, keeping his voice low and calm so as not to startle him. Milo's wolf turned his head and glanced at him, then laid his head back down, his eyes filled with sorrow. Leo sighed as he made his way across the meadow, then sat down on the grass beside his best friend and Alpha.

He ran a hand over the thick fur on Milo's shoulder, gentle and soothing. "I know. I understand," he said quietly. He wasn't sure how he could make this better, but he had to try. He had to help Milo find his true mate and at least attempt to heal. Leo could feel the grief coming from him, radiating from Milo's fur to his hand. "You're not going to find her lying here moping. Let's go to school to get the day over and done with, and if we don't find her at school, then we'll go hunting for her tonight." It was the only solution that he could think of, the sensible solution. It was also one solution that got Milo's depressed butt off the meadow floor and headed to school.

The wolf turned and looked at him, gave a little nod and Leo was able to breathe again. He got up and left the clearing, giving his Alpha privacy to transform back to his human body and dress. Leo was only eighteen, but he had been forced to transform and tackle his Alpha just a few years ago. Back then, Milo had only started feeling the bond to his mate and the rejection implied by her absence. A drunk teenager was one thing to deal with, but a drunk wolf-shifter was quite another. Leo still had a few scars from one fight in particular, but he wore them with pride. He was the Beta to his Alpha, his right hand man, his second in command, and he would do anything for him.

"I'm sorry." Milo's voice met Leo's ears just a second before he stepped to his side. "I just feel so lost when she's gone. I don't know what to do. It isn't normal to feel like this, to have her there one minute and gone the next. The Elders don't even understand it." Milo absently kicked aside a stone, frustrated. He felt ridiculous, pining away for a girl who seemed to be running away from him. Who ever heard of a girl running from her Alpha? From her true mate?

"Then we'll just have to find her and ask her if *she* knows." Leo said. He wrapped his arm around Milo's neck and ruffled his hair teasingly. No one got away with doing that to the Alpha, especially not in front of people, but Milo and Leo had been the best of friends since childhood. All Milo did was laugh and swatted his hand away. He felt better already, knowing that his Beta believed him about the connection with his mate and trusted him to find her. He would not be forced into a union with someone else.

*****

The happiness didn't last forever. Leo watched Milo as the school day began and moved along hour by hour. The longer he watched his Alpha, the more he saw the desperation and sense of rejection returning and growing. It seemed clear that his true mate wasn't at school, but Leo didn't think that was really what was important. Milo was, after all, nearly twenty. It was possible that his true mate was the same age and had already graduated high school, or she could have been older. As far as he knew, true mates could have up to ten years between them. Milo had time to find her, even if she wasn't at school with them. It just meant that they had to work harder.

Leo sat at the lunch table across from Milo and pretended to write out Chemistry homework. What he was really doing was running his mind through the suitably aged girls both at school and in the pack that could possibly be Milo's true mate. When he was finished, he systematically went through the list, crossing out the girls that he knew Milo had regular and close contact with at school. The continued loss of connection between them and the fact that Milo didn't know her name meant that they couldn't have actually met, at least, not long enough for a bond to form. Every girl that Milo had spent more than five minutes with was crossed off the list. What he was left with was a sorry looking list of twenty girls.

Leo picked their names off the list and wrote them onto another page. He could make them out more clearly there. He crossed out five by instinct. The fact that Milo was an Alpha helped. His mate was supposed to be, by fate, someone who could rule beside him, strong and confident, someone who could lead the pack whenever he couldn't, someone intelligent enough to help him with the day-to-day runnings of pack business. Five of the girls on his list didn't fit that profile, so he crossed them off.

The only problem with his list was that no one left on the list really seemed suitable for Milo. And when Leo looked up at his Alpha sitting opposite him, his heart sank. Milo was ignoring his food, gazing around the cafeteria as if any moment now his true mate would pop up out of nowhere and introduce herself. "What about these girls? We could introduce you to them," he offered with a faint smile, trying to cheer him up. Just because he hadn't found his true mate yet didn't mean that it would never happen.

Milo took the list with little interest and let his eyes glaze over the names. "She's not there."

Leo wanted to pound his head onto the table. He didn't know why Milo was being so difficult about this. "How can you be so sure? They're just names. It's worth a try," he said with a sigh. "Just take another look, meet each girl properly to be sure. It won't take long, but at least you'll know."

"She's not there!" Milo growled, throwing the list across the table back to his Beta. Every shifter in the near vicinity turned and glanced at their Alpha, worried and surprised to hear him so angry. It wasn't normal for him to shout at his Beta. Milo lowered his voice, exasperated, and said, "I'll know it is her, just by looking at her name."

"That's not how it works and you know it," Leo said, taking a deep breath.

Unsurprisingly, Milo didn't want to hear it. He got up from the table, shoved his untouched food to the side and grabbed his bag and left the cafeteria.

He wasn't supposed to go anywhere alone, especially not around the human kids, who had no idea who they were or that shifters even existed. So, Leo dragged his butt out of his seat, grabbed his stuff as he shoved the last of his burger into his mouth, and raced after his Alpha like the good Beta that he was.

***

The day had been awful … long, hot, exhausting. Leo hadn't done anything other than run around after Milo, who was trying to avoid him. But Leo didn't bring up the true mate subject for the rest of the day, not until they met in the downstairs hallway of the Alpha's house at eight o'clock that night when they were taking the pack on a hunt.

Leo caught Milo's arm just as he turned to open the front door. "You and I will head off together away from the hunt. We'll go looking for your mate and we will find her," he reassured his best friend. Milo lowered his eyes and nodded, looking utterly terrified.

They proceeded out of the house and down the two front steps. Twenty wolves were standing outside, just hanging around waiting for the Alpha. Leo nearly laughed. If the humans ever saw this, they would think that there was something really odd going on. But the humans never bothered with the house at the end of the village—the pack house. It was just chalked down as "weird" and left alone. He was pretty sure that the humans thought that all shifters were part of some sort of mind-altering cult, but the truth was much more than that. They were family, a community that looked after, cared for and fought for each other on a daily basis. They were a pack.

"Everyone, remember the rules," Milo said in his usual Alpha voice, just an octave or so lower than his normal register, filled with authority. "No one drifts off on their own. You catch it, you kill it, you eat it. No playing games. This is a serious hunt. The Beta and I will be off on our own mission, so I expect you to follow the rules."

Leo watched as all the pack members nodded their heads in agreement. Two people came running toward them, and he noticed that Grene, one of their most respected warriors, was approaching with one of his daughters. He had been in line to become Beta when Milo's father was supposed to become Alpha, but that dream was dead, too. Milo saw them approach and sighed. "Grene, keep your daughter at the back. I don't want her holding up the entire pack," he announced gruffly, staring at the man who had once been his father's best friend and the worthless excuse for a wolf standing beside him. Katarina was pathetic, as a girl and as a wolf. She was short, weak, slow, and difficult. She didn't respond well to authority and she couldn't keep up with the pack or fight like a normal shifter.

"Yes, Alpha," Grene agreed with no argument, his arm around his youngest daughter's waist. He turned and smiled at Katarina in apology for the Alpha's treatment of her, giving her waist a little squeeze, a hug of reassurance. Everyone was laughing at her and the Alpha's demands.

"Katarina, the rules are simple. Stay out of the way, and keep to the back or the side of the pack. Do not interfere," Milo commanded. Katarina nodded and accepted that she would always be treated this way. It was her curse for being weak, she supposed. If she couldn't be like the pack, she was to be shunned.

"Yes Alph," she quickly agreed, even though she wanted to say something else to the arrogant male Alpha glaring at her. He was gorgeous, but that didn't mean that he could treat her like dirt. "You don't have to worry. I'm not coming with you. I'm only here to see my father off to wish him a good hunt," Katarina explained, instantly cutting off the laughter of the other pack members. No one talked back to the Alpha, but she didn't care. She wasn't going to be treated like crap just because he decided that she was worthless, and she didn't feel any shame in meeting his eyes.

Milo approved only of the fact that she wasn't joining the hunt. It was one less person that he had to worry about, especially someone who couldn't keep up, fainted at the first sight of blood, and was so awkward that she would no doubt get herself into trouble at some point. "Good. Keep it that way." The words were an order and everyone knew it. Milo noticed the look in Grene's eyes suddenly harden, even though he was usually loyal and eager to please his Alpha. They looked like steel with a faint blue coating. He knew he'd hurt Katarina and pissed off Grene with the order, but he didn't care. He was Alpha.

Leo was smiling when Milo turned to talk with him. "At least I don't have to worry that she's going to get herself killed out there," he grumbled, giving Grene a minute or two to say goodbye to his daughter and transform before he and his Beta followed.

"What do you expect, Milo? She's the runt. She can't help but be a burden and useless to the pack. At least she's staying out of it," Leo said, smiling at the hope of getting Milo away from the pack on the hunt to concentrate on the search for his true mate. Without Katarina, he wouldn't have to hang back with her as Alpha and make sure that she didn't get herself or anyone else into trouble.

"True. Alright, let's get going," Milo said with a sigh, then allowed his transformation into his wolf to happen, giving little care to the clothes that shredded apart around him. The fibers were natural, as with most things Shifters wore, and would either be gathered or easily disperse into the world of nature to do some good elsewhere.

Once Milo was in his wolf body, he gave a good stretch and glanced at Katarina only briefly to ensure that she hadn't transformed before taking off into the forest, leading his pack.

Chapter 2

Milo's sense of his mate increased with every step. Being able to leave the hunting party behind had been an inspiration unlike any other Leo had before. Milo could feel her, so close and getting closer. His need to find her mounted with alarming insistence. He really felt that if he didn't find her soon, if not tonight, then he was going to go crazy … full on mental hospital, tied to a bed, crazy. She was inside his head, singing some sort of song. He didn't recognize the words or the tune, but it was strangely captivating and he loved the words. It felt like a message from her heart. He knew that it wasn't normal, so he didn't bother telling Leo about it. He would probably just insist he was imagining it, anyway.

"Because as you are to me, I am to you the earth, the moon, the stars, as it is supposed to be.

"We were made to love one another, we were made to understand, to care and feel and hold each other, until the stars collapsed and the earth was black," the voice sang within his mind.

It was frustrating because it was all the things that he ever wanted to hear from his true mate, but because she was singing, he had no way of recognizing her voice. He hadn't heard that many girls sing in his lifetime and it wasn't a tone or pitch that he could associate with anyone's speaking voice. He wanted to call to her, to tell her that he was close, but he had an odd feeling that said if he did, it would scare her off. He had never known a girl to be afraid of him before, but his true mate was afraid of him. He didn't want to frighten her any more by calling out to her that they were made for each other.

Milo slowed to a walk, his nose to the ground as he realized that the sense of his true mate was only getting stronger, so strong that it was beating at his head like the words of her song. He kept his senses open, sniffing around for a familiar scent, just in case something increased the awareness of his mate or gave him some idea of which direction to find her. He knew that Leo was watching him closely, wanting to help, but not knowing how. It was enough that he was there.

He was so unaware of the world around him—his Beta and the forest floor—that his brain jolted the minute his wolf nose bumped into a bare foot. His wolf backed away two steps and when he raised his eyes, it was his anger that made him transform back to his human body. "I thought you said that you were staying at home?" he bellowed as he watched Katarina stand before him, looking utterly terrified. Her eyes were wide and her heart was beating like a drum on speed. Although there were picked flowers in her hand, she twisted her fingers against each other nervously.

"I … I only came out for a walk," she answered honestly. Milo wanted to sigh and rake his hand through her hair because he could hear the tears in her voice. He was the Alpha, he should never have made any of his pack feel inferior or scream at them, but this was different.

"You worthless, stupid little runt!" The words flew out of his mouth without warning and Katarina stumbled back two steps until she had nowhere else to go. She backed into a tree trunk and automatically dropped her flowers to grasp onto the tree. She needed the strength and stability it gave her to withstand her Alpha's fury.

Milo began gasping for breath, not sure why until he felt his chest tighten. His hand automatically went to his heart, gripping his non-existent shirt with panic. His mate was hurt. She was in so much pain. He could literally feel her heart breaking. Then suddenly, the feeling, the sense of her, his breath and half his soul was gone. It was as if she didn't exist anymore. He brought his eyes up to glare at Katarina. This was her fault. She had come along and frightened his mate away and he hated her for it. But through the hatred, there was something much worse that was reaching out to him, crushing his soul. Grief. It was back with a vengeance.

Leo was worried about Milo as it was, but when he looked up at him with grief-stricken eyes, he blamed Katarina just as much as his Alpha did. "She's gone. I can't feel her anymore," Milo whispered, not worrying if Katarina heard him, only unable to catch his breath enough to speak properly.

"Alpha, it's alright," Leo lied, glaring at Katarina as he thought of what she had just done. They had been so close. Milo had been happy as they sauntered through the forest together, searching for his true mate. Now, that was all gone. "Go home. I'll take care of the girl." They had been friends long enough that he knew Milo was in no fit state to face the hunting party. As Beta, he could always claim pack business had brought him home rather than grief.

Milo nodded reluctantly and turned cold, dark eyes on Katarina for one last look of pure hatred before leaving. He took three steps as a human, an unconsciously naked human, and transformed mid stride into a bounding wolf that took off at great speed.

Leo waited until Milo was out of sight and ear shot before striding forward and grabbing Katarina by the shoulders. "Do you have any idea what you just did? The Alpha was searching for his true mate. He had a clear sense of her and then you came bounding into the area and she disappeared," he shouted out of anger, fear, and sheer confusion. Milo was losing his mind because his true mate was playing some kind of sick game of hide and seek and just when he had found her trail and was close to her, it all ended. All of it just went away, leaving him heartbroken, because some silly girl had interfered.

"I'm sorry. I didn't know. I didn't think anyone came here anymore. I was trying to stay out of the way," Katarina said, her words coming out in a rush, trying to hold back her tears. It was bad enough to be hated and shunned by her pack, without having to hear it from her Alpha, too. She barely registered Leo's words. All she could do was to try to show him, to prove to him that she hadn't done it on purpose. Where she was now was just outside of the meadow on her side of town. It was overgrown and wild and, apart from birds and bees, no wildlife ever ventured there because it was too far from the water. How was she supposed to know where the Alpha was going or what he was doing there?

"Why didn't you just stay home like you were told to?" Leo demanded.

"I ..." Katarina couldn't stop the tears any longer. She cried out of pain, grief, and frustration. He sounded so angry with her, but his hatred would never run as deep as the Alpha's. She thought about running away. It wasn't the first time that the thought had ran through her mind. At that moment, she wanted to just transform and take off into the trees, never to be seen or heard from by her pack again. "I'm sorry. I just ... I ..." She couldn't take it anymore. She was stupid and worthless and there was no point in living anymore. Everyone hated her; even her Alpha hated her. Katarina took off at a human run, leaving Leo behind.

He threw his hands up in frustration. She was so weak that she couldn't even face a scolding from her Beta. Leo decided to leave her to it. She could run and hide and face Milo's wrath later. Now, his duty was to his Alpha. He turned and transformed back into his wolf and took off after Milo. The guy was devastated. Leo knew that he would have to make sure that his Alpha was okay and then take care of the hunting party. They could search for Milo's mate again another night, after Milo had punished Katarina for her interference and ensured that she wouldn't do it again.

***

Grene felt Katarina's pain instantly. It slammed into him so hard that he was knocked off his course and into the wolf running next to him. He staggered as he tried to get his bearings, shaking his wolf head to clear it. The wolf next to him glanced at him with worry and he gave a nod as if to say that he was alright. He was instantly met with a caring nudge of concern and then left behind to rest. He couldn't help but wonder why the pack never reacted that way to Katarina when she was dizzy or weak and lagged behind.

He desperately wanted to call out to his daughter, but he didn't dare. The hunting party was going on and he would just anger the whole party. They hated her, the whole pack did. Although he could never understand it, he couldn't do anything about it, either.

Grene changed direction the moment he felt steady again. He could feel Katarina pulling away, running, leaving. It was a father's sense, after many, many years, to know his daughter. Unfortunately, this wasn't the first time that he had sensed Katarina running away from her pack. She had done this so many times before that he had lost count. All he could count on in these instances was the fact that he was fast and strong and Katarina was blinded by emotion. He ran flat out, in the direction that he could sense her. After what felt like hours, he finally saw her.

There was a streak of silver between the trees and he knew that he had found her. She was running as a wolf, fast, sure, unerring in her path. She ran in a straight line away from the pack and their land, following her instincts as she tried to leave her life far behind her. Grene pushed a burst of speed, knowing what she was doing. It was so dangerous that his heart skipped a beat, even in his wolf body. Unfortunately for him, Katarina was a marathon runner while he was a sprinter. He could already feel the heaviness of his wolf feet. He would need to stop in a little while to rest before he could run again, but he couldn't risk it. Katarina could run for days without stopping, as he guessed, was her intention now. She veered to the left ahead of him, just as he had feared she might. He forced his exhausted legs to catch up to her … at any cost.

Grene watched, terrified, filled with pain as his little girl's wolf stopped at the edge of a cliff. They were so far from home that it would take all night to get back, once he had rested and recovered. Katarina wouldn't want to go back and she would stop him if she had the chance. He knew that he had to be very careful.

He could hear her wolf howling, a sad, heartbreaking cry of distress. Inside the sturdy wolf body was a frightened young girl, screaming in pain and crying as she contemplated the worst. He slowed to a walk as soon as he reached the cliff edge and approached her cautiously. The moment he was by her side, he nudged her head with his own, offering love and comfort. Two sad eyes met his and he saw the determination that she had to end her life, to leave her pack behind, to spare them the shame of having to acknowledge her. She thought of herself as worthless, so useless to her people that she would willingly throw herself off a cliff to save them the burden of carrying her on their shoulders.

Grene transformed, needing his voice as he sat, hunched beside her, gently stroking the fur on her little wolf head. "You cannot leave me, Katarina. You are my daughter. I love you and the pack will grow to love you, too," he promised, keep his words positive and encouraging, making sure to keep his voice low. She looked away over the cliff, not sitting down, not lying down, not moving a muscle. She just stood in her tiny wolf body, half the size of his, whimpering. "Your mate will love you, Kate, he will be yours. You just have to tell him."

Katarina had known who her true mate was for years, but she had never told him. She was too ashamed of herself to ever say the words. Grene knew her heart and her wishes. She just wanted to be alone, to never take a mate, because it was easier to be alone than to be hated. She thought herself such a burden to her pack that the very idea of taking a mate, any mate, tore her to pieces. She felt unworthy of having a mate, of being able to enjoy the simplest pleasure of a wolf shifter.

Grene would never truly understand how his daughter felt, but he stayed with her, hoping and praying that she would rethink her wish to leave him. "I need you, Kate. Your sister needs you. The world needs you," he insisted, lowering his voice to a whisper. The little wolf turned and brushed his cheek with her muzzle, making him smile. Tears were welling up in his eyes from fear. She hadn't moved, not in any way that he could be sure that she wouldn't leave him.

He could feel her pain increasing, her hopelessness mounting. He stood up and backed away three steps to give her space to breath, to transform if she wanted to. Grene watched her, cataloguing every twitch, every snuffle, everything that might tell him what her intentions were. He could feel his wolf gathering strength. He could run her home if she just believed in herself. "Come with me, Kate. Come home. We will talk about this in the morning. You don't have to go to school," he offered, trying anything he could think of to get her away from the dangerous ledge.

Katarina turned and looked at him, so full of sadness that he couldn't detect any other emotions in her. She moved and he told his instincts to calm down. She was turning away from the ledge. Her wolf was walking toward him. Her beautiful eyes rose to look at his and she nudged her wet nose into his hand. Grene smiled. Then, before he could register the acceptance in her eyes, she turned and ran off the cliff, throwing her little wolf body off the edge.

***

Grene surged forward, transforming as he went until his front two paws were over the edge, digging into an uprise of jagged rock. He caught the scruff of Katarina's wolf neck in his mouth and froze. She wasn't heavy, but he was balanced precariously. Then, he felt something shift in his head, a sense of warmth and strength that he recognized. Help had come just when he needed it. If he went over now, he was going with Katarina, leaving behind another daughter. But with that presence in his mind, he at least knew that if he and Katarina couldn't be saved, then his eldest daughter would be looked after.

Do not worry. You know I would never allow Katarina to die. The voice reminded him of a vow made long ago. Carlton, a man that he should rightly hate but felt nothing but brotherly love for. He could hear the hard edge to his voice, the strength and determination to save Katarina. The precious gift that they both cherished. *She is my life. My savior. You know how much I love her,* he promised. Grene held onto the inner strength and used his strong wolf hind legs to dig into the dirt at the top of the cliff. He put all his weight on his back legs and heaved, while Katarina whimpered. His grip on her was loose, just enough to hold her, but not enough to hurt her.

It took tremendous effort, but finally, Grene backed onto the ledge of the cliff and flopped down to the ground in exhaustion. Katarina was still clamped in his mouth, but he refused to let go in case she tried to run again. Once she was back in her human body, she would cry for hours and hide away from the world, but she would be safe. And the guilt would sweep in and she wouldn't try to kill herself ever again. He knew her well enough to know that. At least, until the next wave of desolation struck. Grene held her in his wolf jaws and carried the little wolf all the way back home.

He took the back way, through the forests and then in through the back door of the house, covered from human eyes by the darkness. The hunt and the other shifters had long ago ended their day and gone home. For now, Katarina was safe and not even the Alpha could try and punish her for her self-sacrifice ... if he didn't know about it. He stayed in his wolf form right until the moment he reached Katarina's room, scratching at the door handle to open it. He walked her inside, gently lowered her wolf to the bed and left the room.

He dressed for bed, and returned to Katarina's room, knocking lightly on the door to make sure that he could enter. Katarina's voice, soft and full of tears, called him in. "I'm so sorry," she confessed, standing still at the other side of the room, already dressed in a pair of pink pajamas.

He wanted to scream at her, to tell her how selfish she had been to throw her life away for nothing. He wanted to tell her how wrong she was about her opinion of herself and remind her of all the people who loved her and would miss her if she was no longer in the world. Instead, Grene opened his arms to her and let out a sigh of relief as she rushed to him. "Don't ever scare me like that again. I can handle you running away from the pack. I can even handle the tears and the screaming in pain, but I will never be okay with you thinking your life is worthless," he said, letting the tears fall into her hair as he held her tightly in his arms. The fear was still there that maybe one day he couldn't stop her, that he wouldn't be able to reach her in time to save her. Without that mental assistance and the help that he received from Carlton, he wouldn't have been able to save her tonight.

"You mean so much to me, Kate. So much to a lot of people. What would Josanna do or feel if I had to tell her that her sister had thrown herself off a cliff? Did you ever think of that? Did you think of the ripple of agony and despair that would go through every member of our pack?" Grene asked, scolding her. He needed her to understand how wrong she had been to let others make her feel worthless. She was more precious than anything else in the world, and not just to him. There were those who loved her, and would one day love her in the future. She meant so much to him that he couldn't let her throw her life away.

"They wouldn't care, Daddy. They would probably throw a party."

"Don't ever say that!" he demanded angrily. He wasn't sure if he was angrier with Katarina for suggesting it or for the awful thought that it might actually be true. The pack might never care if anything happened to her. They might actually rejoice. It was a harsh reality that he didn't want her being aware of, but she was too smart for her own good. "I know that they don't understand you. I know they never can, but don't ever think like that. Maybe they don't appreciate you now and maybe they don't understand how special you are, but if you died, the entire pack would grieve for you. I know they would."

Katarina wasn't convinced, but she kept quiet and held onto her father, shocked to her very core at the thought of what she had almost done. She hadn't been thinking clearly at all, but the grief was getting too much to bear. It had been going on too long, for too many years. It hurt too much.

Grene let out a deep sigh and tried to change the subject. "And what about your mate? Have you thought about what this would do to him? How he would feel if you were gone from this world?" he asked, heartbroken to think of the consequences if she had gone through with her attempt. So many people would have suffered; nothing would ever have been the same again … and it would be his fault.

"At least then he would be free to unite with another. He could find someone worthy of him. someone decent, someone like him who he deserved to have standing by his side," Katarina said.

Grene could feel the conviction in her words, the absolute belief that she would never be worthy of her mate. She honestly would rather die than to tell him that they had been made for each other to make each other complete. He couldn't understand it, but there were many things about his daughter that he didn't understand, many things that he never could. He had to accept that.

"You're wrong. This kind of pain would crush him. You know it would. I know he doesn't deserve you, Kate, but you have no right to go against destiny. No right," he said with a sigh, gently stroking her hair. There was silence between them for a long time, not a whisper, not even the rush of the wind on the window. Just complete stillness. The only movement in the whole room was Grene's hand gently lacing through his daughters hair, trying to soothe and comfort her.

"I'm very tired, Daddy. Can we talk tomorrow?" she asked calmly.

He pulled back and held her gently by the shoulders. "Of course, darling. Get some sleep." He kissed her forehead. "Goodnight, Katarina. Sleep well." Then, he left the room, gently closing the door behind him to what he knew would be a restless night. As soon as he was gone, the dam would burst and she would cry herself to sleep. Tomorrow he would take the day off from work and keep her home from school so that they could talk. They needed to be together, to work through her emotional insecurities; he needed to keep her safe.

***

Carlton took a ragged breath and reached out with a shaking hand to the teacup on the tray before him. He had been enjoying a quiet night in, reading a book, when he felt his world shift. Katarina had scared the living daylights out of him. He was just lucky that he had connected with Grene in time. He took a sip of his tea, trying not to spill it, then he placed the cup back onto the tray.

"Brogan, I need you to ensure that I am not disturbed," he commanded, glancing across at the figure standing in the corner of the room. Brogan went immediately into action. He left the room, giving him space.

Carlton closed his eyes and focused on reaching out to the Elder Constantine within his mind. Constantine's thought processes were light. Clearly he was catching up on some sleep. *Hello, old friend. I need a word,* Carlton said within his mind.

Anything I can do, he replied instantly, sounding alert and ready to help.

I am afraid that Katarina has fallen, Carlton said, giving his friend one moment to register the shocking, devastating words, before continuing. *The grief is consuming her. We must act.*

You know she will fight it. Constantine sounded as if he had expected his request, so he was honest.

I know. But I also know that she will die if she continues on this foolish path that she has chosen. I would no sooner let her die than I would kill myself. Carlton let out a sigh and rubbed the bridge of his nose wearily. *We must do what we must, even if it is against her wishes.*

Will you accept responsibility for this?

Yes. Blame me, if you must. He chuckled to himself in the darkness of the room. He had always known that Constantine would do as he asked. *I will not watch her suffer any longer,* he said with sadness in his heart.

Very well. I will act tonight, he agreed.

Thank you, Constantine. You are a true and loyal friend.

To the end, Carlton, as we swore. A fondness for the Elder reignited in his heart. It had been a long time since they had last seen each other, but their loyalty never faded. They both knew the truth and, as protectors of that truth, they had created a bond.

Love Bites

Yes. Thank you, again. Carlton broke off the contact and lifted his cup of tea for a last drink. He would need to sleep soon to recharge his energies. He didn't want to be caught off guard by another emergency and not be strong enough to assist.

***

Milo sank onto his bed, feeling empty. His heart ached with real, solid pain, but he knew that it wasn't his own. His mate was in terrible pain. He didn't know if it was emotional or physical; he just knew that he couldn't help her cope with it until he found her. He *needed* to be with her, to make it better, to protect her.

He had returned home alone and faced Leo for five minutes, silently assuring his Beta that he was feeling better. Then, Leo had left him in peace. But he couldn't help noticing that even when he was with his friends and his Beta and his family, he still felt alone ... entirely alone. He didn't care who his true mate was, where she was or why she kept hiding from him. All he wanted to do was to love her. He wanted to be with someone, to feel whole, to do his duty to his pack and his mate.

The phone rang and he let out a breath. He didn't want to talk to anyone but he knew he had to get up and answer it or else it would wake his sick father down the hall. Milo dragged himself off the bed and into the living room of his suite. The phone was buzzing on the coffee table and he reluctantly picked up the receiver and put it to his ear. "Alpha Milo," he answered.

"Milo, it's Elder Constantine. We need to have a word." The voice answered, and Milo instantly sank down onto the sofa. He didn't want to talk to any Elders tonight. He didn't want to have this conversation, but he had no choice. The Elders practically controlled every Alpha in their care. He would have to pay attention, do as he was told, and pray to

God that it all worked out in the end. He needed to stay calm, focused, and remind them that he was searching for his mate, but it wasn't going to be easy.

"I haven't found her yet," he explained apologetically.

Constantine sighed. He hadn't called to check on his progress; he knew there was no point. "I'm sorry, Milo. But frankly, we don't care. You are an Alpha. You need to be mated and united and you need to have an heir. You know your choices, so decide. Now," he demanded.

Milo knew the choice the elder spoke of: was he going to keep searching for his true mate, as was his right as a shifter, and leave behind his Alpha title to do so, or would he accept his responsibility to the pack and take on another mate?

"I'm not giving up my pack," Milo answered honestly. He knew what they were asking him and he knew that the words were going to cause mayhem with his emotions, but he had no choice. On the spot, when asked, there was only one reasonable option.

"Then you leave us no choice. The Elders have chosen a mate for you," Constantine explained, then quickly said goodbye and hung up. Milo put the receiver down and sat in his room, feeling empty. He couldn't think, couldn't function, he couldn't move. All he could do was feel. The only emotion open to him was absolute and utter pain. Eventually, fear swept through him, then, the gut wrenching sorrow. Soon enough, he was curled up on the sofa, grieving for his true mate.

The End

Girl on Fire
By: Kim Stevens

Chapter One

Smoke clawed the midnight sky, hiding the stars and casting a shifting shadow across a full silver moon. The air was perfumed with smells of burning wood and lost memories. The once peaceful neighborhood was now clogged with wide-eyed, bewildered spectators clinging to young children or each other. All eyes were on the crackling fire so no one noticed the young girl standing on the sidewalk.

***

"Ishia, wake up," the elderly woman pushed open the door, banging her cane on the wall. "You're going to be late, sleepy head."

The woman was spooning oatmeal into a bowl when a girl with tousled black hair and rumpled pajamas stumbled into the kitchen, wiping her eyes.

"Oh, you're awake?"

"Obviously," the teenage girl mumbled, collapsing onto a chair.

"Are you nervous about starting college today?" The woman chuckled, placing a bowl and spoon in front of her granddaughter, then turned to set the kettle on to boil.

"Nope," Ishia replied, leaning an elbow onto the table while poking the oatmeal with a spoon. "Why is it called Indigo Flame Academy? I've never heard of it before." She sprinkled sugar over her oatmeal, then took a sip of steaming coffee. The luscious brew tantalized her taste buds.

"It's an Academy for gifted students," her grandmother cautiously replied as she sat on a chair across from Ishia. "I've always said you are ..."

"Special. Yeah, I know," Ishia said, cutting her off, "but don't all grandmothers say that about their grandchildren?" She cupped her hands around the mug and took another sip of her coffee.

"Eat your breakfast. You're going to be late," the old woman ordered.

Ishia shoveled several spoonfuls of oatmeal into her mouth while her grandmother opened her newspaper. After a few minutes of silence, Ishia started to speak. "Will you be okay here by yourself, Nan?"

The woman looked up, smiling. "I'll be fine, love. I'll putter around here ... maybe clean up your room," she said with a wink. "I'm sure you'll visit, if you aren't too busy with classes or chasing boys."

Ishia smiled.

"You'd better eat up. I'm sure your cab will be here soon." She took a sip of her coffee. "Are you all packed?"

"Yes, Nan. I just have to jump in the shower," Ishia said, holding the warm mug in her hands. As Nan busied herself with the local news, Ishia looked around the old kitchen filled with memories: the counter that she used to sit on while baking cupcakes with her Nan and the old table where she tackled her homework. Going to the Academy wasn't her idea, but she wanted her grandmother to be proud of her. This was what her Nan had always wanted for her.

Ishia was brushing her teeth when she heard a car pull up in the driveway. Music blared from the speakers, then was cut off abruptly when a car door slammed shut. Ishia quickly rinsed her mouth and stepped out of the bathroom when her Nan answered the door.

"I'm here to pick up a ... Miss Lightsome," a male voice said.

"She should be out soon," Nan mumbled under her breath.

Ishia crossed the room to her grandmother and a cab driver was standing in the door dressed in ripped jeans and a sweat stained, white shirt under an open taxi uniform jacket.

Ishia reached for her bag, but Nana shook her head, then frowned at the driver. "Young man, can you help us, please?" The driver rolled his eyes, but scooped up the bag with ease and carried it to the cab without a word.

Ishia hid a smile as she followed the driver outside. Standing in the driveway, Ishia looked across the street at a grassy plot of land where a three bedroom cottage with white shutters and a bright red front door used to set, but was now long gone. A cobblestone walkway now lost in knee-high grass that used to lead to a porch and a swing-chair was all that was left.

"They would be so proud of you," Nan whispered in Ishia's ear. Her grandmother's gnarled hand touched her arm, then travelled down to her wrist. "They wanted you to attend the Academy. They wanted the best for their daughter."

Ishia smiled, remembering her loving parents who were taken in a tragic fire. When Ishia was a baby, her parents had bought the cottage across the street from her Nan. Five years later, the cottage had burnt to the ground with no known cause. Ishia was the sole survivor of her family, which included her parents and her little brother.

"I'll miss you, Nan." Ishia looked into her grandmother's kind eyes as tears threatened to spill from her eyes. She hugged her tightly, then slid into the passenger seat of the cab.

Chapter Two

Indigo Flame Academy was several gothic buildings clumped together on a man-made island. A moat at least a kilometer wide circled the campus with an old style drawbridge. Ishia shook her head at the sight. The title of the school was unusual as it was, but the actual sight of the Academy was something else entirely.

The cab driver unloaded her bags, then jumped into his car and drove off, leaving a trail of dust behind. Ishia picked up her bags and was relieved that her Nan hadn't escorted her to the school. She didn't want to be a blubbering mess on her first day of school.

Ishia hauled her bags into the main building and a map was tacked onto the wall near the door. She was scanning it when she heard footsteps behind her.

"May I help you?" a male asked behind her.

Ishia turned around and dropped her bags when she took in the god standing before her. He cocked his head as a delicious grin swept across his rosy, red lips.

"Um," Ishia said, swallowing. "I ... I can't find my room." Her cheeks were suddenly burning from embarrassment.

"What room number were you given?" he asked. When he stepped closer, a scent of ocean spray scented cologne swept over her.

"R ... room 506," Ishia replied, closing her eyes, willing her head to stop spinning. He placed a gentle hand on her arm. She gasped when she looked into his arctic-blue eyes.

"Are you alright?" he asked, watching her cautiously. "Maybe you should sit down before you fall down." He guided her onto a bench seat setting nearby. "I'm Caleb. Caleb Fisher."

Ishia took a deep breath, then raised her eyes to meet his. "I'm Ishia Lightsome." She held out her hand. "It's nice to meet you, Mr. Fisher."

Caleb grinned, making her heart stutter, then slipped his hand into hers. "Please, call me Caleb. I'll show you to your room."

As they walked down the halls, Caleb told Ishia about the history of the school. "The Academy was built in Melbourne in the mid 1800's by Italian stone workers," he said, then glanced at her and smiled. "Indigo Flame is the sister Academy to Azure Inferno Academy in Italy and Blaze Sapphire Academy in America." He caught her checking him out and his smile turned into a grin. "All three campuses look like Gothic castles," Caleb finished, stopping at a wooden door. "Well, this is your room," he announced, pointing to a black plaque with 506 written in gold numbers.

"Thank you." Ishia didn't want her time with him to end just yet. "How do you know all of this?" she asked, removing a bronze key from her jeans pocket.

"I like history," Caleb said. "I'm also the son of the Headmaster."

"Oh," Ishia replied, looking away while her cheeks grew warm again.

Caleb chuckled. "Well, if you need anything, just let me know." When she nodded, he continued, "I'll see you around, Ishia." Then, he turned and headed down the hall. Ishia watched him walk away, then opened the door and dragged her bags inside.

The room was of average size with two single beds in the center of the room, separated by two desks on the wall opposite the door. Above the desks were two windows overlooking the moat. Ishia noticed that one desk was already taken, neat and orderly with pens sticking out of a chipped mug and notebooks stacked on one side. The other desk—along with one of the beds—was bare. Her roommate was already here.

Ishia dumped her bags on the naked bed and unzipped them. She took a deep breath, then turned to open the wardrobe. Shirts and a leather jacket were hanging above three pairs of sneakers. She moved to the next wardrobe and found it empty, except for a stack of plain white sheets, a fluffy pillow, and a woolen blanket. Ishia hung her clothing up then filled the drawers with underwear, socks and toiletries. When she was making her bed, she noticed a logo on the blanket: a blue water drop engulfed in an orange and red flame. Underneath the logo were the Italian words: *In Tra due Estremi.*

She stood back to inspect her side of the dorm room. Everything was neat and orderly. Satisfied, she decided to explore the campus. Slipping the room key into her jeans pocket, Ishia pulled on her jacket and left the room. She wandered the halls and ended up at the Academy map. Scanning the drawings, she decided to take the door to the right leading to classrooms and a cafeteria.

Finding herself in a long hallway, Ishia noticed how silent it was. There were no teachers or students anywhere in sight. She checked the small portholes in the doors and found that every classroom was empty. After checking the fifth room, Ishia pushed the door open and stepped inside.

At the front of the room was a large whiteboard with a teacher's desk to the side. Student's desks formed a semi-circle in the center of the room. But what caught Ishia's eye was something that wasn't found in a normal school: the back wall was made out of glass and beyond the glass was water, reminding Ishia of a huge fish tank. She pressed her nose against the cold glass, expecting to see fish swimming lazily around, but the tank was just like the room ... empty.

Ishia left the classroom and headed down the hallway, passing stone staircases leading to other floors. At the end of the corridor Ishia came across a large board noting different areas of the campus with arrows pointing in all directions. As she swept her eyes over the options, she heard someone approaching.

"Are you lost again?" Caleb asked, grinning.

Ishia was captured by his hypnotic blue eyes. "I thought I'd explore," she said, turning her back to the sign. "This place is strange."

"Really? Why do you say that?" he asked, looking around as if he had no idea what she was talking about.

She shrugged. "I saw a huge fish tank in a classroom. That's not normal." As she spoke, Ishia thought she saw disappointment flick behind Caleb's eyes, but when he laughed she pushed the thought aside.

"Would you like a tour guide?" he asked, changing the subject. He crooked his arm, waiting for her to link her arm with his. "I can show you all the good spots."

Ishia smiled, sliding her arm through his. "Sure, I'd like that." Her head began to spin while the scent of ocean spray cologne overwhelmed her. She must have tightened her grip on Caleb because he stopped walking and wrapped his free arm around her shoulders.

"Are you okay? You look a little pale," he asked, concerned, then pulled her to his side for support. This did nothing to ease the spinning in her head or her pounding heart.

"I ... I'm okay," Ishia stuttered. She took a few deep breaths, then raised an eyebrow. "Are you always this concerned about strange women?"

Caleb's delicious grin brightened his face. "Only the pretty ones."

Blush filled her cheeks as he released her. They headed down the hallway with their arms still linked. Caleb showed her several classrooms, all similar to the one that she had discovered on her own. Then, he guided her down the hallway and pushed open a set of swinging double doors. When they walked inside, Ishia realized why the rooms and hallways were empty. It looked as if the entire school was sitting in this enormous room, tiled white and cluttered with tables and chairs.

"This is the cafeteria," Caleb said as several heads swivelled in their direction. "I'll introduce you to my friends." He let go over her arm, but caught her hand in his. His lovely eyes locked with hers and his smile grew bigger when she didn't pull away.

"Hey, guys! This is Ishia Lightsome. She's new to this school, so be nice," Caleb said when they approached a table with four students sitting around it. Then, he looked back at Ishia. "This is Henry Waters, Emelia Waver, Zac Ashton and Paris Firely."

"Hi," Ishia said, smiling as Caleb pulled out a chair for her. She sat down then took in the faces watching her. Henry's eyes were ocean blue and his hair was short, wavy and black. His arm was draped over the shoulders of a girl with aqua eyes and blond hair with neon blue streaks. Caleb had said her name was Emelia. Paris was sitting on Zac's lap. His eyes were brown and he had long, reddish-brown hair hanging over his shoulders. Paris had deep green eyes and orange hair. Her fair skin was covered in a fine spray of freckles.

"So, what brings you to Indigo Flame?" Emelia asked as Henry played with a lock of her hair.

"Um, my Nan always wanted me to come here. So I guess it's her wish."

"Are you a local?" Paris asked. Her voice held a trace of a Scottish accent.

Ishia nodded. "I don't live far from here. I've never heard of this school, though."

"I guess it's because we like to keep to ourselves," Henry said, pulling a handheld video game from his pocket. "Only certain *types* of people know about the Academies." Henry jumped in his seat, frowning at Caleb. Ishia glanced at him and a deep furrow creased his brow.

"Hey! Why don't we get something to eat," Emelia said, pushing her chair back. She nudged Caleb with her arm, breaking his glare from Henry. "C'mon, let's show Ishia the crappy food Indigo Flame has to offer."

Ishia followed Emelia to the hot food section with Caleb close to her side. Every once in a while their arms would brush against each other, sending shock waves through Ishia. She looked up to sneak a quick glance at Caleb. Their eyes met and a delicious grin appeared on his rosy lips. She was unable to take her eyes away from his until Emelia cleared her throat.

"Oh, you two are so cute. You even blush at the same time," Emelia said, giggling, then turned her attention to the hot food items. While Ishai chose her food, Caleb gave his full attention to rows of hot pies, sausage rolls and cups of potato gems.

A moment later, they were sitting at the table with the others. Ishia popped a gem into her mouth while Paris and Emelia discussed changing the color of Emelia's neon blue streaks. Paris suggested purple, but Emelia wasn't quiet sure. Henry was busy playing his Mario Kart game, while Caleb and Zac were reliving a football game that had been shown a few nights ago.

Ishia leaned back in her chair and took in some of the other students. There was a group with their hair color ranging from turquoise to sky blue. Ishia's eyes landed on a girl with spiky, bright blue hair and piercings all over her face. A few tables away sat a smaller group who were scowling at the blue haired teens. Their hair ranged in various shades from burnt orange to scarlet red.

"Hey, what's got your attention?" Caleb asked, leaning toward her until his shoulder was touching hers. "Are you checking out the other students?"

Ishia looked at him and smiled. "Yeah, there are some interesting hair colors."

Caleb chuckled. "I guess you could say that." When his eyes moved to Ishia's left ear, she froze in her seat. His hand rose as his fingers gently caressed her skin. When he pushed her hair aside, he frowned slightly. She wondered what he had just discovered.

"I ... I should go," Ishia said, quickly standing. Caleb looked at her curiously.

Ishia turned on her heel and hurried through the cafeteria, headed toward the safety of her dorm.

Chapter Three

Ishia was sitting on her bed reading when she realized that the room was slowly becoming dark. Glancing out the window, Ishia was surprised to see that the sun slowly dipping in the sky. She bent the corner of the page and placed the book on her pillow, then scooted off the bed.

Ishia was reaching out for the doorknob when it suddenly jiggled. Stepping back as the door opened, the one person that she didn't want to see appeared in front of her.

"I was just leaving," Ishia said, preparing to sidestep Caleb.

"Wait!" His hand caught her around the waist, blocking her between his tall frame and the wall. "Can we talk?"

"Why?" Her voice came out as a small whisper. Her eyes were trained on the floor. "I should go ..."

"Ishia, please don't ignore me," Caleb said, pressing his body against hers. "I don't know why, but when you left the cafeteria it felt as if I had watched a piece of me walk out the door."

Ishia's breath caught in her throat. No one had ever said anything like that to her before. She looked up and locked her eyes with his. "I feel the same way about you, but I can't explain why. We didn't know each other until a few hours ago."

Caleb placed his hand on her cheek. "The first time I saw you, I fell in love with you," his voice was as low as a whisper. "I don't question it; I just accept it because it feels right." He stared into Ishia's amber eyes. When his lips brushed against hers, Ishia pulled away.

"How did you open my door? I'm sure I locked it after coming inside."

Caleb let out a breath, then pressed his forehead against hers. "You noticed the other bed, didn't you?" he asked.

She nodded, awkwardly.

"I'm your roommate."

Ishia smiled. "You've got to be kidding me."

Without answering, Caleb kissed each of her eyelids then moved down to her lips. Her arms snaked around his neck and pulled him even closer. His tongue gently parted her lips and started to explore her mouth. Ishia's fingers tangled themselves in his dark blond locks. Slowly, she pulled away.

"How is this possible? Is it allowed?" Ishia asked, unable to believe what was happening. Not only was she attracted to this handsome man, he was also her roommate.

Caleb shrugged. "We have co-ed dorms ... and rooms." When Ishia didn't answer, he sensed her discomfort. "Look. I won't push you into anything. And, if you like, I can go to my father to request another room." He looked into her eyes and nodded, then headed toward the door.

Ishia shook her head. "No, don't," she said, catching his hand as he passed.

His eyes met hers. "What are you saying?"

"I'm saying that we just met," Ishia replied. "I need time to process everything. I'm not saying that I don't want a relationship, just not one happening so fast."

Caleb smiled. "I feel the same way." He walked over to his bed and kicked off his shoes. "Let's just take it a day at a time." Then, a mischievous grin tugged at his lips when he added, "I promise to behave myself."

"And not to look when I'm changing?" she asked, giving him a playful smirk.

He laughed out loud at the comment. "Now, I'm not promising that," he joked. Then, he looked into her eyes, melting her heart. "But I will promise to take it slow."

Chapter Four

Ishia woke the next morning and took a deep breath, filling her lungs with the scents of ocean spray and sweat. At first, she didn't recognize her surroundings. She looked around, trying to orient herself. From the other side of the room, she heard light snoring, then suddenly the previous day's events came rushing back to her. The light snoring suddenly stopped and she quickly closed her eyes.

"Good morning," Caleb said from his bed across the room. "Don't go back to sleep."

Ishia looked over and he was lying on his bed, shirtless, with a white sheet pulled up to his waist. "If I wake up, then this peaceful dream might disappear," Ishia said, snuggling into the pillow. She smiled when Caleb chuckled. She didn't know why, but she felt so comfortable with him.

"I'm not going anywhere," he said, pulling the pillow under his head. His blue eyes were penetrating.

Ishia slowly sat up as a huge grin spread across her face. "I'd better get up."

Caleb rose from his bed and gently kissed her forehead. "You're right. We should get up. People will notice if we aren't there when breakfast is served."

Ishia smiled as a devilish grin spread across her face. "I get first dibs on the shower!" Then, she sprinted across the room.

Caleb chuckled as he watched her.

When Ishia had finished showering, Caleb was standing by the wardrobe, pulling a pair of socks from his drawer. He was wearing pants, but his chest was still bare. He reached out and picked up a T-shirt lying on the bed, when Ishia noticed a small tattoo on his left shoulder blade. Ishia crossed the room to take a closer look at the artwork.

"I like your tattoo," she said making Caleb twist around to look at her. "Why did you get a Mermaid?" She tried to get another look at it, but he quickly slipped the T-shirt over his head without a word. "Was it for an ex-girlfriend? Did you get it on a dare?" She smiled, but it slowly disappeared when he kept staring at her. "What?" she asked. "I didn't mean to offend you."

"No, it's not that," he said, taking a deep breath. "I'll make you a deal ... I'll tell you about my tattoo when you tell me about the fire-red streak of hair you keep hidden."

Ishia turned to make the bed. "I…" she frowned when the words didn't come to her.

After she finished making the bed, Caleb sat on it and took her hands in his, forcing her to look into his eyes. "Ishia, tell me," he whispered, gently squeezing her fingers.

She took a deep breath, then sat down on the bed beside him. "I don't know how my hair turned red," she said, avoiding meeting his gaze. "My Nan told me that it appeared after my ... when I was a child."

"You didn't dye it?"

Ishia shook her head.

"What happened when you were a child?" Caleb asked, his voice anxious. When she finally met his artic gaze, she saw that they were troubled.

"It doesn't matter," Ishia said, looking away. "We're going to be late." Caleb watched as she rose from the bed and finished getting ready, ending the conversation for the moment.

"Okay," Caleb said, finishing getting ready, too. "Look, I have to go somewhere. I'll see you in a little while."

Ishia nodded, watching as he left the room and closed the door softly behind him.

***

Ishia entered the cafeteria and saw Caleb's friends sitting around a circular table, talking and laughing. Her heart dropped when she didn't see Caleb with them.

"Hey Ishia! Over here!" Emelia called out when she spotted Ishia standing in the doorway. Emelia waved her arm then smiled as she joined them.

"Hi," Ishia said sitting beside Paris. "I thought Caleb would be here already."

"He is. He's over there." Henry pointed toward the other side of the cafeteria. Ishia followed his finger and saw Caleb sitting beside an older man with the same dark blond hair. "That's the Headmaster's table."

Ishia watched Caleb for a moment until he turned in her direction. When their eyes met, she was the one to quickly look away, suddenly feeling uncomfortable. Ishia knew that she'd have to share her past with Caleb. She hoped that he wouldn't think badly of her.

"So, what's on the menu today?" Zac asked reaching across Ishia to grab a menu. "I hope it's not bacon and eggs again." He opened the menu and scanned the options.

"I don't mind bacon and eggs," Paris said flicking hair over her shoulder. "I hate the pancakes, though." Then, she turned to Ishia and added, "They're more like bricks ... or plates ... than pancakes." She made a face and Zac chuckled.

During breakfast, Ishia tried to listen to the conversations going on around the table, but her eyes and attention always drifted back to where Caleb was sitting. She thought that he looked bored while his father spoke to other adults at the table. When he looked in her direction she forced herself to keep eye contact with him. Ishia was contemplating whether or not to go over to him when Caleb suddenly stood and started to snake his way across the cafeteria toward her and the others.

"Can I sit here?" he asked placing his hand on the empty seat beside her.

"Sure," Ishia said, feeling the others watching her. "How come you left the other table?" Ishia's head started to spin when his ocean spray scent swamped her.

"My father and the other teachers were discussing class subjects. It was becoming tedious." He smiled, but it was laced with concern. Ishia suspected why. She turned quickly away, unsure if she was ready to tell him everything yet.

"So, what are our captors planning for us today?" Zac joked, leaning forward in his seat. "Come on Caleb, share with us, man."

Caleb chuckled, shaking his head. "Sorry, Zac, but the old man had me sign a confidentiality agreement." He looked at Ishia and winked.

After breakfast, Ishia made her way back to her dorm to prepare for her first class when she felt someone following her. When she turned around, Caleb was smiling.

"May I escort you back to your room?"

"Don't you mean our room?" Ishia went to walk away, but he stopped her.

"I'm sorry for ruining the moment this morning. I didn't mean to upset you."

"You didn't ruin anything." Her hand lifted to her hair where she knew the red streak was hidden under her black hair. "I have a past ..."

"So? Who doesn't?" Caleb asked, sliding his hands onto her waist. "I want you to know that I'm here to listen. Whatever you have to say won't scare me away."

"I wouldn't say that just yet," Ishia mumbled. "What do we do now?" She knew it was a feeble attempt to change the conversation.

Caleb laughed as a mischievous grin spread across his lips, but he said nothing.

Ishia laughed, afraid to ask what he was thinking. She could only imagine. "Why don't you show me around a bit more?"

Caleb nodded and released her. "Alright, you win. Come on. Let's go get our stuff and I'll show you to your first class." He held her hand then started to head down the hallway.

Chapter Five

Ishia was getting her books together and listening to Caleb singing in the bathroom, when she remembered to call her Nan. She looked at the clock and shrugged, knowing that her grandmother would already be up. She reached over and grabbed her mobile off the bedside table, then dialled the number. Her Nan answered on the third ring.

"You forgot your poor old Nan, didn't you, young lady?" the old woman said making Ishia smile.

"No, I could never forget you," she replied. "How did it go yesterday?" Ishia leaned her head on her arm.

"Oh, you know, I invited all of my friends over and had a huge party. Then, I went to the movies and threw popcorn at the screen ..." she stopped when her granddaughter started to laugh. "I puttered around the house and missed you like crazy."

"I miss you too, Nan," Ishia said. "The Academy is really nice and the people are friendly. Also, I have a roommate."

"Is she nice?"

Ishia started to respond, but stopped when the bathroom door opened. Caleb stood in the opening, resting his shoulder on the wall. He smiled, then walked over to his side of the room and started packing his backpack for class.

"Ishia, are you there?" Nan asked.

"Um," Ishia couldn't tear her eyes from her roommate. "Yeah, she's really nice," she lied.

Caleb grinned, running his fingers through his hair when he saw Ishia struggling to make conversation.

"Have you started classes yet?"

"Yes, this morning. I have to check my schedule." Ishia closed her eyes and tried to concentrate on talking to her grandmother. "I've met some really nice people. I hope the teachers are friendly, too."

"I'm sure they will be," Nan said. "I'll let you go to get ready for class. Don't be late!"

"Okay. I love you, Nan. I'll call you in a few days." Ishia hung up then sat on the side of the bed. Ishia hated lying to her grandmother, but what would she think about her having a male roommate? No, Nan wasn't ready for that yet, but Ishia silently vowed to tell her later.

"You were talking to you grandmother?"

"Yeah and I became tongue-tied when she asked if I had a roommate." She shook her head, then added, "Come on. We'll be late for our first class."

Caleb laughed. "Changing the subject again?" he teased, casting a delicious grin in her direction, making Ishia's heart stutter. When she just looked at him, he took a deep breath and added, "Fine. Let's go to class."

Ishia laughed, slinging her backpack over her shoulder.

Her first day of classes went well at the academy. After Caleb had said goodbye to her, she spent the morning checking her schedule and trying to find her classes. She breathed a sigh of relief when it was lunchtime, knowing that she would see Caleb.

In the cafeteria, Caleb was waiting for her. "Hey," he greeted her.

"Hey," Ishia replied, happy to see him.

"How was your classes?"

"Fine." Ishia shrugged, then added, "It was a bit rough trying to find my classes, but I'm getting the hang of it."

Caleb laughed. "You'll get used to it."

After getting their lunch, they sat with their friends. Caleb kept looking at Ishia with a concerned look on her face, but she turned away. She knew that he wanted her to talk to him about her past, but she just wasn't ready.

The rest of the day was uneventful with Ishia finding the rest of her classes with ease. Caleb was right. Now that she was getting acquainted with the campus, finding her classes was becoming easier.

Later that afternoon, Ishia was exhausted and had decided to skip dinner. She was just too tired. She looked around the room and Caleb wasn't there yet. She breathed a sigh of relief, knowing that he may push her to talk. She lay on the bed and sleep found her.

She woke to the sound of Caleb coming into the dark room.

"Where were you?" he asked. "I missed you at dinner."

"Sorry, but I was just too tired to go." *Also, I needed some time to myself,* she added to herself, but didn't dare tell him that.

She sat up as Caleb sat down beside her on her bed and brushed his hand gently across her cheek. "No worries. I was just worried," Caleb said then added, "Your first day of classes can do that to you."

"Yes, it can," Ishia agreed.

"Did you find the rest of your classes alright?"

"Yes," Ishia nodded, then added, "I think I'm finally getting the hang of it."

Caleb laughed, then leaned down and pressed his lips against hers.

Ishia smiled against his mouth. "Goodnight, Caleb," she teased. When he pouted, Ishia lifted her hand and poked his bottom lip with a finger. "You need your beauty sleep."

Caleb sighed heavily then stood. "Goodnight, Ishia." He smiled then added, "If you like, I'll go over your schedule with you in the morning so you'll know where your classes will be."

She grinned and nodded as he turned and went over to his side of the room. Ishia watched as he slid under the covers and flicked off the lamp.

***

Sometime during the night, Ishia knew that she was dreaming, but couldn't wake up. Actually, she recognized that it was a reoccurring nightmare from childhood.

Flames licked the sunflower yellow wallpaper while the matching curtains fell in a smoldering heap. The room was suddenly glowing in oranges, reds and yellows while thick black smoke danced toward the ceiling. She couldn't move as the flames jumped around her small body. She tried squeezing her eyes shut, but it didn't work. Then, she realized that the fire burning around her was somehow burning *inside* of her.

When the screams of her family subsided she knew that her life had changed forever. She was about to open her eyes to welcome her fiery end, when she heard her name being called out.

"Ishia, wake up." the voice was close by. "Ishia ... you have to wake up." It sounded urgent. Suddenly, she was desperate to come back to reality ... to escape the nightmare.

Opening her eyes, Ishia instantly knew that something was wrong. When she moved, the sheets were soaked and clinging to her body. Sitting up, she flicked the lamp on and frowned when she saw Caleb lying on the floor beside her bed.

"What are you doing down there?" she asked, swinging her feet to the floor and felt water between her toes.

"I lost the use of my legs for a moment," Caleb said, carefully standing up. He retreated back to his side of the room and pulled out a pair of thick plastic boots from under his bed. "Are you alright?" he asked, sliding his feet into the boots.

"I'm okay ... what happened to my bed?" Ishia stood up and was shocked when she surveyed her bed. It was scorched and the wooden frame was blackened and slightly warped, while her sheets had large holes in them.

Chapter Six

Before Caleb could answer, a loud knock on the door made them both jump. He carefully made his way to the door and opened it to see his father standing before him, dressed in navy blue pajamas and a dark brown robe.

"Father, what are you doing here?" Caleb asked.

The headmaster gazed past him at the water and burnt furniture. "I was alerted to a fire. Is everything alright in here?" Thomas Fisher's azure eyes caught sight of Ishia. "I never agreed to you rooming with one of *them.*"

"Stop it!" Caleb said, turning to see Ishia examining the remains of her bed. "Can we speak outside?" Without waiting for an answer, he turned and stepped out of the room, closing the door behind him

Ishia was quiet, listening to their conversation.

"I asked to room with Ishia. I want to help her ..." Ishia recognized that it was Caleb.

"This was wrong Caleb," Thomas raised his voice, cutting his son off. "She'll do more harm than good. Whatever happened in there could've ended badly. She doesn't even know what you are or what she is!" He shook his head. "I think it would be best if you were transferred to another room."

"Father, I want to stay here," Caleb said, then added, "I love her."

Ishia's breath caught.

Thomas slowly shook his head. "You're eighteen and you just met the girl! You know nothing of love."

"That's where you are wrong. I know my heart better than anyone," Caleb said defiantly. "And even Mother told me about a girl with black hair and a fire-red streak. She knew about my truelove—Ishia—and I'm not losing her because we're different."

"Your mother was on her death bed," Thomas countered. "She didn't know what she was saying ... it was the cancer ..."

"You don't believe that," Caleb cut him off. "She was lucid that day and you were there when she said it. She could see into the future; you can't deny that."

"No, I don't deny that," Ishia heard his father say through the door, then he took a deep breath. "Okay, help Ishia find her true self. She needs a guiding hand and you're the one to do it. Just be careful, son."

"I will, Dad," Caleb said. Ishia heard hard footsteps going down the hallway, fading away.

Ishia quickly turned toward the bed, trying to appear not to have been listening to their conversation.

Caleb entered the room and closed the door, then turned to see Ishia touching the blackened wood. He stepped closer when he noticed that her hands were shaking. "You should get some rest."

"Where?" Ishia shook her head, then laughed without humor. "My bed is practically firewood." She leaned against Caleb's chest when he wrapped his arms around her. "How did this happen?"

"My bed's free," he whispered. "I promise I'll keep to my side." He softly kissed her earlobe.

Ishia smiled then turned in his arms so they were facing each other. "I don't know ..." Then, she yawned, giving herself away.

"Come on," he said, tugging her across the room, guiding her onto his bed, "you need sleep." Then, he added, "I'll be a gentleman."

Ishia nodded, then reluctantly slid under the sheets and lie down on the pillow. He lay down next to her and pulled the covers over them both.

Ishia couldn't help but cuddle up to Caleb, resting her head on his chest. "What happened while I was asleep?" she asked, draping an arm across his stomach. When he stayed silent, she propped herself on an elbow and looked down at him. "Caleb?"

Without a word he closed his eyes, lacing their fingers together on his stomach.

"Why were you on the floor?" Ishia asked.

Frowning, Caleb reached out and flicked off the lamp, sending the room in complete darkness. When she heard Caleb softly snoring, she lay back and stared at the ceiling, wondering what had happened.

***

The next morning, Caleb's eyelids fluttered open and his hand reached out for Ishia. When he felt the bare mattress under his fingers, he sat up and noticed that he was alone. Pulling on the rubber boots he made his way to the bathroom.

"Ishia, are you in there?" he asked, slowly opening the door, but it was empty.

Caleb yanked on a pair of jeans and a T-shirt, then swapped his rubber boots for sneakers. As he opened the door, he was met by two maids who stepped back in surprise.

"Mr Fisher, we were told to come and clean your room," one maid announced.

The older maid peered into the room and exclaimed, "Oh dear!"

"Yeah ... um ... thanks," he said pushing his way into the hall. "Lock up when you leave, please." He wanted to run to the cafeteria and find Ishia, but he forced himself to stick to a fast walk.

His heart was pounding as he reached the swing doors of the cafeteria. When he stepped through the doors, his eyes were already scanning the crowd. After another quick scan, Caleb knew that Ishia wasn't there.

"Hey man, who're you looking for?" Zac asked, approaching Caleb.

"Ishia ... have you seen her?"

Zac shook his head. "Nope, sorry." Caleb started to leave, but Zac stopped him. "Wait ... I think she has a Math class with Emelia and Henry."

"Thanks." Caleb turned and ran down the hallway.

Caleb dodged students in the hallway, moving quickly past the crowded classrooms. When he heard laughter coming from several doors down, he slowed and peered through the porthole. Students were lounging around on desks so he opened the door, making them tense up. They were alone and soon relaxed when they noticed that it was Caleb who had entered the room.

Caleb saw Ishia as soon as he stepped into the room. She was standing at the large tank talking and laughing with Emelia and Henry, who were both leaning their arms on the glass edge while their tails wafted below them.

"Hey, Caleb," Henry said, making Ishia turn around.

"Hi." He kept his eyes on her face while he slid his hand into hers. A smile came to her lips, indicating that he was forgiven for not answering her questions the night before.

"Hi. I didn't think you were going to your classes today," Ishia said.

"I'm not," Caleb replied as someone entered the room.

"Mr Fisher, you aren't supposed to be in here," an older, stocky woman said, setting her books on the teacher's desk.

"I'll be outside waiting for you," he whispered before a woman appeared next to him.

"Mr. Fisher, please leave my class." The short woman crossed her arms over her chest and a deep frown creased her brow. *"Now!"*

Caleb smiled, then escaped the disapproving glare of the teacher.

In the hallway, Caleb took a deep breath as he lowered himself to the floor and leaned back against the wall. He listened as the stocky woman began teaching in the classroom behind him. He wanted to go in and demand that he never leave Ishia's side, but he knew that it would only embarrass her and make his father unhappy. He took a deep breath, not wanting to hear one of his father's lectures.

As he waited for the class to end, he closed his eyes and imagined his mother meeting Ishia. He knew that his mother would have loved her as much as he did. He imagined that she would embrace Ishia and give him a knowing look. His mother was known for her future predictions. She had told Caleb on her death bed that he would meet his true love. He trusted his mother and her visions and missed her dearly.

"Hey, wake up, Sleeping Beauty." A hand gently nudged Caleb's shoulder, making his eyes open. His delicious grin made Ishia's heart skip a beat.

"I woke up to an angel," he replied wiping his eyes, then rose to his feet.

Ishia smiled as a blush rose to her cheeks in spite of herself. "Have you been out here all this time?" she asked, taking his hand.

"I told you I'd wait for you." He raised his free hand and gently touched her cheek. He lowered his head, and gently brushed his lips across hers. "I want to show you something," he said in a low voice.

Caleb took Ishia to Indigo Flame's library. Ishia gasped when she saw a large crystal chandelier hanging above the front table. The walls were stone and archways led to other areas. Shelves were filled with ancient books, standing like soldiers waiting for students to peruse them. Antique lamps lit the odd desk as Caleb guided her to an oak desk away from other people.

"Wait here. I'll be right back," Caleb said, leaving Ishia in the study area with intricately carved wooden chairs. Instead of going after him, she pulled out a chair and sat down.

Ishia was drumming her fingernails on the table top when Caleb emerged, holding a large book. When he placed it in front of her, she looked at the front cover and saw faded golden symbols on a black leather background. The title was in another language.

"What's this about?" she asked, running her fingers gently across a ruby red stone protruding from one of the corners. "What language is this?"

"It's Arabic. You should read it." Caleb sat across the table from her, then reached over to undo the tarnished gold buckles.

"But I don't read Arabic ..."

"The English translation has been added under the scripture." He opened the book and Ishia scanned the first page. "If you have any trouble, then I'll help."

Ishia leaned her arm on the table while her free hand carefully flipped the pages over. "Why do I have to read it? Is it homework?" she smiled, but it slowly slipped away when she took in Caleb's serious expression.

"It will help to answer all of your questions."

Ishia started to read while Caleb's fingers stroked the skin of her palm. When she saw a foreign word she looked up, frowning.

"What's an Ifrit?" She looked at the text and read one of the sentences. *"An Ifrit is an enormous winged creature of fire, either male or female, who lives underground and frequents ruins."*

"You should know your true self," Caleb said cautiously. He held her hand while his eyes watched her confused amber eyes.

Ishia shook her head. "No, this isn't true. I'm a human." She tried to pull her hand away, but Caleb held onto it. "I'm a *human*, Caleb."

Chapter Seven

Caleb stood and moved around to her side of the table. He never let her hand go as he sat beside her. "Listen to me, baby," his voice was low and calm, forcing Ishia to concentrate on his words. "Deep down you know that this is true." His hand reached around to her ponytail and gently eased the band out making her black hair cascade around her shoulders. Ishia froze when she felt his fingers brush past her neck.

"This is the mark of an Ifrit," he said, reaching out to touch her fire-red streak of hair. She closed her eyes trying to block his words, but something deep down told her that every word was true. "I would never lie to you, Ishia."

She swallowed hard, then raised her eyes to meet his. "I know," she whispered. She looked down at the open book, then touched the yellowing page. "Will you stay with me while I read this?" she looked back at Caleb, who smiled and nodded.

Caleb ran his fingers through Ishia's hair when she closed the book and rubbed her hands over her face and looked at him with sad eyes. "I'm a fire demon."

"No, you're not."

"It says it in this book," she said in a dispirited voice, pointing to the cover. "An Ifrit can either be good or evil, but is most often depicted as a wicked and ruthless being ... it's stated in here." Ishia started to flick through the pages, but Caleb caught her hands.

"Stop!" he said, forcing her to look at him. "This was written many centuries ago when Ifrits were like this, but as time passed, the species has become more ... civil," he told her. "Once, they were evil and angry, but now Ifrits are at peace with themselves and their world."

Caleb rested his forehead against Ishia's. "What are you thinking?" he asked while his thumb rubbed her fingers. "Anything at all."

Ishia closed her eyes while she spoke. She didn't want to see the accusations in Caleb's eyes as she spilled her inner most secret. "I killed my family," she whispered.

When he stayed silent she opened her watery eyes.

"Tell me what happened," he finally whispered back. He gently wiped a tear away that had tumbled out of her eye. "I'm here for you, Ishia."

"I was five when it happened," she said in a shaky voice. "I was curled up in bed after spending an hour listening to my mother read to me. I must've woken from a bad dream to find everything burning. My sunflower yellow wallpaper was blackened by flames and the curtains were a burning heap on the floor. I jumped out of bed as smoke covered the ceiling. I cried out for my parents, but they never came." Ishia bowed her head as tears ran down her cheeks. "The fire was burning around me and inside me. I ran outside, right through the fire, and it didn't harm me."

"Ishia ..." Caleb started then jerked back in his seat. He pulled his hands away as Ishia's eyes widened in shock. From her fingertips were six centimeter flames dancing just above her skin.

"Oh, my God!" she watched as the flames glowed bright red and orange. Ishia sat motionless until Caleb licked his fingers and extinguished each flame. He then took her hands and kissed her fingertips while locking his gaze with hers.

"I really am an Ifrit."

"Yes," Caleb said. "Ifrit DNA is passed through lineage, but it can skip generations. Your ability probably came from a great grandparent."

"I don't know how I'll accept this, but I'm glad you were here with me." Ishia leaned closer to Caleb and kissed him on the lips. Her fingers slid into his hair while his cupped her cheeks in the palms of his hands. "Thank you," she mumbled against his mouth.

"You're very welcome."

Later, Ishia and Caleb were sitting in the cafeteria with Henry, Emelia, Zac and Paris when Ishia saw Zac grinning like a Cheshire cat as he ate a steak sandwich.

"What's the grin for?" Emelia finally asked the question that everyone was thinking.

Zac jerked his chin in Ishia's direction. "We have another one in the ranks."

"What?" Henry asked, confused. Caleb glanced at Ishia and saw what had grabbed Zac's attention.

"A red streak is the Ifrit's mark," Zac said proudly.

"Yeah, so I've been told." Ishia lifted her hand to stroke the fire-red streak she usually hid under her hair. Now, she felt that she could show it off proudly.

"Mine's more orange," Zac said revealing his own Ifrit mark.

"So, there are Ifrits, Merpeople and humans at this table," Ishia stated.

"Humans?" Henry asked, confused.

Ishia glanced at Caleb before answering. "Yeah, Emelia and you are Merpeople and Zac, Paris and I are Ifrits. I guess that means Caleb's a human."

Everyone looked at Caleb, who said nothing.

"Did I say something wrong?" Ishia asked, breaking the silence.

Caleb threw her a delicious grin before standing up. "Everything's fine," he said before heading over to the hot food section.

Caleb was eyeing an egg and bacon quiche when he felt a hand on his lower back. He looked up to see Ishia standing beside him. He wrapped his arm around her shoulders and kissed her forehead.

"What would you like to eat?" he asked, rubbing her shoulder.

"I don't know," she said, pulling away. Ishia moved behind Caleb and started to comb through his hair.

He chuckled. Feeling her fingers running through his hair tickled. "Mind telling me what you're looking for?" he asked when she stopped and stood beside him.

"I was looking for your Ifrit mark."

Caleb smiled then turned his attention to the food in front of him. He knew he had to tell Ishia about his true self, but he was uncertain if she would accept him ... after she knew what he really was.

Chapter Eight

When lunch was over, Caleb stood and held his hand out for Ishia, who smiled up at him. She slid her fingers around his then stood up.

"We'll see you guys later," Caleb said to his friends before leading Ishia out of the bustling cafeteria.

"Where are we going?" Ishia asked as they exited out the nearest door, leading outside to the fresh air and warm sunshine. "Caleb?"

"I want to show you something." He took her to a stand-alone brick shed several meters from the lapping water of the moat.

Caleb opened the door, allowing Ishia to see a concrete staircase leading down under the ground. Lining the walls were small circular LED lights that broke through the darkness as they descended the stairs. When they reached the bottom, Ishia was amazed to see that she was now in a large glass tunnel.

"This tunnel circles the Academy following the moat," Caleb said, knowing that Ishia had spotted hundreds of swimming Merpeople. Her eyes were wide while they peered over his shoulder through the glass. He released her hand and watched as she moved closer to the thick, glass wall.

Merpeople swam overhead and around them as they slowly made their way down the tunnel. Oohhs and aahhs came from Ishia as she took in the different sights. Caleb was watching a young girl twirling in the clear water when he felt Ishia stop walking. She was watching him when he turned to face her.

"At lunch, I said that you were a human ..." her voice trailed off as she bit her lip.

"Yes."

"If you aren't human, then what are you?"

Caleb faced the glass wall and watched as Merpeople lazily swam by. He felt Ishia watching him, still holding his hand. When he had chosen the right words, he turned to face her. "It would be easier if I show you." He cupped her cheek in his hand and kisses her tenderly. They were soon interrupted by a loud tap on the glass above them.

Looking up, Caleb and Ishia saw Henry grinning down at them. He started signing. Surprised, Ishia looked at Caleb, who is watching his hands.

"Henry says that we should get a room," Caleb said, then noticed Ishia's raised eyebrow. "Merpeople can communicate with sign language." Caleb signed back to Henry, who nodded then swam away. "Come on," he said, taking Ishia's hand. They head back to the staircase leading to daylight.

Caleb took her to the edge of the moat. Ishia looked into the water seeing only her reflection rippling on the water's surface. When he squeezed her hand, she looked up into his artic blue eyes and delicious grin.

"Go back into the tunnel and wait for me," he said, stroking her cheek.

Ishia nodded, then smiled when he kissed her forehead. As she headed toward the shed, she glanced over her shoulder and saw Caleb striping off his clothes. When Ishia was about to go back over to him, Henry suddenly appeared out of no where.

"This way, Miss Lightsome," he gestured to the shed, then half-smiled.

Ishia laughed as they entered the shed and descended down the concrete stairs. When they reached the bottom, Ishia's attention was quickly claimed by the Merpeople.

"What do you think?" Henry asked, standing beside her.

"This feels like a fairytale ... a story that parents tell their children." She placed a hand on the glass and smiled when a Merman swam past, flicking his ocean blue tale at her. Suddenly, a sharp tap sounded on the glass above them. Ishia looked up and saw Caleb staring back at her. Her mouth popped open as the reality of what she was seeing sank in. He slowly drifted down to her.

She took in his muscular chest, strong arms, and a tail where his legs should have been. When her eyes travel back to his handsome face, wariness was resonating within his piercing, blue eyes.

"I'll tell Caleb what you're saying," Henry said after a moment of silence. Ishia nodded, keeping her eyes on Caleb.

Caleb waited as Ishia took him in, then he started to sign. As he moved his hands, Henry told Ishia what he was signing. "This is what I am. Don't be scared of me."

Ishia smiled. "I'm not scared of you. I think you look ... beautiful," she said as Henry signed for her. Caleb's smile turned into a relieved grin.

"You're accepting my true self better than when you found out about your own true self," Caleb signed.

After Henry told her what Caleb said, Ishia nodded. "It's different. This isn't about me; it's about the man I love. I know that I'm an Ifrit and with time I'll fully accept it, but now I want to focus on you and me."

Caleb moved closer to the glass and placed his hand on it. Ishia smiled and placed her hand over his. "Thanks, Henry, but I've got it from here," she said.

Henry nodded and walked away.

When Henry was gone, Ishia looked back at Caleb. Then, she pointed to her eye and then her heart before pointing at Caleb. He grinned, copying her gestures back to her, then motioned for her to go out the tunnel to the moat.

Ishia exited the shed and looked around, then found Caleb resting his arms on the grass, waiting for her. She hurried over and knelt down in front of him as the sun glittered off his wet skin.

"Now I understand the Mermaid tattoo," she said, leaning forward to touch his left shoulder, then added, "and why you were on the floor after the water sprinklers went off last night."

Caleb chuckled. "It's a Merman ... my tattoo." He reached out and held her hand. "Just add water and my tail appears," he said with a wink.

"So, there really are Mermaids and Mermen?" Ishia asked.

Caleb nodded.

"May I see your tail?"

Caleb shifted his position and watched Ishia's face when he raised his tail out of the water. She leaned forward to see bluish-opal scales glistening in the sun. The fins brushed her arm, causing a bead of water to trickle down her skin.

"So, your legs are under the scales?" she asked, reaching out to gently run her fingers across his tail.

"Yeah. It's like sitting with your legs straight out in front of you and your feet are pointing outwards," he said. "My skin then covers my legs and the scales appear. My feet are the fins." He moved his tail under the water and rested his arms on the grass.

Ishia searched his eyes and realized that he had suddenly turned serious. "What's wrong?" she asked as her fingers found his.

"Did I scare you?" Caleb thought that Ishia still might run, but instead of leaving, she lay on her stomach and reached out to place her hand on his wet, cold cheek.

Ishia smiled when she saw doubt in Caleb's eyes. "I could never be scared of you, Caleb Fisher. I think you're beautiful and I love you from the top of your head to the tip of your tail." She cranes her head, leaning toward him and kissed him, as he placed his hands on her cheeks.

"I love you, too," he whispered over her lips.

And Ishia knew that she was finally home.

The Sisterhood
A Wolf Girl Short Story
By: Theresa Oliver

"*Where have you been, Cathy?*" Roy asked. Rage boiled under the surface as he glared at me with cold, dead eyes.

"At work," I answered nervously, carrying a bag of groceries into the house, then gingerly shut the door of our mobile home with a sigh. *So, it was going to be one of those nights,* I thought to myself.

Suddenly, Roy slammed his beer bottle down hard on the wooden coffee table. Beer splattered over the brim as the trailer shook. I jumped, taking a step back. "I called and you weren't there!" he yelled angrily, watching me. His brown eyes reflected the fire burning brightly within the fireplace.

"After I left work, I went to the store," I said, indicating the bag of groceries in my arms. I collected my courage, determined not to let fear show within my eyes. "I don't have time for this. I'm cooking dinner." I turned toward the kitchen, but in a flash, he was standing before me, planting his feet firmly. He leaned toward me, looking up and down my body, as the stench of stale beer wafted to my nostrils. "You've been drinking," I replied, squaring my shoulders, determined not to let him see the fear that filled my sky blue eyes. "Get out of my way."

"Oh, I think dinner can wait," he replied as he lifted a lock of my long blonde hair to his face, then inhaled deeply.

"Get away from me, Roy," I said, brushing past him. "We're not doing this anymore."

But as I passed, he caught my arm, holding it much more tightly than necessary.

"Let go, Roy! You're hurting me!" I yelled into his face, pushing hard onto his chest, but his chest was solid rock, not giving an inch. That was one of the things that attracted me to him when I first met him in high school. He was great to me then, always the gentleman, sexy, with a great body. Roy didn't start showing his true side until about a year after we were married. He started drinking heavily, then soon started pushing me around. And on more than one occasion, he came home late reeking of a certain lady's perfume.

Suddenly, Roy's eyes narrowed. "I asked you a question."

"I don't know what the hell you're talking about," I replied, trying to brush past him again, but he pushed hard on my shoulders, sending me staggering backward.

"You know damn well what I'm talking about!" Roy said, his eyes evil. Then, he grabbed me hard by the throat and pushed me against the wall. "Where the hell have you been?"

"I told you!" I said as tears slowly trickled down my cheeks. "I went to the store when I got off work at the diner!"

"You liar!" Roy yelled into my face, gritting his teeth as his eyes flared. "Who were you with?" Then, he slammed my head back against the dark wood paneled wall, shaking the whole trailer.

"Get off me!" I yelled into his face, barely squeaking out the words as I tried to pull his strong hands away from my throat. "I'm not seeing anyone, you moron!"

"Moron? *Moron?*" he yelled as his face contorted with rage, animalistic. "You bitch!" Roy yelled into my face, then he threw me hard onto the floor. He watched as I lay shaking upon the floor and replied with a smirk, "Now who's the moron?" Then, he took a step toward me as I lay writhing upon the floor.

"No, Roy!" I yelled, curling into a ball as he took off his belt, then brought it down hard across my shoulders, cutting into my flesh over and again. In a flash, he was standing over me, kicking my stomach with his heavy work boot as I thought, *God, help me!*

But it wasn't God who came to my rescue.

Later that night, after Roy passed out onto the couch, I peeled myself up from the floor with every inch of my body aching and shaking. I made it to the bedroom, locked the door, and fell onto the bed, and pulled the covers around my face and neck. I tried to close my eyes, but images of Roy and what he'd done clouded my mind. *Why didn't you come for me? Why didn't you help me?* I asked God as tears slowly streaked down my face, falling onto the white pillowcase beside me. Then, I silently prayed the Our Father, pausing at the phrase "Deliver us from evil."

Yeah, I thought. *Not tonight.*

When sleep finally found me, safe under the covers, I made a vow that Roy would never do this to me again. I needed strength, and I found comfort in knowing that I would find it … one way or another.

***

"Cathy …" a familiar voice yelled through the bedroom door, between pounding blasts. Faint streams of pale yellow sunlight filled the room. "Cathy, are you in there?"

It was my friend, Crystal. She was crazy, funny, and had been my best friend since grade school. And her long dark hair that flowed past her shoulders and pale white skin with deep green eyes added to her mystique. No one dared to mess with her.

"She's a witch!" one guy told everyone after their first date together. Later, Crystal told me that he had gotten fresh with her and she decked him.

Just sour grapes, I thought to myself, but I always knew that there was something different about her. That was one of the things I liked about Crystal; she was different.

Crystal called herself a psychic, using crystals and Tarot cards to give readings and tell the fortunes of people, but she could also read people. She knew what kind of person someone was and what they were up to within a few minutes of their first meeting. In fact, she tried to warn me about Roy years ago, but, being in love, I had ignored her warnings.

"Cathy! Don't you dare try to shut me out!" Crystal yelled through the door. "I know you're in there! And if you don't answer this door, I'm busting it down!"

"Crystal," I choked out. Every bone and muscle in my body ached.

"Cathy?" she yelled. My voice must have sounded off, because she practically screamed it through the door. "Don't worry about Roy! He's gone to work or wherever he goes, now open this door!"

"Crystal, I'm coming …" I croaked, trying to sit up, but my sides ached. I wondered if he had broken some of my ribs this time.

"Cathy, stay right there," Crystal replied, panicked. "I'm coming in."

"Crystal, don't break down the door. I'm coming," I replied, trying to rise from the bed, but fell back onto it just as quickly.

A moment later, the door opened slowly with a long creak. When I looked over, Crystal's hand was raised and pointed at the door.

"What the hell?" I asked, noticing that she hadn't even touched the door.

"A little trick I learned," Crystal replied with a smirk, then she saw my bruised face. "That son of a bitch! Did he do this to you?"

Immediately, I turned away, trying to hide my face.

Crystal grabbed my chin firmly in her hand and turned it from side to side. "That's it! He's going down!"

"Crystal, you can't kill him! I'll call the police …"

"Yeah, right!" Crystal said, sitting down hard onto the edge of the bed, jostling me.

"Ooowwww," I said, pulling my face out of her hand. "What the hell?"

"Yeah, what the hell is right!" she replied, leaning back against the foot of my bed, taking a closer look at my face. "Cathy, you won't call the police! You've had so many opportunities to call and you never do!" Crystal thought for a moment, then got up and grabbed a black suitcase from the closet and threw it onto the floor, then pulled clothes from the closet and threw them into it at super human speed.

"Crystal, no!" I yelled, forcing myself off the bed. "I can't leave him! He'll track me down and kill me next time!"

Crystal wheeled on me abruptly. "Listen to yourself, Cathy! But you know what? You're right! That son of a bitch *will* kill you next time!" She turned to throw another outfit into the suitcase, then another one onto the bed. "Here! Get dressed. You're coming with me."

"Crystal, he'll kill you, too!" I said, panicked, stumbling out of bed. "I can't go with you!"

Crystal stepped back to look directly into my eyes. Her bright green eyes flared. "Just answer me something, Cathy! Do you want to spend the rest of your life with this guy? Because believe me, it'll be a short life."

"I have no other choice …" I said, gingerly pulling my jeans over my curved legs and hips. Even that slight movement hurt.

Crystal suddenly grabbed my hands and looked directly into my eyes. "Yes, you have a choice. You always have a choice."

My eyebrows pulled together, puzzled. "What are you saying?"

Suddenly, Crystal threw a shirt at me. "Here, put this on! You're coming with me."

I grabbed her arm as she passed, then asked, "What are you going to do, Crystal?"

"Look, it's better if you don't know …"

"Crystal," I said weakly, stopping her with just a hand on her arm. "What are you planning to do?"

"Not me, you." I knew from the look in her eyes that she was dead serious.

"Crystal, no!" I said, trying to stop her long enough to get her attention. "I'm not strong enough!"

"Look," Crystal began, "Do you want to be rid of this guy?"

Slowly, I closed my eyes and nodded my head. "Yes."

"No matter the price?" Crystal asked, looking into my eyes.

"What are you talking about?" I demanded as I slowly slipped into my sandals lying nearby.

Crystal took a step closer. "Oh, I think you do, Cathy." She thought for a moment, obviously wondering how much to tell me, then added, "Did you say a prayer last night?"

"What does that have to do with anything?" I asked, fearing where this was leading.

"Just answer the question, Cathy!" Crystal screamed, taking my hands into hers as she looked into my eyes. "Did you say a prayer asking for help last night? For deliverance from evil?"

"How did you know …" I staggered back, shocked.

"That's what I thought," Crystal replied, then added. "Cathy, did He deliver you from evil?"

I took a deep breath, letting it fill my lungs. "No."

"That's what I thought," Crystal said with a smirk. "You know, if I were you, I would want that son of a bitch out of my life no matter what. Do you?"

I plopped down onto a nearby chair, defeated. "How did you get so strong, Crystal? I just wish I was half as strong as you."

Crystal grinned, incredulous, then grabbed my suitcase off the floor, zipped it up, and propped it against the wall. "You are, Cathy. You just need a little help getting there."

I slowly walked over to her, my eyebrows pulling together. "What kind of help, Crystal?"

"Well, you asked God for help, and He didn't come, so why not ask Satan?" Crystal asked, raising an eyebrow over her flaring green eyes.

"Crystal, don't say that …"

"Why not?" she asked, looking into my eyes. "If it were me, I would want Roy out at all costs … including asking for the devil's help."

"No, it's sacrilegious, Crystal!" I wheeled on her, not wanting to hear any of it. "How can you even say this?"

Crystal shrugged. "It's up to you."

"Okay, okay," I said, taking a moment to collect my thoughts. I looked in the mirror and my long blonde hair was matted, my lip was swollen on one side and a blue bruise was forming around one eye. At that moment, I knew that I couldn't let this happen again. "What do I do?" I asked, turning to face Crystal, not fully realizing the severity of what I was about to do.

"Say a prayer to him, to Satan, asking for his help," Crystal said, her green eyes flaring.

I laughed without humor. "You're serious?"

"Very, but it's up to you," Crystal said, then added, "free will and all."

"Of course," I laughed not taking her seriously, but something told me that she was. "Okay, Satan, please help me."

A smirk appeared on Crystal's face as she waited.

Immediately, I felt something leave my soul, a power, a presence that I had never known I had as my heart sank, turning to ice. "What did you just do to me?"

"I didn't do anything," Crystal corrected. "You did, but you're going to be able to take care of that creep now."

And I knew that she was right. "But how?" I asked, incredulous. "I feel weaker, not stronger."

"No, you feel different," Crystal corrected, then added, picking up the suitcase, "but soon, you'll feel stronger. And right now, you're coming with me."

I nodded, still confused, but followed Crystal as she picked up my suitcase and headed out the door, and I vowed never to come back to this trailer of horrors again. Crystal helped me out to her old Impala and into the passenger seat, then popped the trunk and plopped my suitcase inside.

Crystal slid into the driver's seat and I leaned back against the head rest and closed my eyes. How could I have let this happen? How could it have come down to this? But I didn't have control. Roy had taken that away from me long ago.

"You ready?" Crystal asked, clicking her seatbelt over her chest.

"Ready," I nodded, closing my eyes. I had no idea what was coming or what I was ready for, but Crystal was right. Something had to be done about Roy.

She turned the key and the engine roared to life, reflecting the storm that was brewing inside my soul. As I watched the scenery pass by, I knew that my life had changed forever and would never be the same.

I didn't really pay attention to where Crystal was taking me. At the moment, I didn't care. When the car pulled abruptly to a stop, I looked around and we were in the safety of the woods.

"Where are we?" I asked, looking over at Crystal.

One corner of her lips curled into a smile. "You'll see."

"Crystal," I said, catching her arm. "You know I love you like a sister and I trust you, but what are you into?"

"Oh, I think you already know," Crystal said with a smile. "You've known for a long time."

"Why are you doing this?" I asked, searching her eyes.

Crystal took a breath and looked out the car window, then turned to face me again. "Cathy, you're like a sister to me, too. And sisters protect each other."

I nodded, understanding.

"Here's to the sisterhood," Crystal said, smirking, raising an imaginary glass to me.

"To the sisterhood," I agreed, taking her hand without smiling, knowing that wherever this led, I would see it through … for her, if not for me.

Crystal smiled as her emerald eyes danced, and then she got out of the car and closed the door behind. As I slid out of the car, I felt every ache, bruise, and slash that Roy inflicted upon my frail body. I needed to rest, to let it all sink in.

"Why are we here?" I asked, looking around. We were standing in a clearing and the car was parked on the edge of it. In the center was a fire pit that looked like had been used recently.

"You'll see," Crystal replied as a half smile lit her lips.

I slid to a soft patch of green grass and leaned against a tree.

"Just rest while I prepare," Crystal replied, clearly enjoying herself.

"Prepare for what?" I asked, watching as she threw logs into the fire pit.

"Oh, you'll see," she replied with a smirk, then began chanting, *"Premedora, um stat, al logue rogue, bauche rae bom fa lor. Premedors, um stat, al logue, bauche rae bom fa lor,"* repeating it over and again.

"Crystal, you're scaring me …"

"Shush, you're interrupting the ceremony."

"What ceremony?" I asked, trying to get to my feet.

"You want strength, right? Enough to overpower your enemies?" Crystal asked, looking directly at me as her eyes flared.

"Yes, but ..."

"Then, shush," Crystal replied, as the half smile returned. "You're going to get it for you."

"Premedors, um stat, al logue ..." Crystal resumed chanting, throwing more logs into the circle until there was a huge mound, then she removed a lighter from her pocket and threw it onto the pyre.

Instantly, fire sprang to life, licking eagerly at the logs, devouring them. A blazing bonfire rose to the heavens within minutes ... but it wasn't the heavens that we were invoking.

"Come." Crystal took my hand, helping me to my feet and led me to stand near the fire. "Kneel before the fire, and ask him for your heart's desire, the power to overcome your enemies."

"Okay, Crystal, this has gone far enough ..."

"No, it hasn't," she repeated, taking my hand. Instantly, I felt power radiate from her, and an electric current passed between us, from her into me. "Just ask. I don't want to lose you ... not like this."

I nodded, finding sudden strength within her touch. "To the sisterhood, right?" I asked, looking into her eyes with a weak smile.

Crystal nodded, smiling. "To the sisterhood."

"Premedora, um stat, al logue rogue, bauche rae bom fa lor ..." Crystal resumed chanting, as I fell to my knees.

"Please, give me power over my enemies," I asked into the fire, knowing what I was doing, and that I would pay for this with my soul. "Satan, please give me power over my enemies," I repeated over and again.

Crystal chanted as I prayed Satan's prayer for what seemed like hours, until shoots of pink, red, and purple gently brushed the night sky. Soon, the darkness of night overtook the day.

Crystal fell into a deep sleep, but I continued praying to Satan knowing what I was doing, knowing that there would quite literally be Hell to pay, but I would pay it later. Crystal was right about one thing: Roy had to be stopped and I was going to do it … someway, somehow.

I was growing sleepy when suddenly the fire flared, reaching toward me, growing suddenly hotter. I was tempted to stop, but knew that I had already come too far to stop now. The fire instantly grew to double its height, taller than a man, as shoots of red, yellow, and orange rolled outward, surrounding us, but I found renewed strength and my prayers never ceased.

For a moment, I wondered if I should wake Crystal and get out of there, for fear that the fire was growing out of control, when something stopped me. Fear maybe? Curiosity? An unseen force? I felt myself suddenly fading into another state of consciousness, when a dark figure stepped from the fire. For a moment, I thought I was dreaming, until it stepped closer to me.

She was a woman, beautiful and tall, with coal black hair that hung to her waist and onyx eyes that bore into my soul. She wore black jeans that showed every curve of her voluptuous body, quite modern, and a sleeveless shimmering black blouse that hung loosely at the neckline, revealing just enough of her perfect breasts. She appeared to be in her early twenties and was the most stunning woman that I had ever seen.

"How did you step from …"

"Shush …" the mysterious woman answered in a sultry voice. Then, she took me by the hand and helped me to my feet. The pain that had permeated my body was immediately gone, replaced with beauty and sudden strength.

"Who are you?" I asked, my eyes filling with wonder.

"Oh, I think you know," she purred as one side of her lips curled into a smile. "But the question here is: what do you want?"

My eyebrows pulled together, bewildered.

"Power over your enemies?" she reminded me with a smirk, slowly walking around me, looking me up and down, taking me in. "That is what you asked for, right?"

I nodded. "You're Satan."

Her sultry lips curled into a smile. "In the flesh, so to speak."

"But I always thought that you were a man ..."

She laughed, the sound of wind chimes. "I can appear in any form I choose, male or female, human or animal," she answered, taking a deep breath. "You made a vow to The Sisterhood, am I correct?"

"How did you know ..."

"Well," she said, her voice lowering as she stepped closer to look directly into my eyes. "Just consider me another sister."

I nodded, unsure of what to say.

"Let's see," she said, walking around me, looking me up and down, pretending to think. "You asked for enough power to defeat Roy, correct?"

"How did you know?" I asked, bewildered.

"Oh, I've known Roy for a long time," she said, then ran a sultry hand down my arm. "Do you remember the nights he came home, smelling of ladies' perfume?"

I nodded, horrified.

"Well," she said, leaning in close. "Take a whiff."

Involuntarily, I inhaled her scent and it was the same unmistakable scent that I had smelled on Roy.

She laughed at the expression upon my face. "Roy's been in bed with me, so to speak," she paused for effect, then added, "he's been mine for a long time." Then, she looked directly into my eyes again. "Welcome to the party." She circled me and lifted a strand of my long blonde hair to her nostrils, inhaling deeply.

"Okay, I've had enough ..."

She placed a hand on either side of my face and looked directly into my eyes. They were the most beautiful onyx eyes that I'd ever seen, but they were cold and dead, despite their beauty. "Or have you?" Dominance radiated from her as she looked directly into my eyes, filling my soul with more strength than I had ever felt before. In that moment, her soul touched mine, infusing me with power. Under her amazing power, I surrendered. She pulled back to look directly into my eyes and gently stroked my hair. "Are you ready?" she asked, smiling.

"For what?" I asked, having never felt so much power before in my life.

"For the ability to defeat your enemies, of course," she said, smirking, cocky, already knowing the answer would give as she patiently looked at her bright red fingernails. Then, she looked directly into my eyes again. "Do you want my help?"

"No," I said, backing away as she laughed. I ran to Crystal, trying to wake her, but she wouldn't budge. "What did you do to her?" I demanded, turning back to Satan.

"Yeah, about that," the beautiful woman casually replied, taking a step toward me, then lowered her voice for effect, "I couldn't have her interrupting us if she woke."

"Is she dead?" I asked, horrified.

The lovely woman laughed, sinister. "No, my dear Catherine ... or do you prefer Cathy? Anyway, remind me later to thank her."

I nodded, unable to believe what I was hearing. Maybe Crystal had pulled a prank on me, or maybe this was just a dream.

"Do you really think that this is a dream?" she asked, quite literally reading my mind. "Do you think that Crystal could pull off a hoax this elaborate?"

"How do you know what I'm thinking?" I asked, backing away from her, headed toward the car.

"How do you think?" she countered, quickly catching my arm to lead me back to the fire. Suddenly, all fear left me, replaced by a cold, sinister feeling. Then, she brushed a strand of my blonde hair away from my face to look into my eyes. "I'm Satan, Lucifer, Lucinda … any name you choose; I go by many. Now, do you want my help or not?"

At that moment, I knew that I had a choice … free will, and all. Even Satan could not take away my free will. That moment was the turning point. I knew that I could just walk away and it would be over, but the thought of going back to Roy was scarier than literally facing Satan. "Yes," I nodded. "I don't want to live this way anymore. I want to be free of Roy."

She threw back her head and laughed, a sinister chortle, then looked deeply into my eyes again. "You know, I could take care of him for you. In fact, he chose the path to me long ago. It's just a matter of time before I bring him home to be with me, anyway. But it would be much more fun to let you do it … to let you take care of him." Then, before I could stop her, she placed her hand on my heart and filled it with terror and passion, the most dangerous combination I'd ever felt before.

"Yes, I want your help," I replied, enjoying the dangerous exchange in spite of myself.

"Then, what say you, Catherine?" she asked, looking into my eyes. "Do you want power? Enough to defeat your enemies?" Her lips curled into a lovely smile. "Will you let me join The Sisterhood?"

"So, that's why you chose this form," I said, indicating her female form.

She laughed, dark and sinister, leaning in for effect, lowering her voice, "It was just a formality."

I knew that I was playing with fire, but I was already in too deep. "Yes, I nodded. I want to take him down."

"Then kneel before me and swear your allegiance to me," Satan instructed, taking my hand in hers. Despite her gentleness now, I was well aware that she could be just as ruthless. But I couldn't stop myself.

I fell to my knees, swearing my allegiance to her, to Satan, before I had time to think about the consequences, before the thought of Heaven and Hell could wrestle with each other within my mind. Then, she placed the palm of her hands onto my head.

My body quivered and shook, changing. A power like no other I had felt before filled my soul and my body, but also there was something else that I couldn't explain. My body and soul quivered, shaking, but I kept steady, until Satan removed her hands. Then, she reached out to help me to my feet.

"Feel better, my dear?" she asked with a smirk, looking into my eyes. I nodded and she added, "You know, it comes with a price. I rarely give away gifts such as these for free."

"I kind of figured that," I replied, feeling stronger than ever before. "So, what's your price?"

Satan laughed. "Don't worry. I'll collect at a later time." She held me at arm's length, letting her eyes trail up and down my body. "Yes, you will serve me well." Then, she leaned over, placed her cheek to mine and gave me an air kiss, as women do. When she pulled back, she said, "Well, I must go. Be careful with your power and who you unleash it upon."

I laughed, knowing that now I had enough strength to finally leave Roy. At that moment, I swore that I'd never let any man do to me what Roy had done to me for years. A moment later, Satan walked into the flames, letting them engulf her, as she smiled.

As I watched her go, I felt different somehow. I looked down at my hands and they were sleek, the skin was smooth … beautiful. I felt my hair and it was thicker, more lustrous than ever before. I felt beautiful and powerful, a force to be reckoned with. The pain that Roy had inflicted upon my body was gone, but I knew that there would be a price to pay for this power and beauty. One day, Satan would come to collect, but in what form and at what price? I didn't know.

"Crystal," I bent down and shook my best friend's shoulder. "Crystal, let's go." I looked around and the flames of the bonfire were already dying, but I snuffed the rest out anyway, so as not to set the forest on fire. "Crystal, it's over. Let's go."

For a moment, my heart sank as I feared that the price I'd just paid was my best friend's life, but a moment later, she stirred, then slowly opened her eyes.

"Crystal? Are you okay?" I asked, fishing around in her pockets for the car keys.

"Cathy?" Crystal asked, looking deeply into my eyes. From the look in her eyes, I knew I must have looked just as different as I felt. "Is that you?"

"Yeah, it's me," I replied, helping her to her feet. "Let's go."

Crystal weaved a bit on her feet, feeling groggy. "Was Satan here? Did it work?"

"Oh, yeah," I answered, then added, holding her up under one arm, something I'd never been able to do before. "*She* appeared."

"What?" Crystal asked, confused.

"I'll tell you about it on the way," I said, pulling her toward the car.

She nodded, then let me help her to the car. "I feel like I've been drugged," Crystal replied, as I helped her into the passenger seat.

"No, I think it was something much worse than that," I replied, starting her car. "I'll drive you home."

"Boy, the roles have been reversed a bit here," Crystal replied, letting her head lean against the headrest. Her head lulled over and she looked into my eyes. "You really have changed. You're more beautiful than before, stronger, but there's something else, too." Then, her eyebrows pulled together, concerned as she looked into my eyes. "What did she do to you?"

"Oh, I think you already know," I replied, as my eyes flared, using the same words Satan had used on me.

"What have I done?" Crystal asked, her eyes wide as sudden fear permeated her voice.

"Nothing," I replied, surprised at her sudden change of heart. "By the way, she said that she wanted to thank you for bringing me to her."

"Oh, my God, Cathy!" Crystal yelled, shocked.

"No, not God, Crystal," I said. As I pulled onto the street headed toward her house, I reminded her, "I'm still the same person; that will never change."

"Oh, I think a lot more has changed than you realize …"

"I feel good, Crystal," I replied, pulling into the driveway beside her two-story house. "What? Have you changed you mind?"

"I … I …"

I laughed. "It's too late for that, but don't worry," I replied as I turned off the engine. "I'll never turn on you. We're part of The Sisterhood, remember?"

Crystal smiled weakly, then repeated, "The Sisterhood."

"But I have to tell you something," I said, not knowing what her reaction would be. "Satan is now part of The Sisterhood, too."

She stared at me for a moment, knowing that a true organization had been formed … and it was far from holy. As the old saying goes, be careful what you wish for. Then, she slowly nodded, understanding the enormity of what she had done. After it sank in, her eyebrows pulled together, concerned. "Just be careful, Cathy."

"*We* must be careful," I corrected. "The Sisterhood has begun and is more powerful than you can imagine."

She nodded as tears sprang to her eyes.

Shaking my head at her expression, I laughed. "I'm fine, Crystal! In fact, I've never felt better. Thank you!" I said, trying to lighten the mood. I would think about the consequences later. Then, I handed her the car keys, got out of the car, shut the door, and leaned in through the window.

"What have I done to you, Cathy?" Crystal asked, bewildered.

"What needed to be done," I replied, patting her hand, then added, "It was my choice, Crystal. Free will, remember?"

Before she could answer, I turned on my heels and ran into the woods, stronger and faster than ever before. Then, I poured on the speed, testing it out, darting quickly between the trees until they became a blur. The wind blew my hair behind me as I flew through the forest.

Then I remembered Roy.

I knew that if I didn't tell him to leave me alone forever, he would go after Crystal and someone would die. I didn't want it to be her.

As I ran, the dim light of the moon appeared in the sky, promising to make its appearance upon the night. Suddenly I felt different, but not in a way that I could explain as sweat beaded upon my forehead and arms. Through the woods, I neared the trailer park where I knew Roy would be waiting. I slowed, then stepped from the safety of the woods and walked purposefully toward the trailer. Suddenly, something grabbed my arm and swung me around.

"Where have you been?" Roy demanded, his eyes flaring as his teeth ground together, seething, looking into my eyes.

My eyes suddenly flared red.

"What the hell?" he asked, dropping my arm, staggering backward.

"Yes, Hell is right," I calmly replied, as one side of my lips curled into a smile. I took him in, looking him up and down, wondering how I could ever have been afraid of him and how I could have wasted my life on him.

Roy quickly recovered himself, grabbed my hand, and dragged me into the woods. But this time, I didn't scream for help; I didn't resist. After all, I needed a bit of privacy.

In the safety of the woods, I let him wheel me around to look into my eyes. "I said, where have you been?" Then, he slapped me hard across the face, but this time, I didn't budge. I enjoyed watching the horror fill his eyes. Yes, I knew I would enjoy this very much.

"I've been with Crystal," I replied, smiling a half smile, contemplating how much pain I would inflict upon him. When I looked up, the moon was almost full.

"The witch?" Roy asked, looking into my eyes with fury. "Didn't I tell you never to see her again?"

I casually flung my long blonde hair over my shoulder. "She's my best friend, Roy." I took a step closer for emphasis, looking directly into his eyes. "And you don't get to tell me what to do anymore."

"Since when did you grow a set of balls?" Roy asked, incredulous, looking me up and down.

"Since I met the devil in the flesh," I answered with a smile, then stroked the side of his hair. "And guess what?" I asked as I leaned closer to whisper into his ear. "She's a bitch."

"She?" he asked as horror filled his eyes.

"Yeah," I said, taking a breath, favoring the moment. "Remember the hot brunette that you've been having a fling with?"

"How did you know about that?" he asked, taking a step back.

"Well, she's not who you think," I said, as my lips curled into a sinister smile. "You've been screwing with the devil … literally. In fact, you have been for a long time … in more ways than one."

"You bitch!" Roy suddenly wheeled around and punched me in the stomach, but it didn't move me. I enjoyed the look in his eyes as he shook his hand from the blow. All of a sudden, the bright light of the moon illuminated the woods, allowing me to see Roy with extreme clarity. Yes, I was going to enjoy this very much.

Suddenly, I wretched in pain as my body shook and contorted, bending over from the pain, bringing me to my knees. *What the hell?* I asked, but then realized that was exactly what it was—this power was from Hell.

"What's this?" Roy asked, clearly enjoying my pain, standing over me with a smirk. "A delayed reaction?" He walked closer to me, knowing that he had me, when suddenly my muscles contorted in pain and terror filled my heart. "And don't ever think of asking me for a divorce, Cathy, because I'll never give it to you." Then, he leaned in to whisper in my ear, "I'd rather see you dead."

In the bright moonlight, I looked up past the trees into the sky ... and the moon hanging overhead was full. My body contorted and wretched again, changing and morphing. I looked down in horror and my hands were now covered in black fur. "What the hell?" I asked, almost to myself.

"What the hell is right," Roy replied, taking another step closer.

I was suddenly on my hands and knees, wrenching, feeling my body contort. Black fur suddenly grew from my body, and fangs grew from between my teeth stretching to my chin. I could no longer cry out in a human voice as a guttural growl erupted from my chest through my lips, and my legs contorted into animalistic shapes, like that of a wolf, but I stood upright. I still had human hands, but they were now covered in thick, black fur. As I crouched in the dark shadows contorting, Roy hadn't noticed.

"I came home tonight and saw that a lot of your clothes were gone," Roy yelled, unable to see the metamorphosis now consuming my body. "I'll never let you go, bitch, so don't ever try to leave me again!" Then, he kicked me in my side, but I quickly moved out of the way, faster than the eye could see.

I stood from my crouching position on two legs. Black fur covered my entire body, including my human hands, and a guttural growl erupted from my chest as I took a step toward him.

Roy suddenly fell backward, his eyes wide, unable to believe what he was seeing. "What the hell?" he asked as I took another purposeful step toward him.

As I looked into his eyes, I wondered what was happening to me. What was I becoming? But then I remembered, having heard the stories from the town.

The Ute, local American Indians, called the creatures the wahyapatwin (wa-hy-ya-PAT-win), or wolf man … The Children of the Moon … a werewolf. The stories said that the wahyapatwin attacked the local townspeople, tearing apart their bodies, and leaving no survivors. Now, I was one of them. Suddenly, I knew that if I didn't kill him now, he would become like me with just one bite.

No! What have I done? I cried out within my mind, but what Roy heard was a long eerie howl. I turned my blood-red eyes to look at him, as saliva dripped from the primitive fangs protruding past my chin. I took another purposeful step toward him, knowing what I had to do, seething for the kill.

"No! I don't believe it! What happened to you?" Roy asked, wide eyed as he backed away, then fell to the ground on his back, scooting along the ground away from me, but he never took his eyes from mine.

A guttural, animalistic growl erupted from within my chest.

"No! No, don't!" Roy screamed as I stepped closer, so close that saliva dripped from my primitive fangs onto his white T-shirt as I stood over his body.

Yes, I was going to enjoy this very much, I thought, seeing the terror in his eyes, savoring the moment, remembering the terror that he had inflicted upon me. I grabbed his shoulder with tremendous strength and dragged him farther into the woods so that no one could hear his screams. Within the safety of the woods, I ripped his limbs from his body and tore his heart from his chest, taking my time, enjoying his screams under the light of the full moon.

**

That was five years ago and to this day, no one has ever found his body. After a while, they declared him a missing person. Most people thought that he just ran off, but I assure you, his body will never be found. I got my man, but at what price? For with every full moon, I have to lock myself behind closed doors for fear of terrorizing and murdering the town and everyone in it. But I've kept my word to myself: no man had ever been able to do to me what Roy had done. I've also remained young and more beautiful than ever before, despite my impending age.

Crystal and I still have the bond of The Sisterhood, of which Satan is still a part, but one day Satan will come for us both. Satan had cursed me, but in her eyes, she had done me a favor. One day she—or he—will come to collect, but who would deliver us from evil on that day … when it comes?

One Night to Live
By: Dana Piazzi

Vampires can't go into the sun. They have no souls, possessed by a demon, no longer the human that they once were. Crosses and garlic are sure to keep them away. They can be hurt or killed by holy water, daylight, a stake to the heart, beheading, and fire. Well, who wouldn't be hurt with a wooden shard driven into their chest? All these preconceived notions of vampires are ridiculous anyway.

Rumors are spread and lies are told to fool the human population so that they never know when they actually see one. In reality, they would be clueless that they were talking to a vampire until it was too late.

I know, you're probably wondering why I think I know different. I wish I didn't know, but unfortunately I do. I am a vampire. Well, almost. I was born to my vampire mother and vampire father. Born, not made. We live normal lives, go to school, play with friends, and grow just like a normal human being. At the end of our eighteenth year, we become vampires. At that time, our bodies are fully grown and our minds are mature so nature takes its course and we begin to feel the bloodlust. Our lives change. I can't say I am happy for it.

Contrary to the rumors, I'll still be able to walk in the sun, I won't burn and I definitely won't sparkle, but I will feel blood lust that will change every fiber of my being. I won't care about school work. I will have to say goodbye to my friends. It wouldn't be quite the same, if I bit them all. As far as I know they wouldn't like that, and so I will be on my own. Eventually I will get situated and lead a normal life … well … as normal as a vampire can live. I shouldn't complain. I am happy now. The quarterback on my college team just asked me out. I was headed for a 4.0 GPA, and I had a solid group of girlfriends. But in two days, it would all be over.

***

Casey

The alarm woke me. Today was Friday and my last day as a human. Tomorrow I would turn 19 years old. College student Casey would cease to exist. It was all I could think about. Stretching and letting out a big yawn, I got out of bed. It would be silly to waste my day there. I had so much more that I wanted to do, and none of it involved being in bed. Unless … nah! When Trent asked me out Wednesday it was the first time that anyone had asked me out on a date. For some reason, no one had ever shown interest in me before, or maybe I hadn't been putting out the right vibes to let everyone know that I was available. Either way, I would be completely innocent going into the change.

"Good morning!" my roommate, Angie, said as she started the coffee maker.

"Morning," I responded, dully.

"Why are you so down?"

I couldn't tell her the truth. At this point I wasn't sure if I was going to just go missing or leave a note to say goodbye. Angie would either be worried about my disappearance or angry at me for leaving. Even though I wouldn't be there to face her anger, I hated the thought that she would be upset. I was leaning toward taking the coward's way out. Then, she would be worried. I didn't like that either.

"Hello?" she waved her hand in front of my face, oblivious to my internal debate.

"Sorry," I said, forcing a smile. "I was just thinking about my birthday."

"That should make you happy, lady. I mean it's not like you're turning thirty or anything. You're another year closer to the legal drinking age and Trent just asked you out. I'm jealous!" she said, laughing.

"Yeah. You're right," I replied without much enthusiasm.

"So, what are your plans?" she prodded.

"I have to spend tomorrow with my family," I groaned.

"You don't sound very excited about it," she observed, pouring two cups of coffee.

"I'm really not, but it's unavoidable," I said as she set one of the cups on the table in front of me.

"You never even talk about your family. Is everything okay?" she asked, sliding in the chair across from me.

"Thanks for asking, but I really don't want to talk about them," I said, taking a sip of my coffee.

"Alright, I won't be pushy," she backed down, then changed the subject. "What are you doing today?"

"I don't really have any plans. I have a paper to finish for Sociology." I rolled my eyes internally at my answer. The paper wasn't due for another week, not to mention that I would no longer be there to submit it. There just wasn't anything else for me to do.

"I'm in your class, Casey! I know that paper isn't due yet, so tonight we are going to party!" She jumped off the kitchen chair and started dancing around.

"I'm not sure that's a good idea …"

"Of course it is," she interrupted. "You've never gone to any of the parties that I invited you to, so tonight you're going. We're going to celebrate your birthday a day early."

She was right. I hadn't gone to any of the parties in the past. I was never interested in drinking myself into oblivion and possibly ending up in a stranger's bed. It was never my style. Anyway, I was a total lightweight. I wanted to tell her that I couldn't go tonight. Though, at the moment, a drink to help me forget tomorrow's problems sounded like a perfectly acceptable solution.

"Alright, I'll go to the party," I agreed, smiling. She grabbed my hands and pulled me out of the chair and we engaged in some crazy random dancing.

***

After spending the day getting pampered at the spa, I stood in front of the mirror making sure that I looked presentable. My long brown hair had gotten a trim and some blonde highlights. I had minimal make up on, just a little mascara to emphasize my eyelashes—as a result, my blue eyes looked electric—and a touch of red on my lips. My tight black jeans hugged my curves just right and a silver sparkly tank accentuated my other assets. I was happy with my appearance.

The party was being held at the Kappa Delta house, which was one of the largest frat houses on campus. I usually kept to myself because of my secret, but I actually knew one member there, Trent Walker. He was like a rock star on campus. As far as I knew, he didn't actually play a musical instrument, but it didn't make him any less popular. Girls flocked around him in droves. I couldn't even guess why he would ask me out. I hadn't known what to say when he did. I ended up telling him that I would let him know later. I didn't want to like him if I was just going to leave him. Now, I wondered if I should have lived as much as I could while I still had the chance.

It was weird walking into my first ever college party. Someone had an I-pod hooked into a state of the art speaker system. I'd bet watching movies here was fun. Loud dance music filled the room. There was a small bar in the corner. One of the frat guys was standing behind it pouring drinks for people. I wouldn't want to be stuck with that job. There were people dancing on one side of the room and the rest of the main level was filled with people in deep conversation, or passionate embraces.

"All right, chickie! Time to party!" Angie called over the music. "We're going to knock them dead."

I looked over at my friend and she was wearing tight leather pants that reminded me of Sandy's in *Grease*. She also wore a black tank covered by a low-cut, sheer red shirt. She was definitely showing off her assets. She was a knock out.

Angie and I headed straight toward the frat brother running the bar. "Two beers," she requested.

"Are you ladies twenty-one?" he asked with a smile. They didn't really card at this kind of thing, so I took his words as a sort of flirtation.

So did Angie. She leaned toward him, giving him a good look at her cleavage, pushed up by her Wonder Bra. "We're not," she whispered seductively, "but she turns nineteen tomorrow. Do you think you can help out a couple of girls?"

He stared at her chest and licked his lip. When he raised his eyes up, he gave us a wicked look. "Nineteen, huh? That calls for more than just a beer." He pulled out a bottle of Jose Cuervo. After pouring two shots for us and another for himself, he sprinkled some salt on his hand. Never having done a shot of tequila before, I followed suit.

I licked the salt off and made a face. I wasn't a big fan of doing shots so far. I quickly slung it back. As the liquid burned down my throat, I thought that maybe I would never do another shot again. I closed my eyes as an involuntary shudder went through my body. When I opened them again, the bartender held a lime wedge in his mouth. I reached for it and he pulled back.

"Get it with your mouth," Angie encouraged me.

I leaned in and took the wedge from him with my own lips. As our two lips met for just a moment, I reconsidered. Shots weren't so bad after all. I pulled back with the lime in my mouth and then bit into the juicy fruit to rid my mouth of the tequila flavor. He handed me a beer and then gave one to Angie.

"What's your name?" Angie asked flirtatiously.

"My name is John. Do I get the pleasure of knowing the name of the two beautiful woman asking me?" he asked, flirting with my friend.

Angie blushed. "I guess so," she said, batting her eyelashes. "My name is Angie, and I happen to be very single right now. Meet up with me after you finish bar duty?"

"I will definitely do that," he replied, giving her a sultry glance. Then, she pulled me away before I could tell him my name. I didn't think it really mattered, though. He only had eyes for her tonight.

We danced a little, mostly with each other, but then John showed up and swept Angie away. I stood to the side after that and finished my third beer. I was definitely feeling buzzed, but not enough to carry on random conversations with the strangers in the room. I was just about to leave when a hand landed softly on my shoulder. I spun around to find Trent behind me.

I gave him a once over and admired his medium-length, brown hair. It always looked like he rolled out of bed, but in a good way. He wore a tight black T-shirt that showed off the muscles he got from playing football. Quarterbacks weren't always big, but he definitely worked out. I was sure that if I touched his stomach, I would feel the ripples of a six pack.

"I didn't think you were coming," he said to me, his blue eyes sparkling.

"I changed my mind," I said, smiling. "Thought I would check out how the normal college student lives."

"How do you like it so far?" he asked.

I put my finger on my chin, and pretended to think about it. "Well, tequila tastes gross, but feels good, and three beers is definitely too many for me," I said, smiling.

"Oh yeah?" He took my empty cup and threw it away. Then, his arms wrapped around my waist. "Have you thought about my question?"

"I don't really know you all that well, Trent."

"You know, that's kind of what dating is for," he observed. "People get to learn about each other, then decide whether they want to spend their lives with each other."

"Huh?" This conversation was accelerating a bit too fast for me.

"Sorry, I wasn't trying to go too far too fast," he said, starting to sway slightly to the music. "Listen, I asked you to go out on a date. I wasn't asking you to marry me. I just thought that we could talk."

At that moment, Angie and John came up to us holding more shots. She handed me one and whispered in my ear, "Liquid courage."

"What?" I asked.

"Drink it. Don't ruin your chance with him before you even get to go out. Just enjoy the night."

I nodded, dumbly, taking the shot. Then, they were gone.

Trent held his shot glass up like he was toasting me. "Where's the salt?" I asked.

He chuckled. "This isn't tequila. It's Jaeger. It's not as harsh, I promise."

He downed the drink into his mouth. I copied him and I shuddered at the strong taste, but it definitely wasn't as unpleasant as tequila. We put the glasses on a table and then he grabbed my hand. "Let's dance," he declared.

I smiled at him as he pulled me toward the people dancing with all thoughts of our possible date forgotten. A fast dance song was playing and we danced closely, our hips grinding into each other to the beat. My breath got a little bit shaky and my feelings for this handsome football player grew. When the song ended, he pulled back a little, trying to put out some of the heat between us. Then, a slow song began to play. The bumping and grinding stopped. Hyperaware of him, I nervously put my hands on his shoulders and he wrapped one arm around my waist. We swayed in gentle time to the music.

It might not have been as hot and sexy as before, but I couldn't deny the pleasure I felt being in his arms. I suddenly had a sense of being in the right place just before I had to leave it. I didn't want to miss my last opportunity to experience real life before I changed tomorrow. I took his hand and led him off the dance floor.

"I want to get to know you, Trent. But, we don't have to go on a date for that. Take me to your room," I told him, before the courage I was feeling could desert me.

He yanked me to him and then led me out of the room. We passed John and Angie along the way. "I'm staying here," she said, holding on to John.

I nodded. "That's okay. I have plans for tonight myself." She held up her thumb in approval. I gave her a big smile and headed up the stairs with Trent.

I paid no attention to the dorm room as he led me inside, only that it seemed to be a bedroom within a larger dorm. Before I could look around, he closed the bedroom door and pushed me against it. He paused for one moment, looking into my eyes, and then his lips came crashing into mine. Suddenly, he was everything to me. I had trouble breathing, but I didn't need to breathe. He filled me up with energy and life. His lips parted and his tongue teased my lower lip. I opened my mouth and his tongue slipped in.

All these new experiences in one night were overwhelming. Until now, I had never had an alcoholic beverage and had never kissed anyone, but I had never really wanted to. Now, I wanted so much more. I wanted to crawl into his skin, to be closer to him than I had ever been with anyone else before … closer than I would probably ever be to anyone again.

I entwined my hands in his shaggy layers and tugged on his hair. I pulled back from our kiss, sucking his lower lip into my mouth as I did. He groaned, and I felt a sense of womanly power at bringing this strong person to his knees. I moved my hands from his hair to his abs. Sure enough, the definition of his muscles rippled under my fingertips. I grabbed his shirt and lifted it up over his head as his teeth scraped against my neck.

I knew that I would be doing so much more than that when I became a full-fledged vampire. Suddenly, I almost lost my desire for Trent and would have pulled away completely, when he lowered the straps of my tank. My breasts were a decent size B cup. Some guys would like more, but it could be very convenient sometimes. I didn't have to wear a bra everywhere, and that day I hadn't.

His eyes lit up when he discovered my secret. Then, his mouth was there and I nearly passed out with pleasure. He kissed his way back up to my mouth, and then flipped me over onto the bed. I reached for the buttons on his pants and they popped free. He dug his fingers into my hips, then suddenly pulled away. "No, we can't," he explained.

"Why can't we? We're both single adults. You *are* single, aren't you?" I asked.

"Of course, I'm single. I wouldn't have even kissed you if I wasn't. I don't work that way!" he said hotly.

"Okay, then. What's the problem?" I asked, raising up on my elbows to look into his eyes.

"This isn't how I wanted to get to know you," he explained. "I want to know the real you."

"Wait! Are you gay?" I asked incredulously.

He sprang off the bed, seemingly angry with me. "Trust me, I'm far from gay. If I was, I wouldn't be having this problem right now." I looked where he had indicated the bulge in the front of his jeans and I licked my lips in anticipation.

"Don't do that!" he complained. "I want you so bad right now that I can hardly stand it, but I don't want this to be cheap and meaningless. I want to know what you're really like. You intrigue me. You don't party like a lot of the people on campus, and you don't have a boyfriend, even though you're gorgeous. I see you helping out at the tutoring center and on the hotline, and I just can't help but think that you're a wonderful woman that I want to get to know."

I was surprised by his words. I had no idea that he had been following my life so intently. With very few friends to complicate my situation, you would think that I would notice someone observing me the way that he had.

"You know, you're definitely not like most guys. I haven't dated anyone before, but I've had plenty of offers for meaningless sex … and it's not like I'm not willing with you."

"I'm sure you have," he said, taking a step back, "but I want to show you that I'm not like every other guy at this school. I want us to be so much more than a one night stand."

"Thank you for having so much respect for me and what you think we could be, but I have to be honest. I don't know if I have more than this one night to give you," I informed him. Damn! Why did this have to happen now?

"I don't understand. Are you with someone else?" he asked, stepping closer unconsciously.

"No."

"Are you dying? Suffering from a fatal disease?"

"Not quite," I hedged. Vampirism wasn't a disease. I didn't think so, anyway.

"Are you a top secret government official sent here to keep the calm because the world is ending tomorrow?" he asked as a corner of his lips curled into a smile.

"Seriously?" I asked, completely ignoring the question. As far as I knew, the world would not be ending tomorrow … just my world.

"Are you gay?" he asked.

I laughed at that one. "No."

"Do you have some arranged marriage happening tomorrow?" His guesses were getting closer. I was sure that my parents did have a nice vampire man to introduce me to. We were encouraged to marry within the species. Mating with a normal human and changing that person into one of us was rare. It was possible, but not very likely.

"No," I answered, finally.

"Then there shouldn't be a problem," he insisted.

"Humor me, then. If tonight is all that we have, then let's talk. Let's get to know each other, in case tomorrow doesn't work out for either of us."

"Fine, then let's go out on that date," he beamed.

"It's after midnight. Where are we going to go at this time of night?" I asked.

"Take your pick: Taco Bell, White Castle, or the five-star dining of Denny's." We both burst into laughter at his suggestions.

"Denny's it is!" I decided.

After dressing, I ran my hand through my hair to remove any tangles. "You look great," he told me, kissing me on the cheek. I took his open hand and he led me out of the frat house to his truck. He held my hand for the ten minutes it took to get to the restaurant. Then, he opened the door for me when we got there.

Denny's might not really be five-star dining and really not a place you take a date to, but Trent was making me feel special. I ordered the Grand Slam Breakfast. In a few short hours at dawn, I would be a vampire. During the transition period, vampires didn't crave anything but blood. I wanted one last breakfast while I could still eat regular food.

Once the waitress left, I turned to Trent and asked, "Okay, so what do you want to know about me?"

"I think I'll skip the basics. I want to know your favorite color and your favorite movies, but I want to know more about what makes you … well … you." he said.

"That's a tough question," I said, taking a deep breath and a moment to think. "I don't see myself as a product of anything. I'm a free being making decisions on a moment's notice and making the most out of what life offers me at any given time."

"I don't think so. If you just went with the flow, I would have seen you at more parties and you would have definitely gone off with at least one of those guys offering you a one night stand. In any case, let me break it down further. Tell me about your family," he added.

I put my head into my hands, trying to figure out how much I could tell him. I didn't want to tell him anything, but for this one night, I wanted to be able to be as honest as possible. "My family is very different."

"That's how we all feel," he reasoned.

"Yes, but some are more different than others. They're very close and very controlling," I said. I backed away from the table and stopped talking as the waitress set our sodas on the table.

"Have they hurt you?" he asked after she had walked away.

"No, they're controlling, but not abusive. I grew up very sheltered, knowing very little of the outside world. I was sent to private school from kindergarten through high school. I fought hard to have this year of independence. Tomorrow, they have plans for me that won't include me finishing school or having a boyfriend."

"That sounds a little strange … and mysterious," he said, taking a drink of his soda. "What kind of plans do they have for you? Running the family business?"

"I wish I could tell you, but it's too hard to explain. We have a lot of rituals and traditions, so that's why tonight is all that I have," I explained, sure that I had only confused him more.

"That's not good enough!" His voice began to rise. Thank goodness, the waitress appeared again, this time with our food.

"Thank you," I said, then dug into my pancakes.

We ate in silence for a few minutes. I didn't know what else to say to him, and from the tightness in his jaw, I could only assume that he was thinking about what to say to me. If the world was ideal, I could grab his hand and tell him that I wanted to have a relationship with him. I had only spent a few hours with him, but I could feel that he was someone that I wanted to spend a lot more time with.

Trent finished chewing his bacon and took a sip of his Coke before turning to me. "Listen Casey, I like you. I *really* like you. I know that this is the first time that we've spent any time together and we don't really know each other well, but I feel like I do. I feel a connection with you."

I nodded, hearing him echo my private thoughts. "I wish it was different. The only thing I can do now is to go home and hope that there's some way I can come back. I just can't make any promises."

"I guess that's all that I can ask. I just wish that you didn't have to go home … but I really hope you come back," he said.

"Me, too."

"Are you ready to get out of here?" he asked.

I looked at my half eaten meal, and nodded to him. "Let's go."

Trent quickly paid the bill before taking my hand and leading me to the car. He opened the door for me, and I sat down quickly. Once he joined me in the front seat, he took my hand again and brushed his lips against my knuckles.

"I don't want to let go of you," he informed me. "I need all the time I can get with you. Will you stay with me tonight?"

"I thought you didn't want that from me," I taunted him.

"Very funny! I don't mean I want to *sleep* with you, just stay with me. I want to feel you in my arms all night.

Tomorrow, you'll be gone and I don't know if I'll ever see you again."

My heart broke at the thought of never seeing Trent again. It was on the tip of my tongue to say yes, but I couldn't. It was all so technical and silly, but I was born at seven in the morning. That was my deadline, the end of my eighteenth year. My change into becoming a vampire would literally happen as I turned nineteen. I couldn't risk being in his room at that time.

"I can't stay the night. I'm so sorry." He looked so downcast. "I could come for an hour or so, though."

He looked at me, his eyes smoldering into my soul. "I'll take it," he said.

We drove in silence with a heightened awareness of each other, as a whole lot of sexual tension filled the air. I let out a little sigh, anxious to get back to his fraternity house. It felt like it took a million years.

When we finally reached our destination, we rushed to his room and he swiftly closed the door behind us. The next thing I knew, my back was hitting the wall and his lips were fused to mine once again. His tongue darted across my lips and I opened my mouth as we deepened our kiss. I don't know how long we stood entwined in each other's arms, but finally he pulled away.

"We have to stop," Trent said.

"No," I whimpered.

He kissed my forehead and moved away from me. "I don't want it to be like this. I want you more than you can imagine, but when we're finally together in that way, I want to be able to wake up in the morning with you and know that we can do the same thing the next night."

My heart squeezed in response, hoping that there was some way for his wishes to come true. Maybe I would be an exception to my kind, maybe I wouldn't change tomorrow. Otherwise, this would be the last time that I would see him.

My heart dropped to my feet and my expression matched my feelings.

He grabbed me by the shoulders. "I really care about you, Casey. Come back to me."

I nodded a false promise, and then he led me by the hand to his bed. "Can I hold you for a little bit?" he asked.

"I'd love it," I answered.

He pulled me into his arms and I laid my head on his chest. His hands caressed my arms, and I felt his lips touch my forehead. We lay in silence until his breath evened out and I could tell that he had fallen asleep. I stayed curled in Trent's arms, not wanting to pull away just yet. It just seemed so unfair that I would meet him … just as I had to run away.

I guessed that it didn't matter. Growing up, I was in private schools that catered to my people … vampire people. It just seemed so weird to say sometimes. The whole time that I was in school, I had never met anyone I was interested in having a relationship with. They were all boring, robotic versions of their parents, spouting off their parent's opinions and talking with excitement about their future as vampires, but I couldn't understand their enthusiasm. Where was their adventure, their curiosity? Was I the only one who wished to see what real life was like for other people?

I had just one year to really experience it, to see it through someone else's eyes, and the time went by too fast … within a blink of an eye. That was what it was in terms of how long my life would really last. I felt sorrow for how little that I truly had experienced. All I did was take my classes and keep to myself mostly. All my thoughts had eventually worn me out, and before I knew it, I was asleep too. I was too busy thinking about what I would leave behind to consider why I was leaving things behind in the first place. It was unfortunate for me, unfortunate for Trent … and really, really unfortunate for his roommate.

**

When I opened my eyes, there was a soft light filtering in through the windows. Trent was lightly snoring and I smiled at the sound. Then, my world turned upside down. Pain hit me everywhere. I looked at the clock behind Trent and it read 6:59 am. Panic rose in my chest; I couldn't be here when I changed. My fears and worries were quickly banished when a fiery feeling snaked through my veins like a poisonous drug. My head, chest, and stomach suddenly ached. My hands and my feet burned. I remembered my wish that I would be the exception. It obviously wasn't true. I wanted to jump out of bed and run away. I actually wanted to get to my parents, so that I could be somewhere where people knew what I was going through, but I couldn't. I couldn't move at all. I felt like I was shaking all over. Trent was still sleeping, so I must not have been really shaking. I closed my eyes, as the pain hit a ninety on the pain scale the doctors give you. A tear escaped from my eye and scalded a path down my cheek, and then all at once the pain disappeared.

I sat up and looked around. It was 7:05 am. In just five short minutes my body had shattered into a million pieces and was welded back together by the fires of hell. At least, that's what it felt like. It then occurred to me that I seemed to be hearing things that I didn't hear before. I could hear his roommate moving around outside our door. I could hear people in other rooms getting ready for their day, even a couple giving each other a morning quickie two floors down.

Everything seemed a little brighter. Only a little light filtered in the room through the opaque blinds, but it seemed as if there was full daylight in the room. The last thing that I noticed was a hunger in my belly. Once, when I first started college, I starved myself for two days to get into a really cute dress. Of course, no one noticed me. That was the end of my trying to fit in. The hunger I felt then was sort of how I felt now. only this was ten times worse. I felt like I hadn't eaten in a week.

I got out of bed and did the walk of shame to get to the kitchenette of the dorm room. Lucky for me, the fraternity house rooms were so much better than the regular dorms that I lived in. Each one had two small private bedrooms, a bathroom, a small kitchen, and another tiny area for a couch and television. I just had to walk out of his door to get some nourishment.

I opened the refrigerator, not even considering how rude my actions were, and grabbed an apple. I took a large bite and the mushy fruit made its way down my throat. It tasted good, but it did nothing for me. If anything, I felt hungrier. There were some bagels on the counter. I didn't wait to toast it or for cream cheese, but I ripped into the package and devoured one of them. I expected to feel a little relief. Instead, I wanted to throw up.

Then, the bathroom door opened, Trent's roommate stepped out, and I recognized him. He was the guy manning the bar when we first arrived. "John, right?" I asked.

He looked confused for a moment before recognizing me. "Miss nineteen herself?" he smirked. "Are you looking for Angie? She's still sleeping."

The irony of both of us ending up in the same room occurred to me. I never asked Trent who shared his dorm. Nodding at him, I knew that I had to leave. I opened my mouth to ask him to tell Angie and Trent that I had to leave, but the moment I did I inhaled a deep breath … and realized that I had been monumentally stupid.

I was so hungry and I had tried to eat bagels and apples, when all I really needed lay under the skin of John, Trent, and even Angie. I could feast right now, but this wasn't what I wanted. I crumpled in half with pain and the realization of what I had become. John took a step toward me, and I held my hand out to stop him. Unfortunately, he didn't heed my warning. He took hold of me and lifted me up.

"Are you okay?" he asked.

I couldn't stop it now; I was a slave to my needs. "I'm okay. Sorry for scaring you." I turned to him and made eye contact. If I had stayed at home, I would have been trained on how to do this properly, but now I would have to rely on my instincts. I engaged his mind with mine, hoping that I could do this right.

"I need you to relax, John," I said. Suddenly, his eyes lost focus. "Are you relaxed?" I asked. He merely nodded. "Okay, this won't hurt a bit. Afterwards, you will have no memory of this and no memory of seeing me this morning." He nodded again."Okay, here goes nothing," I said out loud, even though no one was actually listening to me. I leaned forward and sniffed his neck to make sure that I bit into the right vein and not his jugular. Now, my saliva would be able to heal him, but I didn't think I could stop such massive blood flow. When I felt confident, my fangs slid out and I sank them into the tender flesh of his neck.

The moment his blood touched my tongue, I felt relief. I wanted to groan in satisfaction. I could feel a tenuous bond between John and me. I could feel his confusion and also a sense of happiness. He also felt my relief. That could be the reason that he was feeling good. I kept drinking, until a noise sounded behind me. It was the opening of a bedroom door.

"What's going on?" Trent's voice rang out in anger. I pulled out of John's neck. "Are you making out with my roommate?" he asked. I supposed it could look like that.

"I don't believe this!" Trent shouted. "Here I thought that you wanted to sleep with me, because you liked me. Now I find out you were just looking for anyone!"

I froze at the venom dripping from his voice. Hurt snaked through me and I felt guilty. Quickly, I licked the wounds on John's neck so that he would heal, hoping for a come back. It probably wouldn't have been possible, so this might actually be better. A clean break where he thought I had hurt him. He had already hurt me. I worked at trying to get my fangs to retract, but I was still hungry and I had a hard time.

The next thing I knew, another door opened behind me. "What's all the shouting about?" Angie asked.

"Your roommate …" Trent said, accentuating the word roommate with a large amount of hatred. "… was making out with my roommate."

I felt bad for John who was quiet, still under the control of my mind. He would suffer for this, too. I really hadn't intended it to go this way. I thought that I would be safely ensconced in the vampire community by this time. Suddenly, I felt a pair of female claws dig into my shoulder and I was being pulled away from John. "You bitch!" Angie yelled.

John seemed to snap out of it, then. "Hey, what's going on?" he asked, dazed.

Angie spun me around and got into my face. "I really liked him, you know." She slapped John across the face and he looked shocked. Then, I heard a gasp come from the side of me.

Trent gazed at me in horror. Angie seemed to really notice me, then. She drew back, stumbling into Trent. I felt my fangs digging into my lower lip. I darted my tongue out, and tasted the blood that had been staining my bottom lip. I started to panic, and then my teeth did a disappearing act. Both Trent and Angie still gaped at me as if I was a monster. I looked back at a John, who was still perplexed. He hadn't seen my fangs since he had been out of it, and then he was behind me. Perhaps now that the two angry people both knew the truth things could still work out for him.

I looked back at my friends, sad that it all had to end up this way. "I'm sorry, Trent. I fell asleep instead of leaving. I had hoped to spare you from this," I said, indicating my face. "I'm going now. Please, forgive me." I spun around and with vampire speed ran from the large dorm room and created a breeze through the frat house as I rushed out.

***

"You should have never gone to college," my mother said to me. If I had thought I would get any support from her, I was dead wrong.

"Yeah, yeah, Mom. You told me so," I groaned.

"It was such a mistake. We should never have let you go. You put the whole vampire community at risk!" she said, pacing back and forth in front of me. I rolled my eyes, wishing that I could get this lecture over with.

"Mom, I would have left whether you wanted me to or not," I said, then added, "I'm an adult, you know."

"You sure didn't act like one," she hissed. "Now we have to send out some specialists to see if they tell anyone. The reason that we live in peace is because *they* don't know about us." I hated the way she stressed the word 'they,' as if regular human beings were distasteful to her.

"I'm sure that they are questioning what they saw. I healed the guy's wounds, so there's no proof of anything. So, if they go to anyone else, they would probably be put in a padded cell. I'm home now, okay? Can't we just forget about it?"

"I wish it was that easy, Casey," my mom said reluctantly. "If you were here this last year, you would have learned so much more about what was expected of you as a vampire. You would have learned about the dangers that we face. You would have learned about The Hunters."

"What are the hunters?" I asked.

"The question is: who are the hunters," she went on, "and I should think that the description is self-explanatory. They are the humans that have figured out our existence … the humans that don't like that we exist. They think we're parasites."

"Aren't we?" I asked, unable to believe how much my world had changed literally overnight.

"Girl, you're an embarrassment! We might need blood to survive, but we are hardly parasites! We drink bagged or animal blood when we can, and rarely feed directly from humans. Well some of us, anyway!" Again it was back to me and my mistake. "Besides, we contribute to society and the economy. Parasites!" she huffed.

"Okay, then. Are these hunters really that dangerous?" I asked, concerned.

"They've gotten worse over the years. They've actually captured and killed some of our kind," she answered.

I put my head in my hands, trying to sort through all my feelings. I had just had a horrible morning. I really didn't intend to fall asleep at Trent's and I really tried to keep John away from me. Then, I went home ... just to face condemnation. I looked back up at my mom, with her long jet black hair and tight black dress. She looked like a cross between Kim Kardashian and Morticia Addams with her arched eyebrows and flawless, tanned complexion. I wished she could be more like Angie's mom, who visited once a month with cookies and hugs.

"Mom, I can only say that I am sorry so many times. I don't have the power to go back in time. I know that I've made mistakes, but for once, I just wish that you were like other mothers. I wish you would have compassion for me and the mistake that I made. I wish I could just get a hug from you," I told her honestly.

"A hug?" she asked incredulously. My parents had never been very warm to start with, even before my year away. They were a perfect example of why people thought we were cold-blooded. Most vampires were that way. I think they just thought they were so much better than anyone else that they became distant and haughty.

"Forget it," I said. "Can I just get some rest now?"

"For now. The change and the first feeding will make you tired. But when your father gets home, prepare to have this talk again," she added.

When she left my old room, I looked around. It was just as I left it. Plain. I had no pink curtains or dolls leftover from childhood. In fact, I didn't have those things during my childhood at all. There was a twin bed with a black, red and white striped comforter; a writing desk that doubled as a vanity; and one new item, a small refrigerator. I assumed that it contained bags of donated blood. There were donation centers set up just for vampires, and a few well known blood banks that sold their stock if the price was right. If you weren't donating exclusively to the Red Cross, you couldn't be sure where exactly your blood was going.

I fell asleep after that for a few hours and, true to my mother's word, I had to sit through an even bigger lecture when my father returned. If I even had a smidgeon of hope that I could go back to Trent or ask to make him a vampire, it was crushed. Apparently, I was a disappointment to the entire vampire species. He made it sound as if I should be serving time. The idea was moot, anyway. I couldn't imagine Trent forgiving me for biting his roommate and lying about my true nature.

***

Trent

I skipped class on the Monday after Casey left, the first time ever. I never proclaimed to be a goody-goody or even studious. I had a lot riding on my classes, though: my scholarship, for one; my integrity, second. I didn't like signing up for things that I didn't intend to see through to the finish. I might not be the brightest guy, but I took pride in what I had accomplished by myself, and that included my schoolwork. Still, it had been one hell of a weekend and I wasn't up for my daily routine.

I was torn between thinking that I was incredibly naïve about the world that I lived in, or incredibly crazy to think that I saw what I saw. I had really liked Casey. It was strange because I hardly knew her. We had one class together, and I saw her studying in the library all the time. Sometimes, I would sit and watch her. It was almost sickening in retrospect. I had thought that there was some strange connection between us, the kind that they wrote about in all the books that the college girls read here. Instead, it might have just been some sort of super power she had. You know, since she was a vampire.

A vampire! I shook my head at the stupid notion. It was clear that I was crazy, or maybe I had taken a hard hit on the head in the last football game. I've heard of it happening. Maybe I was still unconscious and none of this had even happened, except in my head. Hey, a guy can wish, right? I laughed out loud at that thought. Was I actually wishing that I was in a coma due to a concussion? That settled it, I must be crazy.

After Casey sped out of the dorm like a bat out of hell, I saw the small puncture wounds on John's neck. Just as unbelievable as the wounds themselves was the way that they disappeared within the next five minutes. There was a little tension between Angie and him after that.

"Why did you hit me?" John had asked her.

"I don't know …" she trailed off, her eyes on the door where her roommate had left through.

"You don't know?" he grew a little angry at her poor explanation. "Jeez, I thought you were pretty cool, but maybe I was wrong."

That got her attention. "I'm sorry, I think I got confused seeing you out here with Casey," she explained.

"Casey was out here?" he asked, confused. "I didn't see her."

Angie and I exchanged confused glances. It was a scene right out of *The Twilight Zone.* Or maybe *Twilight.* Either way, something weird had just happened, and I would have given anything to forget it as John had.

"I'm really sorry," Angie told John.

"That's okay," he said, cupping his hand on her cheek. "You can make it up to me." Angie let out a nervous giggle and headed to John's bedroom.

"So, did you hit that?" he asked.

"What?" I murmured.

"Did you nail Angie's roommate?" he clarified.

I looked at him like he was crazy. If I had any feelings left for Casey, they didn't like that John treated her like she was just another notch on my bedpost. I know, I'm pathetic … pathetic and crazy. "No, I did not 'hit' that! I really liked her," I told him, crankily.

"Sorry, dude. I wasn't trying to insult you. I just thought maybe that was why she left before I even noticed her out there with me."

"Forget about it," I said.

"All right. I got to get to my bedroom. Someone needs to 'make it up to me'," he laughed. Then, he was gone. I envied him. He had no memory of what had happened. I didn't know if it was some spell that she had put on him, but he had forgotten all about the encounter. I just wished I could.

That was the last conversation I had with John, the last one I had with anyone. I spent the rest of the weekend and this morning in my bed, staring at the ceiling. Occasionally I would sleep, but each time I saw Casey with her fangs hanging out of her lip and a streak of blood on her lips. Sometimes I imagined staking her. Other times, I imagined licking the blood from her lips. After the first time dreaming the latter, I tried not to sleep again. It was no wonder that I didn't feel up to class today. I didn't think that I had more than an hour of continuous sleep.

I might have stayed in my bed for the rest of the day, too, but there was a knock on the main door around noon. I ignored the first knock. John had left for class that morning, and I wasn't expecting anyone. Then, the knock sounded again. I groaned and slowly rose from the bed like a zombie.

The mattress held an imprint of my body, and my muscles ached from disuse. I only got up because I was worried that John had forgotten his keys. It wouldn't be the first time.

When I opened my door, it wasn't John. Instead, there was a man standing there wearing a suit. His dark hair was slicked back and he wore a pair of shades, even though he was in a semi-dark hallway. "May I help you?" I asked him.

"Yes, I'm looking for Casey Gellar. A few students mentioned that they had seen her with you before," he told me.

The truth was that I had no idea where Casey had gone when she left here. I wasn't sure that I wanted to see her again, but something about this greased up character bothered me. I didn't like the idea of him searching for her. "I did see her Saturday morning. She said that she had to go home, and I haven't seen her since," I said, truthfully.

"Do you know where her 'home' is? It's important that I find her," he explained.

"She didn't tell me. Is there something wrong? Is she in some sort of trouble?" I asked suspiciously.

"I can't really talk about it. Perhaps you can tell me something. Did she do anything odd when you last saw her? Did she exhibit any strange behavior?" he asked.

Besides biting my roommate and running out of the dorm at superhuman speed? "No, she seemed perfectly fine," I lied.

He shook his head in disappointment. It was as if he had wanted her to be doing something bad or that he wanted me to spill some secrets. "I'm not supposed to tell you this," he said in hushed tones, "but she's in some trouble. There are people after her. I'm looking for her so that I can keep her safe."

Casey seemed like she would be able to take care of herself. I was worried about her, though. Something seemed off about this guy. I didn't trust him. I wish I did know where she was, so that I could warn her. "Honestly, we don't know each other very well. Her and her roommate crashed here after a party Friday night, but I haven't talked to her since."

"Oh, it's like that," he said cockily. I frowned at him. "Is her roommate Angela Thompson?" he asked.

Crap! I hoped I hadn't gotten Angie in trouble now. "I think that's her name. I didn't really talk to her much."

"You're sure there's nothing else that you can tell me?" he asked, trying drawing me in, but I shook my head. "Okay. Well, here's my card. If you think of anything, let me know." I nodded and he was off in a flash … maybe a little too fast. I was really worried now.

I looked down at the card. There was no name, and no company name. Just a number. I threw it in the garbage and felt rejuvenated in my nervousness. I jumped into the shower and washed off two days of dirt from my skin. Afterwards, I threw on a T-shirt and sweat pants. I had to get to Angie. I hoped that she didn't tell that guy anything if he found her. I hoped that she didn't trust him, either. We hadn't talked, so I don't know how she felt about Casey. Maybe she would want her to get caught by him … or anyone. I ran for the freshman girl's dorm with my fingers crossed.

When I got there, she was shaking the suit guy's hand. He turned away and I swore he looked right at me. He gave me a smirk, and I turned away from his disturbing smile. I waited for him to disappear into the parking lot, before I called out, "Hey, Angie!"

She turned around and spotted me. A frown formed on her face. I had a matching one on mine as I approached her. "I hope you didn't tell that guy anything," we both said simultaneously.

"What?" I asked her.

"I hope you didn't say anything to Mr. Creepy," she said.

"You gave him a name. I just thought of him as suit guy," I explained. She laughed. "You didn't say anything?" I asked.

"Of course not! She was my roommate and first friend here at college," she said, offended that I thought she would.

"I didn't know if you were angry with her or not, but I didn't trust that guy," I said, taking a breath. "Nothing he said sounded honest to me."

"You felt that, too? I was sure you would have told him something. You were really angry when she left," she said.

"I was confused. I thought I was crazy. I gotta ask you, though. Did you see fangs, too?" I asked.

Angie rolled her eyes at me. "Yes. I hate to break it to you, but you're not going crazy. It looks like our friend, Casey, is a vampire."

"She can't be. Vampires aren't real!" I said loudly, attracting a few strange stares from students passing by.

"You think anyone on campus hasn't heard you?" she asked, grimacing.

"Sorry," I said, looking down. "I don't get it. Casey left the frat house in the middle of morning. Aren't vampires kind of allergic to the sunlight?"

"I guess they aren't or she's gone, but I don't think so," Angie said, then added, "Casey's a smart girl. She would have drained us all before running into the sunlight to go poof."

Somehow, her words were not very comforting. "So, have you heard anything from her?" I asked.

She looked at me suspiciously, then she shrugged as if deciding to let me in on a secret. "She texted me. She said her room and board was paid up until the end of the semester, so I wouldn't have to worry about finding a new roommate."

"That's it?" I almost yelled. I wanted to shake her by the arms, but it might have been jealousy that Casey contacted her and not me.

"No," she sighed. "She said that she was really sorry. That she didn't mean to 'make out' with my boyfriend. As if she thinks I still believe that's what she was doing. Then, she said that someone would be by to pick up her things tomorrow while I'm at class."

I had no classes tomorrow, just practice after three. I could stake out her dorm, and then follow the guy to where she was staying. I didn't think it was that far, but I didn't know. I couldn't skip practice if I wanted to play, but I didn't want to miss my only chance to find her again, either. Yeah, I didn't know what I was getting myself into, wanting a relationship with a vampire, but something deep down told me that it was worth it. There it was again: the chick book feeling. I had to flex my muscles real quick to make sure that I hadn't lost my manliness.

Angie looked at me strangely. "Is there anything else that you want to discuss?"

I grabbed her shoulders and kissed her on the cheek. "Thanks for trusting me with that information. I have to go."

Another strange look was directed my way. "Whatever. Hey, tell John to call me," she added as I walked back to my dorm.

The first thing I did was go to the professor who taught the class that I skipped that morning. "Mr. Walker," he greeted me. "I missed you in class this morning."

"I'm really sorry about that, Professor Yates. I wasn't feeling well this morning. I wanted to see you to find out how I could make up for the missed class."

"Normally, it wouldn't matter, but we had a pop quiz today," he explained. He looked at his watch. "I have another class in a half hour. If you can be there, you can take the quiz then. If not, it will count against your grade."

"I'll be there," I promised.

I ran to my dorm to get my backpack, then rushed back and took the quiz. When I finished, it was three and I was running late for practice. I sprinted there, feeling as if I had gotten my exercise for the day with all the running around I had done. I suited up and earned a scowl from the coach. "Walker, I thought you wanted to play this game!"

"I'm so sorry, Coach. I've had a hectic morning," I apologized. He angled his head toward the other players on the field and I rushed out to join them. At this point, I was exhausted. I hadn't slept well in two days, and I had run all over the campus and back. I wanted to lie down on the field and make Field Turf angels, or maybe just curl up and take a nap. Instead, I had to prove to my coach that I wanted my position and that I wanted to start on Saturday ... especially if I would possibly miss tomorrow's practice. I ran through all the drills like a machine, ignoring the burn in my muscles.

After practice I met with the stern coach and told him that I had a private matter going on, and that I wasn't sure if I would make it to the next practice. He frowned.

"I mean no disrespect, sir. I'm very serious about playing. If it wasn't extremely important, I wouldn't think of asking you to excuse me," I pleaded.

"It has to do with a girl, doesn't it?" Coach Huffman asked.

"Why would you think that?" I asked defensively.

"It always has to do with a girl," he replied, matter-of-fact. Then, he sighed looking at the player sheet and he took notes out on each practice. "You did good today. I don't condone any player missing practice for any reason. I won't guarantee you a starting spot, but if you come an hour early on Wednesday to make up for it, I might still consider giving it to you."

I nodded. "I guess that's all I can ask."

"Damn right! Now go hit the showers," he said grumpily.

I had to take a moment to consider whether Casey was worth all this trouble. Seconds after I thought about it, I knew that she was. Damn those mushy feelings. I swear I might need to see a shrink after this. Even if I hadn't imagined her fangs, I still thought I could be going crazy. I got back to my apartment and fell asleep, getting some actual REM sleep, dreaming of the dangerous girl that I was going to chase down tomorrow. This time I licked the blood from her lips in my dreams … and I liked it.

***

I woke up the next morning a little bit freaked out by the dream that I had and a little bit turned on. I pushed all those feelings aside for the greater purpose. I had to get to the dorm and find a good hiding spot. According to Casey, her family obviously wasn't as open to living life among the rest of us mortals, human beings … whatever they thought of us. I had to convince them that we weren't that bad, or at least I had to convince Casey. Maybe she would take a chance and run away from them for me.

Wearing another pair of sweatpants, this time black, and a black skin tight T-shirt, I nonchalantly leaned against the building across from hers. At least, I hoped it was nonchalantly. I might just stick out like a sore thumb, but maybe I just looked like the college student that I was. I wore a pair of sunglasses and a black ball cap. Yeah, I probably stuck out. I looked down at my Algebra textbook. I had solved a few problems that I once thought were impossible, but I realized that they were nothing compared to the problem that I was facing now.

A conspicuous black SUV with black windows, pulled up in front of Angie and Casey's dorm. Another guy in a black suit got out of the front seat. He was missing the slicked back look of the one who questioned me, but he was a lot bulkier … pure muscle. He opened the rear driver's side door and a beautiful woman exited. She shook out her long black hair. She wore just a tad too much make up, but her body was pretty fantastic, wearing a black dress that accentuated her curves. When she lifted up her glasses, I saw a familiar pair of eyes. It wasn't Casey, but she had the same eyes. This woman was definitely a relative.

I stayed where I was, waiting for them to come back out with Casey's stuff. It didn't take long since both of them were carrying more boxes than normal people carried at one time. They looked heavy, too. I casually strolled to my car which, thankfully, was parked on the street right behind the SUV. The man held open the back door for the woman again and she climbed in gracefully. I darted to my door so that I wouldn't lose them.

I managed to follow them off the college campus, staying two cars behind them so they wouldn't get suspicious. Thank God for all the James Bond movies that I had watched growing up! After a half hour of driving, I followed the SUV off the expressway onto an exit ramp. We drove for five more minutes when they pulled over into a driveway. I stayed in my car as the occupants of the car got out and went inside the house.

I unbuckled my seatbelt and stealthily made my way to the house. I had to search for an open window or door so that I could get to Casey. I managed to get a side window open before I felt a tap on my shoulder. I barely had a moment to recognize slicked-back-suit guy before his fist came toward my face. Then, I didn't see anything … not for a while, anyway.

When I woke up for the second time that day, I was in a slightly dark room, tied to a chair. One eye felt swollen shut and there was a sticky feeling of dried blood on my cheek. A piece of tape was over my mouth, preventing me from crying out, but I made do with shaking the chair as much as I could and grunting wordlessly. Finally, the door opened and the woman I was sure was related to Casey walked into the room.

"Who are you?" she hissed venomously.

"Mmph," I grunted through the tape.

She rolled her eyes. What was it with all the women rolling their eyes at me lately? Was I that ridiculous? I didn't get to ponder that thought for long as she ripped the tape from my mouth, probably taking some skin with it, if my senses could be trusted.

"Who are you?" she repeated.

"Walker. Trent Walker," I laughed at my private joke. Had I really considered myself an accomplished spy?

"Are you with The Hunters?" she asked me.

"Who?"

"Don't play dumb. We know about The Hunters' organization. You've taken some of our people, now we have one of yours. If you tell me what you know, I will kill you quickly. If not … well … let's just say that it's better if you tell me what you know."

I gave her a skeptical look. "I have no idea what you're talking about. If I was part of some super-secret organization, don't you think I would have planned my break-in a little better?" I pointed out.

Her eyes narrowed. I don't think she liked my condescending tone. Well, I didn't like hers, either. I gave her a snarky smile. Then, she grabbed me by the throat. Yep, I was just asking to get killed. For some reason, Casey's gentle nature led me to believe that vampires were peaceful. The door opened, and spots danced across my vision as I recognized slicked-back-suit guy and super-bulky-suit guy.

"Hey boss, what ya doing?" the slicked-back guy asked.

"Killing The Hunter," she answered calmly. The man cracked up. I was seconds from passing out, when she let go to find out why slicked-back found it funny.

"Why are you laughing, Hank?" she asked, narrowing her eyes at him.

Hank. Hallelujah! I had a name for this guy. I could stop thinking of him as suit guy or more recently slicked back guy. I gulped in air. My throat was on fire. "This ain't no hunter, boss. He's Casey's boyfriend, the guy you wanted me to check out."

It occurred to me that maybe this person that looked like Casey wasn't a friendly relative. Maybe that was why they were so violent toward me. "What did you do to Casey?" I choked out.

"What are you talking about, young man? Casey is my daughter. She is perfectly safe," the haughty woman said, glaring down at me as if I were a bug.

"The house didn't look very safe," I said roughly.

"We saw you following us two minutes into our trip," she said, laughing. I guess I really didn't have this spy thing down. "That house was just a decoy so that we could get you out of your car. We are hours away from where we picked you up," she added, treating me as if I was some stray hitch hiker.

"I think the term you meant to use was kidnapped," I corrected her.

"You know, I don't like your tone, young man. I could just kill you now, but I'm afraid that Casey would never forgive me. However, I am not above a little mind control. There are some of my kind that are very adept at getting into the minds of you pitiful humans. They can make you believe anything they want. For instance, when you wake up next, you might think that you are Jimmy Thompson, a stranger from Florida who's just trying to get back home to his family. You won't remember anything about Casey or any of us."

I didn't doubt for a second that she could do those things. Since I didn't want to end up homeless and heading to Florida, I decided to keep my mouth shut. "Geoff," the woman said to burly suited guy. "Get Tom over hear so that he can sweep this boy's mind free of any memories of Casey and his adventure today. And then guard the door so my daughter doesn't find her way in here. It is a delicate procedure."

Just as Geoff made his way to the door, it swung open on its own and in walked the girl herself. The girl I had decided to risk life, limb, and my scholarship for. She was looking at her mom as she talked. "Mom, can I go for a drive? I can't stay cooped up in this *compound*."

Then, her eyes averted to me and she gasped in shock and perhaps horror. Did I look that bad? I wasn't sure, but I guess I kind of felt that bad. "What are you doing, Mother?" she shouted. The next moment, she was kneeling before me, her hands tearing apart the ropes that held me. "Are you okay?" she asked.

"I've been better," I admitted.

"Someone better tell me what the hell is going on right now!" she demanded.

"You are not in a place to make demands, my daughter," the cold woman said.

Casey leveled a glare at her mother that had me reconsidering her sweet nature. Her mother scowled. "Fine. He followed us back from your silly college. You know, there are people after us. We couldn't risk that he was a hunter."

"Now you know he's not so let him go!" she demanded.

"Wait," I said, my throat still sounding as if I had swallowed a cheese grater. "I came to get you, Casey." They stared at me as if I had grown another head.

***

Casey

My mother turned toward Geoff and asked him to get Tom. I knew who Tom was and I wouldn't stand for it. I grabbed the big man by his arm and effectively held him back from the door. Vampire strength could be quite deceptive. We were exceptionally strong, whether we were packed on with bulky looking muscles or not. Some of us were blessed with more strength, some with mind control prowess, and some with perfect looks like my mother's to tempt any stranger into being her prey.

"You're not getting Tom. I'll handle this," I said. I looked at Trent's glassy eyes, staring at me with admiration. He must have been hit really hard. Had he seen what I just did to muscle man Geoff? Didn't he realize what I could possibly do to him?

"Trent, Snap out of it!" I said, snapping my fingers.

He shook his head, and the glassiness left his eyes, at least. "I know this sounds ridiculous and that I should probably get my man card revoked, but even though I only spent one night with you, I love you, Casey."

I felt myself get a little teary eyed at his declaration, but I had to toughen up. My mother chose that moment to butt in and refuel my anger. "You spent the night with him?" she asked in a disgusted voice. I hadn't told her about that part. I had only told her that he had caught me biting his roommate. For all she knew, we were all eating breakfast in the common area.

"Mom! That's hardly the point," I grumbled.

"I think it's important." She reached out her hand as if she was tempted to choke Trent again. I could still see the imprint of her fingers from when she had done before. Between that and the shiner, he was going to look horrible when he went back to school … alone. My mom put her hand down and looked at me, urging me to clean up my mess.

"Trent, I really like you, too. You're great, but you know what I am. There is no place for someone like me out there. Let's not discuss the fact that I could crush you if I hugged you just a little too tightly. I don't live off of cheeseburgers and fries like the rest of the student body. I live off blood, which coincidentally runs through the veins of everyone at school … even you.

"What happened with John was bad enough," I explained further. "I tried to wave him away, but the smell became too much. It's all too much, especially at this stage. I can't leave here. You have your whole life ahead of you, though. You have your family, your schooling, and a chance at pro-football. If it helps, they can bring Tom in just to rid you of the memories of me, but that should be your choice, not my mother's." I glared at my mother for a moment before turning back to Trent.

"Tell me that you don't love me," he whispered, grabbing my arms. "Then, I'll go."

"Oh please, they say the same line from every book and movie since the beginning of time!" I tried making light of the discussion, not wanting to break his heart, and unable to lie.

"There's a reason why they say that, Casey. It gives the main character a chance to reexamine their feelings, so they don't blow what could be the best thing in their entire lives," he urged. Then, his lips descended onto mine. I tasted a small amount of blood as he ravished my mouth with his. I closed my eyes and took one last happy moment for myself.

When he pulled back, he smiled. "You liked that," he insisted.

"You taste like blood," I said harshly. "Of course I liked it."

His face fell a little. Then, he was grasping me again. "I can tell you what you taste like," he whispered in my ear. "You taste like warm chocolate chip cookies. You taste like sunny days and all the happy moments of my childhood. You taste like inner peace and enlightenment. You taste like home. I'm home when I am with you, Casey."

I couldn't take it anymore. The tears started rolling down my cheeks. I think his words would have brought almost any woman to tears, except maybe the staunchest feminist … or my mother. I looked over at her and her eyes were lit with a new light, a new curiosity. I wasn't happy being a vampire. I wouldn't wish it on anyone, but at least I had my family here, as detached as they were. At least I had been prepared for this life from the moment that I was born. There was no way that I could let Trent make this sacrifice.

I pushed him away, crying profusely. "You're right! You definitely need your man card revoked. What's wrong with you?" What was wrong with me? Why was I doing this? "It will never work out for us. Go! Go now, before I go and get Tom myself."

He reached out for me again, but I didn't know what to say to him. Why wouldn't he just leave? I couldn't kick him anymore. I ran toward the door to make my escape.

"Wait!" Trent called out. "You're right. I do need my man card revoked. I don't even care anymore, but you could do me the courtesy of at least hearing me out." I frowned at him but stood my ground looking at him. "I honestly don't know if you mean the things you just said or if you're trying to protect me from something. The kind of connection I feel with you isn't just born out of one person, though. I know what is waiting for me out there. A hundred possible victories on the football field, but no one to share the joy with. The thought of those empty victories makes them hardly seem like wins at all ... not compared to the victory that I would feel by winning your heart. I love my family, but I've found a new family with you. I won't be alone. That other life means nothing without you. I know that you can't leave, but I'm willing to stay here with you."

"Humans don't live in our midst," my mother stated.

"Then make me like you! I would do anything to be with you, Casey," he said.

"Do you really know what you are suggesting, young man? Do you really know?" my mother asked. "You will never see your parents again. Your life in the sport of football is over. You can't go back to that with your new gifts. As a 'made' vampire, you forego all chances of having children of your own. It's never been done before. It's too much of a shock to your system during the change. Pure vampires are made for it, but you are not. Can you really give all that up?"

He looked at me, his eyes gleaming. "Are you with me, Casey?" he asked. I couldn't deny my heart anymore. Neither could I talk through my tear clogged throat. I nodded yes. He looked at my mother. "I can give that all up."

My mother's stiff demeanor relaxed a little, and there was a bit more softness in her expression. "I'm very happy for you, Casey. I know that I seem so cold and forbidding. My mother was that way, too. Within this closed off community, it's easy to become that way. I fear that one day it will happen to you, too. You're like a ray of light in this icy palace. Maybe you can thaw us all out a little bit."

Now she addressed both me and Trent. "The road you are going to walk will be rough. In the past, the few mortals that joined our kind had to be begged, cajoled, and even threatened by the one who loved them. Never has one asked to be one of us. It is a hard life and, as you can see, a somewhat cold life. You two are strong, though, but you're stronger together." Trent tightened his arms around me and kissed my head. "You will be a beacon to our kind to come out of our shells. One day, I think you will be a beacon for the whole world."

Hearing these kind words from my mother warmed my heart even more. I pulled away from Trent and wrapped my arms around her. She gasped in surprise. "Not for a while, though. We have The Hunters to deal with first," I reminded her.

"That is another problem for another day," she said, tightening her arms around me. "I love you, Casey." Another happy tear slid from my eye. Then, my mother took her leave from the room, dragging the smiling henchmen with her.

I turned to Trent, and he gave me an endearing smile. "I'm sorry for what I said earlier," I said.

"I know why you were doing it. You were trying to protect me. I can forgive you," he smiled as he took me into his arms.

"You are so much more man than I deserve. Your card is perfectly safe. I don't know that there has ever been a man strong enough to stand up to my mother, to sacrifice so much of his life and face his feelings the way that you did. I feel all of the things you said. I never wanted to trap you into this life." I snuggled into his embrace.

"I'm not trapped; I'm free," he said, looking into my eyes. "You made me free to embrace all of life's possibilities instead of the road that was mapped out for me."

"You loved football, though," I reminded him.

"Not as much as I love you," he countered.

"That can't be nearly as much as I love you," I teased, giving him a wink.

"Yeah, I knew that you were just in denial, babe. Who wouldn't want a piece of this body?" I laughed at his words. He kissed my lips until I stopped laughing. "So, when will you change me?" he asked in all seriousness.

I shrugged. "It's up to my mother and the others on the council. I wouldn't worry about it right now, though. I can think of a few other things to do with our time."

He groaned and I led him through the building to my room. I hadn't returned for him. Instead, he came to me. I saw no reason to wait. We took the next step into our new life … together.

Rescue Me

By: Stephanie Parke

"This is Rachel Chauvin reporting for WBEX 10, I am at the scene of another murder believed to be the work of the Groom." Her tone was quiet and solemn, her green eyes wide and serious as she described the details of the battered body that had been found in the alley beside the East Baton Rouge parish courthouse. "Detectives are not releasing the victim's name at this time, but they believe that this is the work of the same suspect who has perpetrated the last three crimes. Detectives are asking that anyone with information in this case please contact the police immediately." She took a deep breath and looked straight into the camera, hoping to ensure the attention of the public.

"This suspect targets young, single, professional women. Detectives are asking that any young female living alone in the city take extra precaution until this criminal is caught. As you can see from the scene behind me, detectives are working around the clock to catch this criminal.

Until then, police ask that you be vigilant." The blue and red lights cast an eerie, otherworldly glow on her face, deepening the dark shadows behind her eyes. She looked back at the crime scene and then into the camera. "This is Rachel Chauvin for WBEX 10 News."

The camera went black and Rachel sighed, rubbing her

grimy eyes. She turned back toward the crime scene and her stomach clenched. From where she stood, she could see the leg of the dead woman peeking out from under the sheet. Rachel shivered when she thought of the condition that the poor girl was in when she had arrived on the scene. The body was naked with marks of torture evident on every inch of her exposed skin, then carelessly tossed aside, wedged halfway under a dumpster. Her left hand had a burn across its third finger in mockery of wedding band, marking her as the fourth of the groom's victims. The police had quickly covered her with a sheet, but Rachel had seen too much. She shivered again in the warm night as the image rumbled through her brain.

A feeling of unease trickled down her spine as she surveyed the scene. The leaves of the hanging Spanish moss draped across the steps of the courthouse, sending shadows across the grey stone of the building behind her in the darkness of the night. Rachel pulled the lapels of her jacket close together as the coroners loaded the victim into the van with a muffled thump. She shook her head as the feeling of being watched washed over her again. She knew that it probably had a lot to do with the story she was covering, but for the last several weeks Rachel had felt probing eyes watching her on a regular basis. She'd done the things she'd suggested to the public, but the feeling of hot breath on her neck as she walked into the house or phone calls in the middle of the night with no one there had become a common occurrence. Of course, the police didn't believe her. They thought she was simply spooked … but Rachel knew when she was being followed.

Rachel told herself that she was just being silly. Then, a voice screamed in her head that sometimes what seemed impossible was often quite possible. Rachel had grown up hearing the stories of her voodoo-priestess grandmother and she had seen her share of the incredible, both as a child and as an adult. The supernatural seemed to have a way of finding her no matter how much she tried to hide from it.

"I'll go back and file your report," her cameraman, Justin, said with a smile as he broke into her thoughts. He put the last of the camera equipment in the back of the van and waved a hand in front of her face, trying to get her attention, but she continued to stare off into space. "Earth to Rachel … you coming?"

Rachel sighed, watching the police still milling around the scene. Detective Carlson was working behind the tape. She stood straighter, trying to look unfazed as she said, "Nah, I'm going to stick around and see what I can get from my source." Justin looked at her doubtfully, but Rachel ignored it.

"Rachel," he said cautiously, "did you just hear your own report? This guy's dangerous."

He surveyed the area, glaring suspiciously into the darkness. He was younger than her and new to the area, but they'd become fast friends. Justin, his wife, Callie, and their three small children had become her new family. And for someone with so little, it meant the world. She gave herself another shake and smiled at him.

"Okay, mom," she teased, trying to sound confidant. She shoved a strand of her long, brown hair out of her green eyes and shoved it behind one ear. She straightened herself, trying to look professional. Due to the events of the night, she felt bogged down and ready to give up. "I'll get a ride home from one of the uniforms when I finish, or I can always get a lift from Don."

Justin hesitated, scratching his wavy blonde hair with an uncertain smile before slamming the door and jumping inside. "Just be careful," he said with a worried look that tugged at her heart.

"Tell Callie hello for me," she said, smiling as he pulled away. After he faded from sight, the darkness embraced her fully. Her face fell as she ambled toward the police tape, taking in the scene. She straightened her jacket, drawing herself up to her full height of 5'3, which was not very impressive. Don cringed behind the crime scene tape, eyeing her walking toward him.

Rachel felt a satisfied smile tug at her lips for the first time since the call came in.

Rachel's father had been a police officer for twenty years, but was killed one night in a robbery gone wrong. Emile Chauvin had adored his wife and only child. He'd spoiled them both, never letting her mother handle anything. As a result, the bottom fell out of their universe after he died. He had left behind a grieving widow and a six-year-old child who didn't know why her world had just ended. His partner, Don, had stepped in, taking the place of her father. She and her mother had come to lean on Don and his wife heavily—maybe too heavily. Her mother, Nadine, never fully recovered. She found it difficult to care for herself, let alone a child. Nadine had killed herself three years later. Rachel became a nearly catatonic nine year old, who had gone to live with Don and his wife.

With no other living family that she knew of, she'd lived with Don and his wife until she became of age. Then, she'd done the most shocking thing of all for the child of a cop: she'd become a reporter. Don had understood, but it was hard for him to tell her no when she needed information on a case for a story and she used it to her advantage. He affectionately called her the pit bull. Don knew that if he didn't give up the goods, she'd badger him until he did.

Two hours later she waved goodbye to the police officer who dropped her off at the steps of her apartment. In front of the door, she fished around in her purse for her keys and cursed her own stupidity for not putting them where she could easily find them. She shivered as a chilly late night wind blew up the back of her jacket, slithering up her spine. Rachel rubbed her eyes as she captured the keys in a tired gasp and sighed as she consciously let herself think about Rider.

She'd been fighting his ghost all day in her mind and pretending that she wasn't was the hardest part. Unfortunately, she had never been good at resisting him even when he was only storming her thoughts. Over the last two months, his image had battered her mind, along with his smell, the memory of his touch … it was driving her crazy.

She had slept little to none since he had disappeared, but when she did, Rider still haunted her. It was getting to the point now that her makeup girl was beginning to give her grief about the huge dark circles under her eyes. She was beginning to crave what little sleep that she could get just so she could see Rider again. She took a deep breath and looked back over her shoulder as the same feeling of being watched washed over her again.

Over the last two months she had to live without Rider knowing that someone was following her. At first she'd thought that it was in her head, but then she realized that the footsteps she heard behind her late at night stopped when she did. When she turned, she didn't see anyone, but that didn't make the feeling of sick unease go away. At her front door, she reached up and unlocked the deadbolt. She had never been one to leap at every little sound, but the cold feeling kept creeping up, taking residence inside of her. It terrified the hell out of her.

After she'd been assigned the coverage for The Groom cases, she was sure that it was why the creepy feelings kept coming over her … but you never could be too careful. Unfortunately, there simply wasn't enough evidence to get full time protection, even with her connections. The Baton Rouge police department was simply spread too thin. *Not that I want it,* Rachel thought to herself as she stepped into her apartment. She could take care of herself.

She paused for a moment, allowing her eyes to adjust to the darkness. She tried to tell herself that her nervousness was due to a lack of sleep. She looked around her apartment, breathing hard. She wasn't used to being afraid, but since Rider had pulled his vanishing act and the groom had begun his little killing spree, nothing seemed normal. She sighed, pushing the thought aside. She felt less vulnerable, almost safe inside her apartment. She walked across the room and peeked out the curtains, but, as always, saw nothing. She stumbled to the couch and plopped down hard, placing her head in her hands and gave in.

Immediately, Rider's image flashed through her mind and her heart crumbled. A tear ran down her cheek as the familiar ached took over. It was pathetic how little it took to rip her apart, no matter how hard she tried to prevent it. She kept the pain hidden most of the time, but it was always there in the back of her mind. No matter how many times that she tried to ignore it, it was still there. She could almost feel Rider's touch, feel his lips on her skin. For those few moments, reality seemed to slip away and she was with him again.

Rider had stormed into her life when she was twenty and she'd fallen in love with him immediately. His long, brown hair and hazel eyes had attracted her, but it was his demeanor and sweet Texas twang that had won her heart. Rider had rescued her from a sure death at the edge of a knife blade one balmy summer evening when she drove to meet a source.

Rachel had known that meeting the little weasel alone in the dark was a bad idea, but it had been too juicy a story to pass up. Getting the dirt on a dirty politician in New Orleans had been the biggest story of her life and this was her only chance to get the information she needed for the case. The Politician's butler was getting nervous. She found herself wishing that she had refused to meet him, but she really needed the information. The night sky opened up and she was soaked in minutes as she waited. She shivered in the dark, getting dirtier by the second.

Rachel had realized that the meeting was a trap when the air had changed. Something felt off; everything was just too silent. Her grandmother had always said that she had the second sight. She had called her the little medium. Rachel had spent years resisting the idea, but she'd wished that she'd listened as she stood in the cold darkness shivering with silence surrounding her. Suddenly, a beefy arm slid around her from behind and the shining blade met her throat. The sharp point of the blade made her sweat with fear and she knew that there was no way out.

She had struggled, but the man's burly arms had crushed the air from her lungs as the blade caressed her skin. She knew that she was going to die … and she was furious.

Suddenly, a shape rushed from the darkness and jerked the man away from her. His screams echoed off the walls of the alley and then fell silent in almost the same instant. She felt as if she had been watching the scene from outside herself. It had happened so fast that she barely had time to register it. The knife bounced off the wall and hit the ground with a clattering sound that made her skin crawl. She'd gripped the wall, her fingers digging into the gritty surface as she tried to stand. She'd hit the wall hard and she'd been hazy on most of the details. She'd always wondered how he'd been there at just the right moment, but all that she had remembered thinking for sure was that he had the most beautiful eyes that she'd ever seen.

He'd approached her slowly, breathing hard and Rachel had memorized him as if she had no choice. His long brown hair had pulled lose from its binding and he'd reminded her addled brain of some kind of animal stalking her. Her head hurt like a bitch and she was currently seeing two of him, but he was without a doubt the sexiest man she'd ever seen. He had approached out of the darkness and caged her with his arms. She could hear his hissed breathing and felt the heat rolling off him in waves. She had tilted her head back and looked up into his beautiful hazel eyes and had been lost. He smiled crookedly and picked her up as if she weighed nothing. Rachel had felt her heart beat faster as he'd held her against his strong chest and, for a strange moment, she'd been sure that he was going to kiss her. "Thank you," she'd muttered just before she'd fainted. Rider had never let her live it down.

She'd wondered and rolled it over in her mind as their relationship grew and when the undeniable, animal passion between them had exploded they had become lovers. Rachel had never been so happy and for a while wrapped in his arms, his naked body pressed against hers, she'd been able to cram her questions into a tiny box inside her mind. She had pushed down her natural curiosity because she wanted him. No matter how much she loved him the pieces simply hadn't added up and her reporters mind and thirst for knowledge hadn't let her. She'd worked it until she'd put it all together. Rachel had realized eventually that Rider had been in that alley because he'd been following her. Rider had actually been a friend of her Dad's and had vowed to protect her.

Rachel hadn't been sure what had surprised her more, the fact that he'd known her dad or the fact that he was a vampire. Either way, the moment she'd seen his glowing eyes and fangs, he'd tried to bolt. Rachel had stepped in his way demanding answers and he'd been forced to confess what he was. Rachel had been afraid, but her past had shown her that not everything was as it seemed. She'd tried to talk to him but he was so sure that he would kill her because of his darker nature. No matter how she'd tried to convince him to stay, he'd disappeared.

Rachel banged her head on the wall as she remembered herself on her knees begging him to stay, and the pain when he had left anyway. She shook her head to clear her vision as she pushed Rider to the back of her mind into that tiny box and forced her heart to stop bleeding before she died from the pain. After he had disappeared, she hadn't heard from him and all of her massive resources had failed to find him. Rachel simply wanted a chance to tell him that she loved him, but she didn't know if she would ever see him again, at least, not while she was awake.

Rachel wiped her nose on her sleeve and stood. She slid the second newly installed deadbolt across and stopped when she caught her own gaze in the mirror. She wondered if it was possible to be dead and not know it because the circles under her eyes made her look like a phantom instead of a living, breathing woman. Rachel pulled the skin under her eyes tight and sighed. It did no good. She rubbed her eyes as Rider's smile danced in front of her closed eyelids, wondering if he ever missed her or thought of her at all.

***

Miles away, Rider placed the last bag in the car and slammed the trunk shut. He leaned against the hood and sighed, letting the cool night air rush over him. He ran his hand through his long brown hair, thinking of Rachel. He knew he looked like shit. Rider hadn't felt this bad since a hole was blown into his chest by the local sheriff with his Winchester rifle. Rider and his brother, Jess, had been members of the James gang. They had died late one night outside a local whore house. He and his brother had been ambushed when one of their men turned traitor. The result was a hole in his chest as big as his fist. Rider watched the cruel joy in the eyes of the sheriff as he watched him die and prayed for revenge. He had gotten it later that night after he had been transformed into a vampire.

He rubbed the grit of the road out of his eyes and sighed heavily. He knew he should stay away; that's why he had left after all. He wouldn't take what he so badly wanted, and what she willingly offered, but something about her entranced him. She had awoken a part of his soul that could deny her nothing. He loved her and needed to be where she was, even if he could only stand in the shadows of her life, but he couldn't stay away. He'd lived 131 years on the fringe of normal life, but for the chance to simply protect her, he knew he'd take a chance of getting his long dead heart stomped. He'd stayed away for three months since the night she'd found out what he was, but she was under his skin every moment like a sweet itch that he didn't want to scratch. Her soul called to him across the distance and he was done fighting the pull; three months was enough. She was in his veins like a drug and he couldn't get enough of her. He jumped into the car, slammed it into gear and headed off into the night ... back to his Rachel.

***

The night shifted, growing quiet, like the calm before a storm, but Rachel didn't feel it. She was lost in dreams of Rider. In her dream, he was driving in his car and she was right there beside him. She looked at him and smiled. Damn, she missed him. She slid over toward him and ran her hands over his long brown hair. She brushed his neck with her lips and he shivered. He sighed and kept driving, unable to see her beside him. Rachel smiled as she saw a highway sign and realized that was he headed toward Baton Rouge, back to her.

The dream faded, leaving her alone in her dark bedroom. Rachel wiped her eyes and sat up, cocooned in her blankets, looking out the balcony window. She picked up the phone to dial Rider's brother, Jess, to see if he'd heard from him, then she slammed the phone down. She hated feeling this need, but it clawed at her. She drummed her fingers on the bedside table and finally gave in. She picked up the phone again. Rachel shivered as she was met with silence instead of a dial tone. Rachel's brow furrowed in confusion and, more than a little fear, as she clicked the receiver, trying to get a tone. Rachel's hand was still on the receiver when strong hands clasped her from behind, covering her mouth, blocking her ability to scream.

His hold on her body was like a vise. No matter how hard she struggled, she couldn't free herself. A sickeningly sweet whisper slipped past her ear and she felt her heart drop as she heard the hissed words roll off his tongue like silk, "This won't hurt a bit."

Suddenly, a needle was rammed into her arm. The fluid raced through her veins like fire. Rachel struggled against the drug and the man holding her. He was big, but she wouldn't give up. She slammed her head back and heard a satisfying crunch followed by a husky scream. Her brain screamed in fear, but she felt her strength begin to fade fast as the drug raced through her veins. His grip loosed, but she could barely move her head. Abruptly, he pulled her from under the covers and the hand covering her mouth slipped away, as she was almost dead weight.

Rachel thought quickly as she dug her fingers into the soft flesh of her wrist, drawing blood, praying that it would help Jess and Rider find her. As the darkness began to finally close in around her, she bit down savagely on her captors hand and screamed.

***

Ten miles outside of Baton Rouge, Rider felt a presence beside him and turned expecting to look over and saw Rachel. He felt a breeze drift over his hair like a caress and felt lips drift down his neck. He could have sworn he felt her. He breathed deeply and decided that he must be losing his mind. He shifted in his seat and adjusted his jeans. He could swear he smelled her perfume, Forever Red, inside the car. He sniffed the air again, feeling the pain twist in his gut. Suddenly the presence was gone. As it began to fade, Rider felt dread come over him like a shroud. A scream—unmistakably Rachel's—echoed in his mind. Rider stomped on the gas, hurrying toward Rachel as he dialed Jess's number.

The phone rang twice before it was answered. "Jess," Rider said quickly without preamble. "Rachel's in trouble." Silence drifted from the other end of the line weighing heavily on his chest.

Jess wasn't sure what to say, but in true Jess style he said the first thing that came to his mind. "So, the prodigal brother has returned," he said trying for casual. Rider heard the rustle of leather as Jess sat down in his favorite desk chair. "Where the hell have you been?" Rider's temperature rose and his eyes stung as they began to glow. Suddenly, severe pain shot through his abdomen. He reached down and felt his stomach, but nothing was there. The phantom pain shot through him again as a sick feeling raked over him. Dread spurred him on and he felt impatience rush over him as another pain shot through him. "I don't have time for this," Rider growled down the line, "Rachel's in trouble."

Jess put his feet up on the desk to admire his new black boots. You can take the cowboy out of Texas, but you can never completely take Texas out of the cowboy. He sighed deeply. He shifted his weight and the leather of his chair creaked again. "Your little Cajun is fine," he said softly, sounding bored. "I left her at a crime scene a few hours ago, safe and sound. She got a ride with a uniform." Jess sighed as he sat back, not sure whether to be happy or pissed at Rider.

"Not like you've cared about her much these last three months, anyway. You stuck me with babysitting the human," he said, licking his fangs, thinking of all the time he lost watching her.

"You're lucky I like her or I might have had her for lunch." Jess chuckled trying, for awkward humor, but stopped short when Rider growled down the line.

"Shut the hell up!" Rider growled viciously, cringing as another pain shot through him. "I love her but I had to let her go. She's better off with a normal human." Rider felt his heart tear, barely able to say the words that had haunted his every moment for months now.

Jess leaned forward, concerned. "Ri," he said quietly, "about Rachel." He broke off when Rider growled again.

"I don't want to hear about it," Rider groaned, chocking back the pain in his heart and his gut. "All I know is that she's in trouble, damn it! It's my fault, Jess. I should've been here."

Rider felt impatience creep upon him as time slipped away. With every second, the pain in his body grew worse and the dread in his heart doubled.

Jess cringed at the certainty in Rider's voice, but asked anyway, "How do you know?"

"Because," Rider growled as he clutched his stomach again. "I can feel it. Meet me at

Rachel's." Rider hung up and threw his cell phone on the seat beside him as he sped through the night, praying that he wasn't too late.

***

The world swung wildly and came into focus in slow motion. Time seemed to stand still in the darkness as Rachel tried to focus her vision. A weak scream pierced the air and it took her a moment to realize that it was coming from her own lips. She stifled the scream, but realized that she was too late. She tried to move but found that her hands were bound together, linked to a chain threaded through a metal bar in front of her. She ran her fingers to where the chain was connected and felt bars. She cringed as she realized that she was in a small, metal cage. She yanked at her hands and cringed at the streak of pain that followed from the cut on her wrist. She found herself unable to move her hands more than a few inches.

Panic rose up within her and a sharp, tearing pain ripped through her abdomen. She panted, unable to catch her breath, willing the pain to pass. A dim light flicked on somewhere in the room, assaulting her eyes and Rachel cringed back from it. The cage swayed as someone moved near. Rachel tried again to focus, but found that she could see nothing but blurry shadows in the light. She whimpered again as fear skated down her spine and her stomach twisted again. Rachel bent double as cold hands suddenly stroked her cheek. She jerked away as far as possible in the small cage as the pain once again faded, leaving her sweating and praying for salvation.

The hand followed her retreat and stoked her face tenderly. The smooth cool texture of his hands made Rachel's stomach heave as she crouched, withstanding the touch with nowhere else to go. "Poor Little Rachel," the slithery voice hissed, "so confused and lost. I expected more from you." The small chuckle he gave as he finished speaking made her cringe.

She whimpered again, but managed to keep it inside this time, even though fear was choking her. "Why can't I see you? Why am I hurting?" she demanded, even though her throat was raw and the pain racking her body seemed to have increased tenfold. Rachel reached inside for her reporters calm as she pulled her chin away and demanded, "What did you do to me?"

The soft laughter came again, floating out of the inky blur that was her vision as the fingers slid back along her jaw line, lingering on her skin in a sick parody of a caress, making Rachel's skin crawl. "Don't worry, sweetheart," he said in a sugary-sweet tone so reminiscent of the dead serial killer Max Stanford. "It's just the drugs I gave you, but they will wear off in plenty of time." The silence following this statement made the pain in her stomach pale in comparison to the fear that she felt rolling through her.

Max Stanford had been the spoiled son of one of two of the cities wealthiest families and he'd felt himself entitled to everything, including the right to kill. Max had murdered fifteen people before he had been caught. He showed no remorse. Rachel had reported on the case until his death by lethal injection. Max had become obsessed with her through her newscasts and he started to contact her with voice messages and letters from prison. Rachel was glad when he'd died. Now, hearing his voice slither through the darkness made her want to puke. Someone like that did not deserve to come back from the dead and she prayed in this case that she was wrong.

"In time for what?" she demanded as the blur in her line of vision faded and the light flickered off again.

The voice slithered through the darkness, a hiss that wrapped itself around her until she felt the air squeeze out of her lungs. "In time for us to play," came the amused reply as the voice receded into the darkness. "It wouldn't be fair to my current opponent to begin our game before I've finish the one I've begun." The voice dropped to a sick, singsong whisper as the door creaked open and drifted shut.

Rachel chocked back a sob as her blurry vision became dark and her stomach cramped up again. She hunched over as much as possible and prayed. She prayed for help and found herself wishing that she could see Rider one more time. Pale and delicate classical music trickled through the air as a scream split the darkness. The pain and despair in the scream was almost palpable, making her blood run cold.

***

Rider's car screeched to a stop outside Rachel's door and he jumped out almost before it stopped moving. He raced around the building and jumped easily to her balcony. The door was open and Rider felt his heart drop inside his chest as he stepped inside. He made no noise as he crossed the carpet toward the bed. The night seemed unnaturally still as if it were holding its breath, making his skin crawl. He leaned over the bed, noticing its rumpled sheets and the overturned phone. He picked the phone up and found no dial tone. Swearing loudly, he turned to examine the rest of the room when the smell hit him.

He turned toward the scent and saw the stain on the carpet. He leaned toward it and breathed deeply. The darkness crowded around him as an image of Rachel came into view, playing like a ghostly movie behind his eyes. He saw Rachel lost in sleep. She was smiling, and he couldn't help but smile a little himself at seeing her again. He looked closer and a frowned as he noticed the dark circles under her eyes; they looked like they had been there for some time. She looked sad and tired, even though she was asleep. She woke up crying and Rider reached out to her, knowing that he was unable to touch her. He watched her smile and reach for the phone lifting the receiver. She frowned and clicked the receiver and was still frowning at the phone when the hands grasped her from behind. Rider launched forward to save her, but only met the cool sheets of the bed as his hand grabbed at the air. The phantom shadow jerked her against him and injected her with a needle. She struggled and managed to crack him in the face with her head before she began to fade as the drug took control. Rider felt proud as he saw the phantom Rachel stab her nail into her wrist. The shadow carried her away, but she made sure that the blood dropped on the carpet behind them as they left the apartment. He growled as his vision cleared and he raced toward the balcony door, following the scent. He jerked the door open and stopped short as he came face to face with Jess, who had an eyebrow raised questioning.

"Come on," Rider replied, then led the way back out the balcony into the night, not giving him a chance to do more than jump with him.

Rider landed on the street with barely a sound. He opened himself up to the night and breathed deeply. He picked up the scent outside the apartment and followed it down the street.

He had barely taken three steps when another wave of pain hit him. He bent over, trying to breathe, bracing his hands on his denim clad knees, but nothing helped. He heard his name, a soft whisper in the late night wind and for a moment he could swear that Rachel was close enough to touch. He looked around but found himself standing in the darkness with Rachel nowhere in sight. He breathed deeply again and caught a scent that was distinctly Rachel's. His heart raced as he caught Jess's eye and nodded into the darkness. Without a word they sped off, as a burst of preternatural speed pushed him toward her.

***

The darkness seemed to crowd her from every direction. Rachel breathed deeply, trying to remain calm. The music still played and the screams kept time in a gruesome symphony. She was unsure of how long she had been alone in the darkness. It all seemed to run together, confusing her mind. Panic rose within her chest as the screams from the other room faded away, and she suddenly found herself holding her breath, waiting.

Footsteps echoed in the darkness and light permeated the room, shining directly in her face, making her cringe away. She blinked as she heard the footsteps come closer as her eyes adjusted to the dim light. Her captor moved out of the light and Rachel was able to see him for the first time. She frowned as she took in his normal looking face and average build. This was the type of man who would fade into any background, not a man you would remember easily, yet something about his cold, gray eyes reminded her of Max. He leaned down by her cage and smiled. The sick twist of his grin turned his face into a ghoulish specter.

"There now, Rachel," he said with a sardonic chuckle. "I told you that your sight would return in time for our games. Not what you expected, hum?" He chuckled slightly at her disbelieving look. "I get that a lot," he tisked. "My last opponent is winding down, but I wanted you to see the grand finale, to get a taste of what you're in for." He leaned in and Rachel saw the needle in his hand. She struggled to pull away, but her hands were bound and chained.

"No," she said in a half sob struggling against the bonds. "Why are you doing this?" He smiled again and Rachel felt the needle pierce the back of her hand. Immediately, she felt weak but didn't feel the fire like before. She looked at him with sluggish eyes as he slowly opened the door.

He unhooked the chain holding her hands and tugged viciously, pulling her from her cage. "Because I like to play with women like you." He punctuated his statement with another jerk on the chain, dragging Rachel closer. "But women like you don't like to play my games." He paused jerking her against him. "And I love a challenge ... just like my dear brother, Max. But you? Your different," he said with another tug on the chain. He studied her with a sick smile. "You watched my brother die and you liked it." He said the words slowly and they marched over her skin like ants. His hot warm breath washed over her and Rachel gagged as the drug kicked in.

She struggled to pull away but he laughed Max's laugh. She reared back and glared at him as best she could with the drugs coursing through her. "You're damn right I did," she spit at him with as much venom as she could manage. "Your brother was a sick animal and he needed to be put down." Rachel's head spun with the knowledge that Max had not been an only child as reported; he'd had a brother. Rachel felt woozy as she fought against the drug, but she was barely able to stand. She swayed as he dragged her out of the room and down a dingy hallway.

His heavy breathing and quick stride reeked of anger.

"Bitch," he screamed loudly as the back of his hand crashed into her face. Her head snapped so hard that she wondered if he was going to kill her right here. His fists pummeled her anywhere that he could reach and he kicked her in the ribs several times when she fell to the floor. She heard the crack of at least a few ribs as she struggled to breathe.

"You will pay for that," she said through clenched teeth.

He jerked her to her feet and she barely registered the institutional gray walls and cracks in the ceilings that dripped rain. As he dragged her along the dim corridor, she fought against it but the lethargy was catching up with her, making her as limp like a rag doll. The room swayed as he placed her on a table. She shivered as the cold steel of the table penetrated her shirt and he tightened the straps on her hands and feet. Rachel raised her head with great effort. Panic rose up inside her as she studied the leather strips holding her to the table. Her captor paced back and forth, anger radiating in every stride. Her eyes scanned the room and landed on the eyes of her captor. He stopped pacing. He closed his eyes and listened as sounds of *Vivaldi's Genius* filled the room.

Her captor visibly calmed down as a wide, creepy smile spread across his face. He crossed the room and bent over her, stroking her hair and face with his cold, clammy hands. Vomit rose in Rachel's throat as she tried to pull away. "I wanted you to see the end to this little play," he whispered in a sick singsong voice. He moved closer and his hot breath blew on her ear, making her stomach roll. "It'll build the anticipation for what is to come." He gave her ear a light kiss and moved away. Rachel followed him with her eyes as he crossed the room. He flipped a switch and a new song, *Beethoven's Fifth Symphony,* filled the room. He sighed and moved to a table directly in her line of vision. The woman strapped there, a brunette like herself, met her eyes, dull and lifeless.

Rachel began pulling on the straps holding her down with a sick feeling for what was coming next. She began to pray and cried out for Rider, screaming his name inside her head. The woman tied on the other table whimpered weakly as their captor raised a wickedly sharp blade and placed it on her skin, and this time Rachel couldn't help it ... she screamed out loud.

***

Rider and Jess raced through the night, following the scent of Rachel's blood on the pavement. Rider's head pounded, but he felt panic rise even faster once the pain faded. He looked at Jess and shook his head. "I can't find the trail," he growled. "We have to find her now!" Rider's thoughts were a jumble as he frantically searched the streets, trying to keep his panic in check. A moment ago, it was as if she had been leading him, but now he was filled with an empty void. He was cursing himself for staying away so long, for risking her safety because of his stubbornness. He had failed her.

Jess shook his head as he looked at the sky, which had faded from deep night to the dark gray of predawn. "Ri, I'm calling for backup," he stated with worry etched on his features. "We need help." He began to dial his cell phone, but Rider stopped listening. He lifted his face and smelled the air, desperately searching for the scent of her blood.

His breath caught in his throat as he caught the scent again. It was faint, but it there all the same. He started moving in her direction when a scream ripped through his skull. Rider groaned and he felt his blood ran cold.

The scream came again and it took him a moment to realize that this time it was not in his head. His eyes iced over and his gums tingled as his fangs erupted in his mouth. Rider met Jess's glowing blue eyes, then they sped off toward the sound.

They reached the dilapidated warehouse just as the sound faded away. It had many narrow corridors, but Rider had no problem navigating it. His blood pulsed through his veins as a force urging him on. He felt as if she were there with him leading him to her. He heard the music drifting down the hall, its sweet melody clashing with the screams that were now resonating over it. Rider ran faster than he thought he ever could, ignoring the scent of blood that got stronger with every step. His breath shuddered in his throat. Fear ran through him when he suddenly heard Rachel whisper his name. He reached the door and gave it a swift kick. The door gave with a crash, bouncing against the far wall, exposing the room to view.

Rider rushed in and stopped short, taking in Rachel's terrified eyes and the man across the room holding a sharp blade to the torso of another woman strapped to a table. Rachel weakly cried out his name. Rage, cold and hard, engulfed him until he saw nothing but the man's death.

The man holding Rachel captive barely had enough time to register his entrance before Rider jumped on him. The man managed to raise his arm that was holding the blade, but was too late. Rider met his arm with such force that the bone shattered, jabbing through the skin. The man's eyes widened in shock as Rider pulled him close. He cringed back from the demon staring out from Rider's face.

Rider saw red as he choked the man in his iron hard grip. He leaned closer as he growled, "Don't ever touch what's mine. You will never hurt anyone again, asshole!" With a feral growl, he picked up the now screaming man and broke his back with a sickening snap. Rider pulled the man back up and bared his fangs preparing to strike. The restraining hand on his arm stopped him and he took in Jess's face. "No brother," Jess said softly "Let me, this isn't you, let me help you." Rider breathed hard and tightened his grip, the monster inside fighting for its right to take the man apart. The monster howled and beat at the cage Rider was barely holding it in. Rider was fighting so hard to keep himself form tearing the man apart because he knew from experience that he could barley handle the consequences when the vampire within him got everything it wanted. Jess tugged gently at Rider and he regained enough control to toss the man to Jess. Jess hefted the man and with a hiss and a snarl before quickly tearing the man's throat out.

The man's eyes, glazed over with death, registered a sick fascination as his life's blood drained away. Jess threw the man's dead body to the floor as Rider raced to Rachel's side. He jerked the straps holding her away as if they were paper, then pulled her into his arms. Rachel sighed as she felt Rider's arms encircle her, feeling for the first time in a long time that she was safe and where she needed to be. She buried her face in his shirt and inhaled his raw masculine scent, a unique combination of sweat, leather and warm man. Her heart raced, even with pain racking her body. She snuggled closer.

Rider held her, trying to be gentle, cursing himself for leaving her alone. He couldn't believe that he had lived without her for so long. She was like the sun, brightening his darkness, and he had failed her. He kissed her hair and cradled her closer, careful not to hurt her, and she felt as if she had just entered Heaven. She pulled back and looked into his glowing eyes and gently touched his face, as if memorizing it. She didn't seem to care about the fangs erupting from his lips. She only saw him for the man that he was inside, and he loved her even more for it.

"Why did you stay away so long?" she whispered, trying to put her heart into her eyes, unable to mutter more than a few words.

Rider pulled her against him, trying to absorb her into him. He was unable to answer and looked across the room to where Jess was checking on what was left of the other woman lying on the table. He met Jess's eyes and sighed into Rachel's hair when Jess shook his head from side to side, confirming his worst fear; they were too late to save the last victim. He promised himself that no matter what, he would never leave Rachel again. Her safety was his first priority.

"I was stupid, I guess. I'm so sorry," Rider said huskily, as his voice caught, fighting the urge to cry. He'd been alive for well over his allotted human lifetime and he had only cried a handful of times in his entire life. The last time had been when he'd held Jess when he died in his arms. No matter how he tried to stop the tears, Rider felt them slide down his face anyway. "I should have been here for you."

Rachel smiled weakly, placing her bloody hand on his face to turn his face toward her.

"Rider, you're here now. That's what really counts." She forced him to look at her and, reluctantly, he did. "But I will have to kick your ass if you ever leave again."

Rider smiled despite himself as he stroked a hand down her face. "You got it," he said as he gently pulled her closer. "I wouldn't want to piss off the boss."

Rachel relaxed against him and laid her head on his shoulder. "Just so that we understand each other." She closed her eyes and breathed in his scent, feeling safe and right for the first time in months.

"Well," Jess said wryly, wiping his mouth with his hand. "Very nicely done." He gave the body of the murderer a quick, hard kick and smiled at Rider as his eyes faded to brown and his fangs retracted. "I like it, but he's not my usual vintage. Serial killer always gives me a stomach ache."

Rider placed another gentle kiss at Rachel's hairline, chocking back a laugh. The sounds of the approaching ambulance broke into his thoughts and he began to look for a place to set her down, but felt her grip on him tighten. He slipped his arms back around her and pulled her back against his chest.

"I'm here," he said softly as he watched Jess dump chemicals from the killers sink around the room. He dumped extra on the killer and gave him a hard final kick. They had to make it look like they were just getting out of the building in the nick of time when the police show up. They had to hide the state of the killer's body. It wouldn't do for the humans to find the body with its throat ripped out. Jess stepped over to the woman on the table and closed her eyes. Then, he covered her with his coat and picked her body up gently. Rider knew that Jess would never leave her here, especially not after finding his wife murdered in a similar way over a hundred years ago.

Jess held the girl's body close as if it were nothing, then pulled out his lighter. He smiled sadly as he stepped away and flipped the lighter open and nodding toward the door. "Get going, I'm right behind you," he said quietly. Rider smiled sadly as he nodded to his brother, then pulled Rachel against him he nodded and moved toward the door. He slipped out as the unmistakable whoosh of the chemicals caught fire. Jess slipped out and they ran for the door. The fire hit a gas line and the building burst into flames as they stumbled out the door. They hit the ground hard and Rachel moaned. Rider pulled her on top of him cushioning her with his body. She smiled down at him weakly and he lifted his hands and caressed her brown hair lightly.

Love Bites

"I've got you," he whispered quietly, wondering how he could have gotten so lucky. "I won't let anyone hurt you. I'll never leave you again."

"Promise?" she asked quietly, her voice hoarse from screaming.

Rider sighed and smiled, then tucked a strand of hair behind her ear and ran a finger across her split lips. "I love you," he whispered quietly, then added, "I'm not going anywhere." He smiled and pulled her head down on his chest. Rachel smirked at him as Jess grunted softly. Jess slid to the ground beside them with the groom's last victim held tightly on his lap. He had been unable to just leave her on the ground. They all cringed as the building blew.

"I love you, too," she whispered softy. She snuggled against his chest, breathing deeply of the scent that was distinctly his. Rider sat up and pulled her close as they watched the building burn.

He looked over at Jess cradling the dead woman and knew that he had been very lucky tonight. He had almost lost Rachel, which was something that he could never do again.

***

By the time she was released from the hospital, Rachel knew that she could never go through anything like the last few months again. Rider was in her blood, a part of her that she simply couldn't live without.

She planned her seduction carefully, making sure that her body rubbed his every time he helped her up and down and making sure to leave the door to her room cracked while she dressed. He'd come in several times and she'd looked at him with open invitation but he'd simply turned and walked out. Her Victoria's secret collection had never had such a workout.

By the time she'd been out of the hospital for two

weeks, she knew that she would have to push harder to get him to break. He was holding back on touching her. He kissed her gently, as if she was breakable. He was fighting it with everything that he had. His south Texas upbringing kept him from taking what they both wanted. He was resisting for her sake. It was too bad he was going to lose.

Rider groaned as he pulled his key out and prepared to open the door to the apartment. He sniffed deeply and his fangs lengthen as the scent of her drifted to him. He smelled the scent of her shampoo and the night blooming jasmine lotion she used all over her delectable body. He slammed his head against the door. She was driving him crazy. He knew what she wanted, what they both wanted, but he wouldn't risk hurting her. He wondered if he should just put the stuff inside and run, but he knew that it wouldn't help. He couldn't go very far from her. Eventually, he knew that he would give in. He growled, knowing that it was just a matter of time.

He growled and called his vampire back, pulling the monster inside the cage. His fangs sank back into his gums as he opened the door a crack looking around suspiciously. Rider thought that the coast was clear as he ambled into the living room. It was empty. He let out a relieved sigh as he set the bags down on the small, granite countertop and began to unpack them. He was almost done when he heard her cry out.

Rider ran faster than he ever had before and made it to the bathroom in record time. He plowed through the door and scanned the room so quickly that he seemed like a blur. Rachel smiled as the door bounced off the wall, cracking the plaster, but it was totally worth it. Rider's eyes met hers across the small bathroom and he knew that he'd been had. Rachel stood leaning one slim hip against the vanity with an evil smile on her face.

Rider tried to get away, but when he looked into her sparkling green eyes, he knew he lost. "Okay, darlin'," he said softly, his twang deepening as he stepped closer. "You asked for it." He flashed her a fanged smile and she found herself turned on, but speechless. He stalked her across the room so fast that she almost didn't see him move. She shivered as he grabbed her hand and pulled her against him. He slid his hand into her long, brown hair and cupped her head in his massive hand, positioning her for his kiss, then plundered her mouth, taking everything. She moaned and pushed her naked body against his, more than ready.

Rider gave in. He simply couldn't help it. He lifted her and she wrapped her legs around him, struggling to get closer. Rider growled and carried her to her bed, then laid her down to admire her against the forest green bedspread. She opened her arms in invitation and Rider answered her siren's call by stripping down and covering her body with his own.

Rachel smiled as she arched her body against him, urging him on to possess her. Her head spun with delight. She moaned as he made love to her and she knew now was the moment to offer herself and demand that he make her his forever. She arched her neck and pushed up against him, seeking his lips. His fangs were barely sheathed as he loved her and the moment he felt her skin against his teeth, he tried to pull away.

Rachel gripped his hair, holding onto him, not allowing him to pull away. He growled and stopped moving inside her. "No," he growled as he saw the demand in her eyes. "I will not damn you to this life." He jerked back and found himself surprised at the strength in her grip as she refused to let him go. She wrapped her legs tighter around him and pulled him back down against her naked skin.

"So, you would rather damn me to a life without you?" she asked fiercely, almost growling herself. "I can't do it again. Every minute without you was a nightmare for me, I won't live like that again. That's not a life."

Rider looked down into her eyes, warring with himself. He knew what he wanted. God! He wanted her forever, but he couldn't take the chance that she might not make the change. And how could he damn her to darkness and make her a blood sucking monster? Rachel didn't know what she asked; he'd seen many good people not make it.

"No," he growled softly jerking free. "I won't do that to you. This life is not for you." He put his head in his hands and massaged the back of his neck where she'd ripped some hair away when he had pulled free. He could hear her heavy breathing, could smell the tears and anger rolling off her, but he knew that this was the only way. He had to make sure that she had a life, even if it meant that he had to be out of it.

"You don't get to make that decision for me," she said with a snarl as she sprang from the rumpled sheets. "I make my own choices and, after what I've been through, I chose you. So, get used to it." She stomped over to stand in front of him and put her hands on her hips, looking fierce.

Rider stood and met her beautiful green eyes. God, he loved her, but he simply couldn't watch her transform into a monster, couldn't let her lose herself. He ran his hand over her cheek and stepped toward the door. "I won't do it," he said softly. "You deserve better." His hand closed around the door knob when her next words cut him short, raising every vampire sense that he possessed.

"If you leave, I'll find someone else to do it."

The words cut into him, creating intense pain at the thought of anyone else touching her, turning her. He turned back and looked at her, searching for the truth in her eyes. His inner vampire growled when he found it. She was dead serious.

"Don't," he said quietly, trying to keep the monster who was demanding he claim her under control. "You don't know what you're asking." The vampire wanted her and was shaking the cage inside him harder than ever before. It wanted, needed, to claim her forever, and he wanted to let it.

Rachel shook her head and stepped closer, she sensed that he was weakening. She had to find just the right crack in his wall to get him to cave. Eyeing him thoughtfully, she shrugged her shoulders. "If you make me," she said softly, her words dripping seduction as she stepped up and rubbed against him. "If you don't want me enough to claim me, then I'll find someone who will."

Rider groaned and felt his walls begin to break. The crack started small at first, but the vampire saw his chance and sprang out with a roar. Rider's eyes began to glow in the darkness and Rachel knew she had him.

"I love you and I won't let you run away from me," she said softly as his head slammed back against the door. His glowing hazel eyes met hers and she saw the fangs lengthening, ready for the vampire to take over. Rachel smiled and pulled him down for a kiss, ready for anything.

Rider growled and kissed her hard. He knew that he was being selfish, but he couldn't let her go. He had no life without her and he couldn't go on living without her. He'd been alone too long. He moved his lips down her cheek to her neck and the vampire cheered loudly, but Rider reined him in one last time. "Are you sure, really sure, that this is what you want?" he growled, his voice straining with the effort to restrain himself.

Rachel smiled, pulling him to her throat, offering him everything. "I want you. I want this," she said softly, waiting for him to take her.

Rider growled again and pulled her against his chest. He looked deep into her eyes and let the vampire out as he carried her back to the bed. He laid her down and lifted her head in his big hand cradling her as his mouth caressed her throat. Rachel began to burn as his mouth closed over her neck, and the sting as his fangs sank in.

Suddenly, she was floating, twisting, burning as he claimed her. She fought against it, but that she knew she had to go through it to be with Rider ... and he was worth it. "I love you," she whispered softly as she let herself go and felt herself fade into darkness.

***

Rachel woke hours later and was ravenous. Rider helped her feed and watched her, looking for signs of the rogue vampire. He had held his breath as he watched her over the day and a half that it had taken her to change. He'd found himself praying for the first time in years that she wouldn't go rogue, for he knew that he wouldn't be able to end her life if she did. She'd smiled at him when she woke and pulled him close. Her green eyes glowed brighter than ever and her white fangs glistened on her red lips. He thought she'd never looked more beautiful or more like herself, and he saw no hint of a rogue vampire.

She kissed him and wrapped herself around him, hungry for more of him and finally feeling alive for the first time in months. He made love to her with a ferocity that he had never been able to exert when she was human. Rachel held on tightly, gave him everything and took everything, As his whispered words of love floated over her, she couldn't help wondering how she had gotten so lucky.

Hourglass
By: Vanessa Hancock

Eva's eyes closed, and she heard Jonathan screaming, "Hold on!"

Where was she going? Was she dying? The darkness felt soft and damp. Was it raining?

"Jonathan, can you hear me?"

"Hold on to my hand! Don't let go!"

His voice sounded muffled as if someone had a hand over his mouth, and then there was silence. The darkness welcomed her. Looking down at her hands she wasn't even sure if there was ground beneath her. Was she floating? Shuffling her foot, she felt a cold rock. So, she was standing, but where?

Just as slowly as the darkness had come, it began to fade to grey. Her eyes were blurry, but she could see that someone was standing before her. She had heard stories of loved ones welcoming others in death. Could this be her mom and dad? For so long, she had lived without them … too long.

The blurry person laughed with a deep, grave sound. This wasn't family.

"Who are you? I can't see."

"Dear child, hold out your hand, and I'll take you where you need to go."

Eva leaned forward with her hand outstretched, and as her eyes focused, she snatched it away. The horrifying creature standing before her was nothing like she had expected.

"Am I dead?"

"Yes, beautiful, and I'm here to guide you to your new home."

"But I thought that when you die, you go to someplace wonderful." Hearing a wretched screeching, Eva looked up. Thousands of winged creatures similar to the one before her polluted the sky. "What is that?"

"It's harvesting time, and I send the troops out when I know the air is thick with evil. As for going to someplace wonderful, why would you think that YOU deserve to go to such a place? You've listened to just about everything I've ever told you to do, my star pupil. Well, you listened to everything except when I told you to dump that stupid boy that thought he could change you and love you."

"I don't want to go with you. Send me back."

The creature of death laughed, stepping closer until Eva smelled his foul breath. "You chose this path, and now you must pay. Time is up."

"There must be something that I can do that will keep me from having to go where you're taking me. I imagine that there will be suffering in that place ... endless suffering. If I'm out of time, then give me something to do. Let me work for you."

The creature began to ponder her proposal. "You might do fine as a guardian of time. You see, each of you humans is given a certain number of heartbeats. See, this was your time." He held up an hourglass. Each of you has a certain amount of time to do what you have to do in order to not end up with me, and yet here you stand. I win! Isn't it fascinating?"

"So, what would I do as a guardian of time?" Eva asked.

There are many people out there who are on the verge of time, a time when they can cross over and be free of me. You can be sent out to make sure that when it's their time to go, they never choose the good over the bad."

"I'll be responsible for everyone's suffering to escape my own?'

"Look at you learning so quickly, my precious darling!" The creature snarled touching her face. "With your beauty and relentless kindness, you'll have people following you right off a cliff if you want them to. Your job will be to keep a watch on the hourglasses, and when you see that time is almost up for someone, you'll be sent back to Earth to manipulate and destroy them. Here's the catch: when time is running out, the other side sends out reinforcements, too. There may be a battle or two for a soul who could turn; but for the most part, if they haven't changed, chances are they won't listen to anything good going in their thick brains. Your part is relatively easy. Go, influence, and if they die in front of you, take their hand, and bring them to me. I'll do the rest. So, what do you say, sweet cheeks?" the creature asked, grabbing her face.

"I'll do it."

Instantly her clothes vaporized, and she was suddenly dressed in a long, flowing gown. Twirling, she forgot herself and smoothed her hand over the fine cloth.

"Amazing, isn't it, how quickly your plight is forgotten with something of worth?" the creature snarled.

"I've just never worn anything so fine."

The creature spun her around and waved his hand before them. Suddenly, a dark hall lit with dripping candles enveloped them.

"This is your new home. It's better than what I've led others to. Never doubt that, my dear."

Eva looked around and the endless walls of hourglasses containing the heartbeats of every living soul on earth that might one day join them here … but they still had a choice.

"Just so you don't get any brilliant ideas of escaping your assignment, I cannot kill your precious Jonathan, but I can ask permission to torture him a bit to … let's say …

strengthen his faith."

"I'll do as I'm told. Just leave him alone."

"Want to hear his pathetic voice one last time?"

Eva began to shake, not knowing what was coming. The creature waved his hand above his head and the darkness parted briefly. Eva could hear sirens and, suddenly, her hand felt warm. Jonathan was still with her, holding her hand. So, she wasn't dead. She was in an ambulance.

"Jonathan!" Eva screamed.

"Eva, I love you!" The darkness closed over her. She suddenly felt her hand grow cold, and through the thick dark air she heard the heartbeat monitor in the ambulance flat-line.

Eva turned to the creature, and said, "He heard me!"

"That's right. There's nothing like a little false hope to completely ruin someone's day."

Eva felt chilled, then warmed, then chilled.

"Oh, that's rich! They're using the paddles on you. I'd love to step in the ambulance and say, 'that's enough boys, she's with me. Now, go bother someone else.' That might cause a fantastic accident." The creature contemplated for a moment.

"No, don't! Jonathan's in there. Leave him alone, and I'll do whatever you ask."

The dark creature pulled an hourglass from the wall. "Here you go. Get to work. Time's just about up for this one, and you'll get a nice battle for her soul. I can't say that you'll win," the creature said, stopping to take a deep breath, then added, "and losing is atrocious. The big guys who you will be battling for her soul will just about tear you apart. And let me just say that if she is taken by them and you don't have a scratch on you, I'll personally take you to the lowest part of this place will give you a ring-side seat to watch what I'll do to Jonathan and everyone else you love."

"Agreed," Eva said, snatching the hourglass. At once, the floor shifted beneath her and she was suddenly in someone's home.

A woman sat on her couch and it appeared that her chest was hurting. She rubbed her palm across her heart and squeezed her arm. Picking up the remote control, she turned up the news. Abruptly, another pain shot through her.

Eva said out loud, "So, a heart attack is about to whisk you away." The woman couldn't see her, but she could hear her words within her mind.

The woman said, "Oh no, this must be a heart attack!" She got up to search for the phone, but it wasn't where she had thought she laid it. Another pain suddenly hit her hard, buckling her knees.

"This is it for you. Time to go," Eva whispered.

"I'm not ready to go," the woman yelled.

Eva stumbled back when two giant men in white shook the house as they suddenly appeared beside her. One knelt beside the woman and whispered, "Just believe."

"Oh God, help me!" The woman yelled.

"Confess to your Lord," the other giant in white whispered.

"I need you, God." The woman was holding her chest tightly as if it were about to explode.

"You don't have to listen to them," Eva said aloud.

One of the men in white turned with his sword drawn. "Silence, you."

"You don't tell me what to do here!" Eva spat in his face.

The other creature drew his sword and slashed it across her arm. "You will hold your ground, young one."

Eva stepped forward, just to be defiant. The giant in white lashed his sword again through the air, and Eva stumbled backward feeling blood trickle from her cheek. With his sword pointed in her direction to keep her on the ground, the giant stood ready to attack her again. The other knelt beside the woman and whispered in her ear.

Eva couldn't hear what the woman said, but she saw a smile spread across her face. Then, her body went limp and she died. The giant in white beside her reached down to take the woman's hand and lifted her out of her body. The woman looked back at her lifeless form. "Thank you for helping me to see the way. I don't think anyone ever told me what to say to get myself right."

She turned and looked at Eva, smiled and waved, then disappeared with the white giant. The other giant was left with her. He stepped closer. "You and I will meet again, no doubt, but I warn you now, today is mild to compared to how I will fight you for a soul."

Eva thought quickly and asked, "Can other humans hear you?"

The white giant laughed. "You never did."

Eva looked to the ground. "And now I'll pay for that forever, but with your help, I might be able to escape this."

The white giant leaned forward. "It's too late for you. You belong to darkness now … forever."

"Have you ever tried to help someone cross over?" Eva asked.

"There's never been anyone who asked to try," the white-winged creature replied, then added, "You have an easy job, hateful and horrible, but easy."

"This is not me; it's not who I am," Eva begged. "I don't want to cause people to suffer, but I have to do this to protect my Jonathan. You have to go to him and warn him. Tell him that I'm being held captive. Tell him that he was right all along, and I'm sorry that I didn't listen. Also, tell him I love him."

"I know this Jonathan. He is a mighty warrior for our side. He does a lot to advance our Kingdom."

"Then, you'll go to him?"

The white giant thought for a moment. "I've often wondered if there is a way to redeem yourself after death, but let me just say that it's never been done. I don't see why it would start with you."

"I want my life to mean more in death," Eva answered.

The white giant nodded. "If nothing else, you will be entertaining," he said as a smile curled his lips. "But I won't give up my battle with you. These precious souls are my job to protect."

"Understood. Just please go to Jonathan and ask him to help," Eva begged.

"I can appear to Jonathan as a normal man," the white creature said, lost in thought, then continued, "In fact, I've always enjoyed walking around among humans. They are a curious lot, and when they do a simple, kind deed for me, it usually causes their hearts to grow. It's my favorite thing to do. People need the hope in helping others." The white giant paused. "I'll help you, but you have to keep this between us, or what will become of you will be worse than anything you've ever imagined."

Eva hugged him before she thought about what she was doing. Suddenly, the white giant felt a portion of his strength leave and he stumbled.

"Did I just do something to you?"

"It's just the light and the dark usually don't hold onto each other like that. It causes a strange shift in the air," he explained, straightening himself. "Now, be off with you! My suggestion is to limp when you return. Take the hourglass. The sand is finished."

The white giant vanished, and she was instantly back in the hall of hourglasses. She collapsed on the floor wiping the blood from her cheek.

The dark creature walked to her. "Nice battle scar. It suits you. Now, time for another."

"I don't get to rest?"

The creature laughed as he took another hourglass from the shelf and shoved it to her. "Rest? Dear no! Your choice was to work and that's forever child." He laughed as he pushed her forward.

The room shifted and she was instantly standing on a bus. A woman was rocking back and forth, sobbing. She whispered quietly, "I should just kill myself."

Eva whispered to her, "How about we get some coffee?"

The woman was startled, thinking that she was alone. "I'm sorry. I shouldn't have said that out loud."

The bus came to a halt, and Eva pointed outside. "So, coffee?"

The woman nodded.

They sat together at an outside table, and the woman spilled out the story of her life, telling Eva about her cheating husband, her abusive boyfriend before him, and the news that she had just received this morning.

"Wow, I don't know if I could have lived through that," Eva said, sitting back in her chair. "I'm not too good at this sort of thing, but I have a friend that can tell you about hope. Would you like to talk to him?"

The woman nodded.

"Give me your cell, and I'll call him." Eva instructed, and the woman handed Eva her cell phone. She quickly dialed Jonathan's number and swallowed hard.

"Hello?" Jonathan answered.

"Jonathan, it's Eva," Eva said, thinking quickly. "I know it's hard to believe, but I've been sent back. I'll explain later, but right now I need you to tell this sweet woman that I'm sitting with about how to find hope. She wants to kill herself, but she needs a light that I can't give to her. Tell her, Jonathan, and I'll find a way to talk to you later."

Eva handed the phone to the woman, and she looked at Eva as she listened to Jonathan. She spoke quietly, "Yes, she has brown hair and brown eyes," the woman replied. "Yes, that's her completely." The woman continued to listen, and Eva watched as tears rolled down her cheeks ... and she started praying.

"Thank you, Jonathan," the woman said. "I guess the hardest thing is dealing with the fact that I have cancer. The doctor said that there was nothing more that they could do, so I thought that I didn't have any purpose. Now, I can at least share what you've told me with my entire family. Thank you, Jonathan." She paused. "Yes, she's still here." The woman passed the phone back to Eva.

Eva began talking fast, trying to explain as much as she could to Jonathan.

Jonathan replied quickly, "If all this is true, then when you don't return with her, you'll be punished."

Eva started crying. "Oh, Jonathan, he threatened to punish me and you! What have I done?"

"You just keep finding ways to talk to me, and we'll figure this out. Don't worry about me. I've battled this for years, and I won't give in knowing that the stakes are higher now. We'll beat this, Eva. I don't know what the end will be, but I won't give up until I know that you're free."

The ground suddenly shifted underneath her feet. The creature was behind her and the dark hall loomed before her. Then, the whisper she dreaded to hear filled her ears, "You failed me! Now, it's time for Jonathan to suffer … and all because of you. Then, we'll try this again. But first, you'll get to see the show, and I must say, it's going to be a doozie just for you!"

The wall in front of her changed abruptly, and she could see Jonathan getting out of his car at his apartment. He unlocked his door and started to go in, but stopped. His apartment was demolished. Someone had broken in and robbed him. He stood frozen in the doorway, wondering if they were still there. When his dog didn't greet him, his heart sank.

"Luke!" Jonathan yelled. The dog didn't come. Jonathan slowly walked through the mess and he found Luke in the kitchen, dead. Jonathan dropped to his knees and began to cry. Luke was given to him by his grandfather just before he died. He lifted the dog and headed toward his truck.

"You were a good dog. I'll miss you," Jonathan said through his tears as the picture faded.

Eva was crying, too, but never said a word.

"Oh, did that break your heart? Pathetic humans! That was just a taste of what I can do. I can do plenty to him, too, but that's only if you decide to fail me again."

The creature took another hourglass from the shelf. "Back to work, Missy. Time to harvest."

The ground suddenly shifted, and Eva was in a car with a young man. He was driving too fast. Crying, he held his cell phone and said, "When you get this message, I'll already be gone. It's easier this way. You won't have to worry about me upsetting your life anymore." He tossed the phone in Eva's lap as he increased his speed. The young man said out loud, "Just get your courage up, man. You can do this. That curve is just ahead. That should do it. Just don't lose your nerve."

Eva was silent. She didn't want to be in the car when he killed himself. She didn't know what would happen to her in all of the destruction.

Suddenly, two white giants appeared in the back seat. One spoke aloud, "Stop the car. You are worth more than this."

The young man shook his head. "I'm through with trying! I don't matter!"

The white giant leaned forward. "Love is real, and you can have it if you'll stop the car."

Eva remained silent. The other white giant winked at her and then said to the man, "Your life has purpose. Remember how you used to love your family? Remember life before you left home. It's time to forgive."

The young man was crying, and the curve was just ahead. He floored the gas and the car went sailing over the edge. Eva screamed, and the young man turned to look at her. Their eyes connected just before impact. Eva felt nothing, but had to watch as the young man was tossed about. The white giants looked at her with great compassion, and when the car stopped moving, she saw that the young man was dead.

"I didn't say anything. Why did he not listen to you?" Eva asked, trying to understand.

One white giant disappeared and the other sat with Eva. "Just because we show up doesn't always mean that they will choose to go to the light. He's known the truth for some time, but continued to walk in darkness."

"Like me," Eva said, sighing.

"Yes, like you," the white winged creature replied. "Now, it's your job to take him. His soul is yours."

"I don't want to lead him there," Eva said, suddenly crying.

"You don't have a choice. He isn't welcome where I'm from."

"Why was I not led like the ones I go after?"

"You hardened your heart to us long ago," the white creature said, looking at her with kind eyes. "With the dark that surrounded you, your soul was already on the path. You didn't need a guide."

Eva suddenly felt colder. She looked down and felt small compared to the white giant.

Eva picked up the young man's cell phone. "Am I able to use this?"

The white giant nodded. "Be quick."

Jonathan answered, "Hello."

"Jonathan, I don't have much time, but I'm sorry about Luke. I love you, and I'm sorry for anything that might happen to you. I'm here with someone who is coming to visit you. Just listen to a man named …" She looked to the white giant.

He spoke low, "Sam Godwin."

"Listen to a man named Sam Godwin," she said into the phone. "He's from the other side, and he's coming as a human to talk with you."

"Eva, I love you," Jonathan replied. "Be strong, and don't worry about me. No matter what the dark has to bring, I'll fight it until the end."

"I've got to go. I love you, Jonathan."

"Love you, too."

Eva ended the call. Tears streaked down her face as she reached out her hand to the young man.

"Time for me to go," whispered the white giant. "I'll see you soon, Eva."

Eva nodded. When she touched the young man's hand, he immediately grasped hers. He sat up out of his body and looked around, "Am I dead?"

Eva nodded. "I'm here to take you away."

The young man caressed the back of her hand. "You're beautiful. I'll go anywhere with you."

Eva blushed, realizing that the dress she wore revealed too much of her. She squeezed his hand and their surroundings shifted. They stood together still hand in hand appearing in her hall of hourglasses. The dark creature stood before them.

"Oh look, you're still holding hands. She is beautiful, isn't she?" he asked the young man.

All he could do was nod, and he squeezed Eva's hand tighter.

"Thanks, you precious beauty," the dark creature said to Eva. "It seems that he didn't listen to all the do-gooders begging him in the end, but most never do." The dark creature picked up a twisted horn and blew it. Out came a deep, low sound that summoned two winged creatures. They flew in and scooped up the young man.

"Don't let them take me!" he screamed, holding onto Eva. "I want to go back! I'll do better, I promise!"

The winged creatures lifted him higher and his fingers scraped Eva's hands, trying to hold on. She stood there crying, but all she could do was to watch the hideous creatures take him away.

"You can't get attached to them," the dark creature said to Eva with a sigh. "He liked you, though. Maybe we should use that more. Your looks can go a long way with men on the brink of decision. Many a good man has fallen into darkness because of some random pretty face. Men are truly weak." The dark creature laughed.

Eva felt sick seeing the terror in the young man's face before he was hurled away. In the distance she heard him screaming, and her skin prickled.

"Ah, the sound of the beginning of eternal torture," the dark creature said, his lips curling into a sneer. "There's nothing like a good scream to wake up the mind."

Eva remained quiet.

"Here you go, dear. Time to fetch another worthless soul," he said, shoving another hourglass into her hand. Suddenly, the ground shifted under her feet. Eva sighed heavily. She would get out of this. She would escape. She would see Jonathan. But, for now, it was harvest time.

A barroom materialized around her. Colors shone from the neon signs as the darkness shifted into the chaos of noise and haze. Looking down at her dress, Eva was shocked to see what she was wearing. The tight shirt revealed too much of her and the short skirt made her feel uncomfortable. "So this is what you think will make someone choose to go with me?" she whispered.

The bartender slammed a bottle on the counter, and Eva turned, startled by the noise.

"Get to work, Missy," the bartender said, smiling.

"What did you just say to me?" Eva asked, glaring at the man.

The bartender's face changed, softening. "I said, would you like something?"

"I'm still thinking," Eva said, trying to compose herself. A man sitting on the last barstool stood up and walked over to Eva, but she tried to ignore him.

"Well, you look like you want some company," the man slurred, leaning close to Eva's face. The smell of alcohol on his breath saturated the air around her.

"No, I just want to leave," Eva said, turning to leave.

The man followed her out the door. "Hey, I was talking to you," he said, grabbing Eva's arm. "You're a sweet thing that could make this night a lot more fun."

"Let me go!" Eva said, clenching her teeth as she snatched her arm away.

The man stumbled backward and fell against a car. "I'm sorry. I don't usually act like this, but my wife just left me for a younger man. I thought that I could get someone as easily as she did. I have to go." He fumbled for his keys and unlocked a truck parked nearby. He fell once, trying to get into the cab of the truck, and Eva realized that this was the man that she was sent to harvest.

"Don't drive. You're too drunk to drive," Eva said, running to the truck.

"You want to drive me home?" the man asked, smiling.

"No, just don't do this," Eva replied, trying to take the keys away from him. He held them up above his head. "You can have them for a kiss."

Eva stood watching him, feeling defeated. "Just don't drive."

"Why not? No one cares what happens to me anymore," he said angrily.

The man pushed her away and climbed behind the wheel. The truck revved up and he spun out of the parking lot. The cab suddenly glowed with white light, and Eva knew that the others were with him now, trying to convince him to accept the good that they offered. The truck sped toward the intersection without slowing down. Eva stood frozen, unable to take her eyes from the scene. An eighteen wheeler came barreling through the intersection just as the truck ran the red light and crashed into the driver's side, tearing the truck in half. Eva screamed, but no sound came from her.

Three points of light rose from the truck and Eva watched them ascend. The ground rumbled under her feet and the air shifted once again. She realized that her feet were coming off the ground and at once she was flung to the ground. Jarred and breathless, she looked around as the room filled with hourglasses materialized. The dark figure towered over her and snatched her up by the arm.

"It appears that you don't have it in you to drag men to their deaths as I thought. You will play the part or your precious Jonathan will suffer," he said, breathing onto her face.

"I'll not become what you want me to," Eva whispered.

"You will harvest the next soul, or I will call to have you taken away." He raised his hand and an hourglass flew from the shelf to his grasp. "You tell your buddies to stay away or this will be your last outing, deary."

The ground shifted under her feet and she was suddenly in a hospital room. A pregnant woman held the rails of the bed.

"Something's wrong! Call the nurse!" she screamed out in pain.

The man at her side held the call button and pushed the button repeatedly. "Hurry! Just hurry!" he yelled.

The woman looked at Eva. "Who are you?"

"I've come to help. Don't worry about anything," Eva whispered.

"Who are you talking to?" the man beside her asked.

"The girl in the corner," she said, pointing to Eva.

"There's no one there, dear. Just stay with me. You're going to be fine," the man said, suddenly panicked. "The baby will be just fine."

"He can't see me, and he can't hear me," Eva whispered.

"It doesn't matter if I die," the pregnant woman cried.

The man grabbed her hand. "But I want you to live."

The nurse came rushing in to inject her IV with medication.

On each side of Eva lights began to glow. The two white giants appeared and the woman's eyes widened, then closed as she fell back onto the bed.

"She's dying!" the man yelled.

"Sir, step back. We'll do all that we can," the nurse yelled at him.

"She's going to die, no matter what they do," the white giant said, standing beside her. "It's just her time, but the medication they gave her may sedate her too deeply before we can talk to her." The giant that had talked to her before grabbed Eva's arm. "You can help her. She's too weak to hang on alone, but if you go inside and help her, her soul can be spared. You'll be trapped there and, when you don't go back to where you came from, Jonathan will surely pay, but I'll go to him to help."

Eva nodded. "How do I go in and help her hold on?"

"We can put you in." The giant nodded to the other and they took Eva by the arms and lifted her over the woman. "Take a deep breath and close your eyes."

Eva had the sensation of falling and then felt smothered and hot. She tried to open her eyes, but couldn't. She whispered, "Did it work?"

"Who are you? Where are we? I can't see? Help me!" the woman yelled in the dark.

Eva reached out and said, "Find me. Take my hand!"

The woman grabbed Eva and hugged her. "Get me out of here," she cried.

"I don't know how to get out of here, but I can help you hold on. Let me explain." Eva then told the woman her story, what happened to her and what happened in the hospital room.

"So, we're stuck in my body? Are we in my mind? Are we dead?" the woman asked, crying.

"You're not dead," Eva said. "Listen. You can still hear the beeping of the monitor, and someone is talking. It must be your husband."

"You mean, we're still in the hospital room?"

"Yes," Eva said quietly. "And I'll be here with you until you wake up."

"Well, the man in the room isn't my husband," the woman replied. "He's my brother. I don't have a husband, and this baby was not planned. My brother talked me into having it, and he said that he would raise it. I just wanted it to be over, but when the time came for the abortion, I couldn't do it. I walked into that clinic and cried the entire time that I was filling out the papers. I got up, walked out, and called him right away. He agreed that day that if I would have this child, he would raise it as his own. This way, I can still be in the baby's life, but I wouldn't have to take care of it. I can barely take care of myself, much less a kid.

"Now, he's in that hospital room, wondering if either of us will make it. How horrifying that must be for him! It's a little girl. He's been so excited about having a daughter. He even has her nursery at his house ready for her," the woman said, crying softly.

"I'm so sorry that you are going through this," Eva said. "I don't even know your name."

"It's Melodia. Isn't that a horrible name?" She laughed. "My friends call me Mel."

"Well, Mel, it's good to meet you, and I'm glad we're in this together," Eva said, trying to sound reassuring as she squeezed her hand. "You're the first person I've really had a chance to talk to since …"

"Since you died?" Mel asked.

"Yes," Eva said, "that's a weird thing to be able to say, but yes, since I died."

"This all sounds like some sci-fi movie that we're all stuck in. Do you think that your Jonathan will come when he finds out you are here?" Mel asked.

"What good would it do for him to be here? Once you wake up, I leave and go back to that horrible dark place," Eva whispered.

"If I don't wake up, if I die, do I have to go with you?" Mel asked. "Will the baby?"

"The white giants are ready to take the baby if you die, but yes, unless you accept their path, then you will have to go with me," Eva said.

"I don't understand their path," Mel replied. "No one has ever told me how to follow the way that they believe. I thought that it was about being good and acting a certain way."

Eva sighed. "I thought that too for a while, until I met Jonathan. He shared the truth with me, but I was too selfish to accept it. I held back, thinking that I had plenty of time. The thing was, time was the gift that I didn't appreciate … until it was taken from me. Now, time is suspended and an eternity of service in darkness is all that I have." Eva took both of Mel's hands. "Sit with me, and I can tell you all that Jonathan told me. I've heard what the white giants share with those about to die. I can help you to follow their path."

Mel sat down in the darkness, but no longer felt afraid. As she listened about grace and forgiveness, she understood and believed.

***

Jonathan sat on a park bench thinking and didn't notice the man approaching.

"May I sit here?" the man asked.

"Oh sure, I don't mind," Jonathan said, continuing to look ahead.

"Jonathan, I'm Sam Godwin," the man said in a quiet voice.

Jonathan looked around with wide eyes. "You've seen Eva!"

"I have, but there's more going on here than you can imagine. You know, she heard all that you tried to tell her. She knew the truth in her heart when she died. She lives the truth more now than most people who claim to know the light … as we beg so many," Sam said.

"Wait … who are you … really?" Jonathan asked, standing up.

"I don't want to frighten you," Sam said, trying to reassure. "Let's just say that I keep good company when I'm not persuading people to make that one important eternal decision."

"But Eva is dead? Are you from the other side?" Jonathan whispered.

Sam laughed. "I do love when your kind call it the other side. That side—as you call it—and this side are merely one, yet you are unaware. We, meaning those like me, wander freely among you. We help when needed, we take when necessary, and those like me are sent to help in the final act of bravery. The choice. One final shot at the bright light, so to speak," Sam said with a sigh. "That's harder than you think. People still want things their way when the other guy is just waiting to torture them for an eternity."

Jonathan sat back down, remaining quiet.

Sam noticed the shocked look on Jonathan's face. "Eva sure loves you, you know? I don't just walk around your world eating ice cream. She asked me to come here. She wanted to make sure that you were safe. When the one in charge of her finds out what she's done, there will be no stopping him. He's ruthless and completely entertained by the suffering of others. You won't stand a chance."

"What do you mean, 'what's she's done'? Where is Eva?" Jonathan asked, worried.

"I showed her a way to help someone who was dying … a single woman who has been hospitalized due to complications in her pregnancy," Sam explained. "I was sent there with another to help the young woman to see the way of the light and to help her make the choice to believe before we take her and the baby. Eva showed up and was there to convince the woman to deny us and follow her, but she's a good girl and couldn't ask her to do it. She would have been punished this time, but I thought of a way to keep her here temporarily, and, for the moment, she won't have to return to her job of harvesting souls for the darkness.

"The woman was about to die, but we took Eva and immersed her into the woman's soul. They share the space now. Eva will be there helping the woman to hold on until I get you back there. She'll be able to hear you, and when we wake up the woman, Eva will be able to talk to you before the woman dies.

"There is however, one path that Eva can take that I haven't shared with her yet, and I'll explain it along the way. We must hurry, before the darkness invades that woman's soul and Eva is banished into a deep darkness for eternity." Sam stood up. "Time to go."

"My place isn't too far from here. How far away is Eva?" Jonathan asked, hurrying along the path.

"The hospital is about two hours away. I think her master was keeping her close to you so that she could be near if you needed to be used to persuade her to keep working. It's easier to travel a shorter distance in the spiritual world. Not much thought has to go into short distances for him. His work is much harder than ours," Sam said, walking in time with Jonathan. "I could take us to the hospital the easy way, but I thought a nice chat along the way will do you some good."

"I want to know all you can tell me about how to help Eva," Jonathan said. "I'll do what I have to do to save her … at any cost."

Sam smiled. "That's why you'll be able to help. She's going to need convincing and you'll be the only one who can."

***

"Mel, you've been quiet. Are you afraid?" Eva asked.

"I was thinking about what the doctor just said. You heard him, didn't you?" Mel asked. Her voice was shaking and she began to cry.

"I heard, but we're still here, so there's hope. There's always hope. I've seen that, if nothing else." Eva took her hand and held it tightly.

"Well, if they can just save the baby, I don't care if I die," Mel said softly. "That baby is the best thing that I've ever done. I knew that I couldn't care for her, and I don't want to raise a baby. I was a drug addict, and I'm not even sure who the father is. Now that I know she'll be taken care of, I don't really want to go back. Just help me to hold on until the baby is ready to come out, and I'll go with the white giants. Can you tell them for me?"

"I won't have to tell them. Once you've chosen, you don't have to go with me," Eva said quietly.

"You're going to be in trouble then, aren't you, because of me?" Mel asked, taking her hand from Eva's.

Eva took her by the shoulders. "You listen to me. I made my choices and I'm paying for the things that I've done, but you were given a chance to do the right thing. Now, your baby will grow up with your brother loving her as his own, and you will be at peace. You are the only person I've been able to talk to about everything, and I will gladly take whatever punishment comes, knowing you don't have to go with me."

Mel spoke in a whisper. "No one other than my brother has ever cared about me. I won't forget you, Eva." She stopped talking and took Eva's hand again. "Listen, there's someone in the room. I don't know that voice. It must be a new nurse."

"I know that voice. It's Jonathan!" Eva shouted. "Sam brought him here. He's here!"

***

Sam and Jonathan walked into the room where Mel lay on the bed, unconscious. Her brother stood up and extended his hand. "I'm Mark. May I help you? Do you know Mel?"

Sam looked at Mark. "I knew of your sister, but I just need to talk to you."

"Are you the father?" he asked Sam.

"No, and neither is Jonathan," Sam replied kindly. "We have something to talk to you about, and something to say to Mel."

Sam sat down and began to explain all that he could about what was happening. Mark sat listening silently, and then he stood up with his hands on his hips. "You expect me to believe this?" Mark demanded. "This just sounds like some crazy scheme that Mel cooked up to get me to leave so that she can get rid of the baby."

"That's just it, Mark," Sam reasoned. "The baby needs you. You need to be here to make sure that everything is taken care of properly. You can't leave. You have to stay and tell Mel goodbye. She's going to be okay with me. I'll make sure that she finds her way. It's my job." Sam took him by the arm. "When Mel wakes up, you will have a small amount of time before she has to leave, and you can tell her goodbye. We'll leave and then Eva will birth the baby. If you agree to take the baby and let Eva go with Jonathan, then everything will be fine. You have to believe what I'm telling you, and you have to give me room to work. Mel is going to come with me. It's her time, and there is no changing that fact, but we need to help her now."

Sam backed away from Mark and Jonathan, and began glowing. His common clothes shifted before them into a bright white smock. Wings unfurled behind him and spanned the room. Slowly he began to fade until there was but a shadow of him in front of them. "We don't have time to waste, Mark. It's time for her to go. Either you believe what you are seeing, or you will miss saying goodbye to Mel," Sam said. "Now, don't interrupt me while I explain all of this to Eva. She has a choice to make."

Mark stepped back. Tears streamed down his face as he realized that this would be the last time that he spoke to his sister.

Jonathan stepped closer to the bed, not wanting to miss anything.

Sam began to speak, "Eva, listen to me."

Eva said, "I can hear you."

Jonathan yelled out, "I'm here!"

Sam turned to him and said, "Be silent."

Jonathan stepped back, his heart pounding in his chest.

"Eva and Mel, I need you both to understand what's about to happen," Sam firmly said. "Mel, it's your time to come with me. I know that Eva told you about truth and faith, and now it's time. You've made your decision to follow a path of light, and when I take the hand of your earthly body, you'll feel it. Grasp hold and don't let go. I'm going to pull you into the hospital room, and you'll be able to say goodbye to Mark.

"Eva, I need you to be completely aware of what is about to happen. You will stay in Mel's body and birth the baby. Mark will take the baby as his. Jonathan is here to accept you in Mel's bodily form, but I must warn you. You have crossed over, and you will be hunted. Right now, your current location is not known to the world of darkness. We have set up a shield for everyone to be protected. You will have to fight this, and the only way to do so is to keep fighting for the light. There are so many out there that need what you have shared with Mel. You will see deeper into the spiritual world than others because of what you have endured. You will be able to see the dark and the light in the lives of those around you. You must fight for the light or be consumed by the darkness. I explained all of this to Jonathan, and he is willing to stand by you and do whatever is necessary to help you survive. Life won't be easy, but my dear, you will have life! You'll be able to see me from time to time and, because you have found a way to escape your position, there will be another to take your place. The darkness has been angered, but where there is darkness, there is always light. Light is the life you will share, the life you will fight for."

Eva shook with fear and uncertainty. Mel turned and took her by the shoulders. "Fight for others like you fought for me."

"Sam, I'll do whatever I have to do to have a second chance," Eva said, crying.

"Mel, I'm ready for you," Sam said. Then, he reached out and took Mel's hand. Mark watched in disbelief as she clasped hands with the incredible being before him.

Slowly, like seeing your breath on a cold day, the spirit of Mel sat up from the bed, leaving her body behind. She stepped onto the floor and looked at Mark. Mark stepped forward and stopped, looking at Sam.

"Time to say your goodbyes," Sam said softly, knowing the depth of pain Mark felt.

Mel's spirit and Mark stepped toward each other and as soon as they embraced, Mel materialized for a final time.

Mark cried and said, "I love you, little sister, and I promise that I'll be a good daddy to your little girl."

Mel whispered, "For the first time, I'm not afraid."

Mark stepped back and continued to hold her hands. Mel began to glow. "You look beautiful."

"I love you, Mark. It's time for me to go," Mel said, smiling with peace.

Mark nodded. "I think I'll name the baby Melody."

Mel smiled, and a single tear rolled down her cheek.

Sam spoke softly. "Jonathan, I'll be back. I need to take Mel to her new home." He reached for Mel's hand. Immediately, she began to fade until she was gone.

Mark and Jonathan remained quiet for a moment. Mark spoke first. "That was amazing."

Jonathan whispered, "I'm still trying to sort out all of it in my mind."

Mark nodded.

Sam appeared once again beside the hospital bed and said, "I'm going to need you two to step back. I need to wake up Mel's body." Then, Sam lifted his hands and smiled as light brightened and settled over the bed. With a sound of rushing wind, the light was absorbed into the body before them, and her eyes flew open. The monitor began to beep, and immediately a nurse was at the door.

Moving to the side of the bed, the nurse began to talk quietly. "Can you hear me? Honey, can you hear me?" She turned to Mark and Jonathan. "I need to call the doctor. I'll be right back."

When the nurse was gone, Jonathan stepped forward. "Eva, can you hear me?"

Eva spoke softly, "Yes. Oh, Jonathan, it's really happening. I'm here. Everything feels strange, but I'm here. I didn't know what to say to the nurse."

Mark stepped forward. "You're going to have to respond to the name Mel, or they will think you're crazy."

"That's right. You can't call me Eva," she said. The baby moved and Eva gasped. "Oh, Jonathan, I felt the baby move."

"It won't be long until you deliver. Are you sure that you can do this?" Mark asked.

"I know I can do this. I'm just so sleepy," Eva said closing her eyes.

The doctor entered the room with a nurse. They immediately began taking Eva's vitals. "Well, nice to see that you're awake."

Eva nodded. "Am I going to be okay?"

"You're much stronger than I thought you were," the doctor smiled. "It seems that today is a day for miracles. I don't even understand how you could be awake."

"How's the baby?" Eva whispered.

"She's just fine, and we'll keep you here until it's time to deliver," the doctor said, smiling kindly. "You're too weak right now to deliver. We'll need to get your strength up and see how things go. I'll schedule the C-section as soon as I know you're ready."

Eva touched her rounded belly as her entire abdomen tightened. "The baby is moving again."

The doctor looked at the monitor. "No, honey, that was a contraction. We have you hooked up to a monitor. See that little rise in the line across the paper? That signals that you just had a contraction. The nurses will keep a watch on your monitor at their desk. No need to worry. We might be having that Cesarian before schedule."

"Why do I have to have a Cesarian?" Eva asked.

"I'm just not sure that you're strong enough to give birth."

Eva sat up a little and held her stomach holding her breath. "Oh my goodness," she said. "I feel like my breath is being squeezed out of me."

The doctor looked at the monitor. "That's a big contraction and that was way too close to the other one. I need to check and see if you are dilating," he said, then turned to Jonathan, "You'll need to step out."

Eva looked at Jonathan and said, "I need him to stay, if that's okay."

"It's fine with me," the doctor said. "Just rest on your back and let's see what's going on."

Within a moment, the doc removed his gloves and put his hands on his hips. "Well, you've gone from five to ten centimeters in a very short time. Here comes another contraction. Just hang on. It looks like this baby is breaking through the meds. Evidently, she wants today to be her birthday."

Eva reached out to Jonathan and he stepped up to take her hand. "I won't leave you."

The nurse came rushing through the door. "It looks like we've got some action going on in here tonight."

The doctor looked to the nurse. "Have room three prepared for her C-section."

"I want to have her in here!" Eva spoke loudly. "Please, let me do this. I want to."

The doctor put his hands on his hips and Eva leaned on her side. "I don't think it's a choice anymore. Something feels really strange." She held her abdomen and closed her eyes leaning her head back. "I feel like maybe I should go to the restroom before anything happens."

The doctor stepped closer. "Let's see if that's a good idea. Lie back one more time."

The nurse buzzed the nurses' station and announced, "We're ready in here."

The doctor laughed. "Well, that baby is on her way out. She's crowning." He turned to the nurse. "Call Mark and let him know."

The nurse left the room and others entered instantly, flitting around doing things that Eva wondered about but didn't ask. *Maybe it was best to not know,* she thought. Her abdomen tightened again and it felt as if she couldn't breathe. "Jonathan, the baby is coming," Eva shouted. "I can feel her moving through my body!"

The doctor lifted the hospital gown. "There's no time to break down the bed!" The nurse came to his side and raised the back of the bed. "Now, when I tell you to push, you're going to push and keep pushing until I tell you to stop. Understand?"

Eva nodded and looked to Jonathan. He kissed her on the forehead. "I love what you're doing," he said. "I'm right here."

When the doctor said to push, peace washed through Eva's new body. A faint glow beside her let her know that she wasn't alone in this. Her favorite white giants were there to give her strength. They reached across her abdomen and touched her. Suddenly, her body began to shake and she felt the baby move farther down.

The doctor looked up, smiling. "You do a couple more pushes like that and we'll have her out in no time. Breathe for me. Breathe, take a deep breath and push!" Eva held onto the bedrail and knew that Sam Godwin had taken hold of her hand. The doctor was smiling as he motioned for Jonathan to look. The door opened and Mark came in, crying. Once again her body shook with a force that Eva knew she'd never be able to describe to anyone, and she knew the baby was almost out.

The doctor laughed. "You've got this! Breathe for me, and … push!"

Eva leaned up slightly, screaming out in pain, and then felt as if everything inside of her simply was gone. Within seconds, a baby's cry filled the room. The doctor made the necessary clip, and the baby was separated from the umbilical cord.

The nurse put a blanket in Mark's arms, and the doctor laid the baby in the blanket. Mark looked up at Eva, nodding as tears of joy ran down his cheeks. Eva nodded back and turned to Jonathan. He kissed her on the cheek and held her close. The nurse motioned for Mark to come with her. Mark looked back as he left the room, and Eva realized that he was looking at Mel's earthly form for the last time. She smiled at him, and he nodded a final goodbye.

Mel had asked for Mark and the baby to be allowed to leave the room so that she wouldn't have to watch them together and want to hold her. Eva was thankful to watch them leave. Even though the baby wasn't hers, she still felt connected to her. A tear rolled down her cheek and Jonathan wiped it away.

He whispered, "You're brave, and I love you."

Eva whispered back, "I love you, too."

The doctor had grown solemn and finished all that he needed to do with Eva. The nurse was cleaning up around her, asking her questions that she didn't know about Mel. It all seemed so unreal, and several times the nurse had to ask if she heard her. Eva was glad that Mel was in a better place and not having to go through the pain of giving birth to such a beautiful little girl … and then having to let her go.

Before long, Eva was in a different room and Jonathan was asleep in the chair next to the bed. She stared at the walls around her, and for the first time, realized how exhausted she felt. Her eyes closed, and she drifted into sleep. The darkness surrounded her instantly, and Eva felt cold. Something grabbed her arm and she felt hot breath on her neck.

"You didn't think you could get away that easy, did you?" the dark creature asked.

Eva struggled to get free, but she knew that she was trapped. "Let me go," she whispered.

"You will never be free of me." Her captor laughed in her ear.

She gasped, and her eyes flew open. With her heart racing, she raised up in bed. "Jonathan!"

Jonathan came to the bed. "What's wrong?"

"I was dreaming, or at least I think I was dreaming," Eva said, looking up at him with fear in her eyes. "I was back where I came from, and the one who was in charge of me told me that I would never be free."

Jonathan took her face in his hands and kissed her gently. "You listen to me," Jonathan said. "I know what Sam told me, and I believe him. You have been given a second chance, but you will have to battle that darkness forever. Don't you ever be afraid again. I'm here with you, and we will do this together. No matter what you see or hear, we'll face it together."

Eva nodded, and Jonathan motioned for her to move over. He climbed in the bed beside her and held her until she fell asleep again.

After the doctor gave her the go ahead the following morning, Eva was released to go home. Walking out of the hospital, Jonathan reached out to take her by the hand. "Together."

Stepping out into the warm air, Eva's hand began to tingle. She looked down and saw an image that she wasn't ready to share with Jonathan just yet. A sword that radiated with the light of the white giants faintly materialized in her hand and then disappeared. Darkness swirled around her and then faded in the sunlight. She knew that Jonathan had not seen anything, and that in the days ahead, she would have to fight for her life and for the souls of others.

Eva looked to Jonathan, squeezed his hand and said boldly, "Together."

Annie

By: Ashlea Burns

Annie sat by the lake waiting for her best friend Zoey, as she had something really important to tell her. Zoey had told Annie during the prom the night before that they could talk today. It was the day before graduation, and Zoey was leaving the state to go to college. If she didn't tell her now, she may never get the chance to tell her again.

As Annie looked across the calm water, she thought back to six months before … when her life was changed forever. Annie had been suffering from severe headaches, but hadn't done anything about them. She never told her parents because she thought that it was just from stress … until the day she blacked out and was rushed to hospital. It was then that her life took a drastic turn. She was dying.

Annie's mind came back to the present as she skipped a rock across the water. Annie was getting a little impatient waiting for Zoey, so she decided to meet her halfway at the old oak tree near the other side of the lake toward town. She sat under the tree, thinking of her best friend.

She regretted that she hadn't told her best friend about her terminal condition, but she didn't want her to worry. No, she would wait for the right time, but she knew she had to tell her soon. After all, Zoey was more like a sister than just a friend. Ever since she had started dating her brother, Marcus, Zoey was practically a member of the family.

She waited until dark, but Zoey hadn't arrived. When Annie rose to her feet, the earth around her began to spin under her feet and she fell to the ground. Suddenly, she saw an otherworldly, bright light and her soul lifted from her body and moved toward it. She knew that she was dying and had made peace with it. Extreme joy and peace filled her heart and she was happy, for the pain was no more, but she couldn't leave her best friend or her brother behind.

***

Zoey had been dating Annie's brother, Marcus, and couldn't be happier that they were together. Annie knew that she could watch over them as their relationship grew, and she hoped that she would be able to watch over their children, as well, but would she get the chance? Or would her dying affect everything?

When Annie passed away, she found herself in a strange, white room. Everything was white: the walls, the floor, even the ceiling. She thought that it was sort of a waiting room between this world and the next. As a result, Annie wasn't quite sure what to do or what was expected of her.

"Hello," a friendly voice said, coming from behind Annie. "I guess you're stuck here, too." Annie turned around to find another girl standing there that was not much older than she. "I'm Ally."

"Um," she said still, a little shocked. "I'm Annie, where are we?"

"Good question," Ally said, walking toward Annie. "As far as I can figure, we're in limbo."

"Limbo?" Annie asked, confused.

"Yeah," Ally replied. "You know ... sort of a 'between space' ... like where souls go that haven't crossed over yet."

"Oh, I see." Annie replied. "So, why haven't we crossed over yet? Is this some sort of waiting period or something?"

Ally started laughing. "Haven't you ever watched movies where a ghost had unfinished business when they died so they couldn't cross over? That's why they haunt places," Ally replied as she sat on the white floor.

Annie finally understood. She still had unfinished business on Earth with Zoey and, until she was able to finish it, she couldn't cross over. Fear, trepidation and amazement ruled her as she ventured through this strange dimension, and she wasn't sure how it all worked.

"So, what's your unfinished business?" Annie asked as she sat down on the floor across from Ally.

"Well," Ally began, looking away from Annie. "I told my boyfriend that I wanted to break up because I was in love with someone else, then I was going to tell the other guy that I loved him, and … well … things kind of went badly. My boyfriend got mad and pushed me down the stairs. I don't think that he meant to, but he did. The next thing I knew, I was here." Annie just looked at Ally with horror and shock. "So, I'm guessing that since I never told the other guy that I loved him, it made me come here."

"That's horrible," Annie said, looking at Ally's sad face. "I'm so sorry."

"It's alright," Ally said. "I've been here for a few years now and have finally accepted it. I know I'll cross over one day. I've learned how to write notes to the living and soon Andrew will know how I feel about him."

"Really?" Annie asked, surprised. "You can write notes that humans can see?"

"Yes," Ally replied. "It's simple to do. It's just hard to get them to accept that it's from someone that's dead."

"Oh, I bet," Annie said, then fell silent. Since she was now a ghost, could she walk through walls now? Could people see her or feel her presence? It was all so overwhelming. She looked down and was delighted that she could see people on Earth, but was filled with concern when Zoey found her lifeless body under a tree by the creek. At first, Annie didn't think it would affect Zoey so much, but the next day when she left town, she began to worry. Zoey wasn't set to leave for college for another three months.

She followed Zoey to a small town called, Rich Creek, trying to find out why she had left her home of Cloverdale and why she had left Marcus. Annie and Marcus had seemed so happy together, they had talked about making a life together after they both finished college and had decided where they wanted to settle down. Annie couldn't figure out what would possess Zoey to just leave without telling Marcus. Annie watched Zoey for over a year as she pushed herself farther away from her family and all the people she loved. *Why was she doing this?* Annie pondered. *What has happened to my best friend?*

As the next few years went by, Annie tried reaching out to Zoey. She wanted so badly to tell her friend that she was there with her.

Annie used what she had learned from Ally about writing notes to try and reach out to Zoey, but nothing worked. Zoey would find the notes, but would automatically throw them away. Annie didn't know what else to do, but she knew that Zoey must know deep down that she was with her, at least in a spirit.

"I wish I could figure out a way to tell Zoey," Annie said, sitting in the white space in Limbo across from Allie. "The notes aren't helping any."

"You'll find a way," Ally replied. "Look at what we've learned so far! We've discovered how to write notes and even go to different places without being all ghost creepy."

"That's true." Annie said as both girls laughed. "I would've been stuck here forever had you not showed me how to 'pop" in and out of limbo. The only thing that sucks is that we still can't talk to humans."

"Yeah, it'd be so much easier if they could see us ... like in those crazy movies that we used to watch where the ghost appears to the living," Ally said with a chuckle.

"Oh yeah!" Annie replied. "That would be so much cooler. We need to find a way to pop into human form or something." Both girls laughed, hoping that it was possible.

Being in limbo wasn't so bad for Annie until Ally resolved her unfinished business, found peace, and crossed over. As a result, Annie spent the next year trying to find a way to resolve her unfinished business and find peace so she could cross over, too. Annie tried to expose herself to Zoey, but there was something keeping Zoey from seeing her. Before she died, she knew that ghosts could appear to the living, but she had no clue how to do it. Zoey could sense a presence that wasn't normal in the room, and she hoped that Zoey would put the pieces together, but to no avail. Annie even tried telling Zoey once that she was there by leaving a note saying, "Zoey, this is Annie. Please, believe me." But even that hadn't worked.

One day as she watched Zoey studying an invitation to her sister Julia's wedding, it hit Annie: this was her chance to get Zoey and Marcus back together. She tried to call Zoey on the telephone, which was a waste, because the living can't hear the dead over the phone. Annie knew that Zoey would go back to Cloverdale for the wedding. That was her chance. She had to make sure that Marcus told Zoey the truth behind her death and that she wasn't responsible. Annie felt better, knowing that her plan was set.

Annie watched as Zoey reunited with her family after five long years and was surprised that she hadn't gone back to visit in the past. There was a lot of emotion between Zoey and her mother. It was heartbreaking to Annie to watch and felt that she had been the cause of her long absence.

Annie knew that she had very little time to get Zoey and Marcus together, so she began her plan. First, while Zoey was sleeping she found some paper and a pen on the desk and wrote a note to Zoey. She had tried to do this before and had never got any emotion or response from Zoey, but maybe this time would be different. Annie didn't want to write the whole story out so she kept it simple and just wrote, "Don't blame yourself." Annie hoped that this would at least intrigue Zoey enough to find out who left the note.

The next morning, Annie watched as Zoey got up and discovered the note. She was excited that she might finally understand, until Zoey balled it up and threw it away. Apparently, Zoey had thought that her mother had written the note, which didn't help Annie. Luckily, Annie had thought of a plan 'B'. Even though Annie didn't know how to show herself to Zoey, she *did* know how to transfer her thoughts through a human. The only problem was that the human had to be a believer of supernatural activity. If he or she didn't believe in ghosts or spirits, then it wouldn't work. Lucky for Annie, Zoey's sister, Julia, was just that type. She believed in possession, spirits, ghosts, and the power of the unknown, so Annie was able to use Julia to get in touch with Marcus. Granted, Julia wouldn't remember any of it since Annie would be possessing Julia. Perfect. So, Annie used her body to call Marcus and tell him that Zoey was in town.

Annie watched as Zoey opened the door and found Marcus standing there. The shock and fear was evident on Zoey's face as she stared at the man she still loved. Annie knew that she had to mend their hearts and get them together or she would be stuck in limbo forever. Things seemed to go well until Marcus tried to tell Zoey the truth.

"What happened to Annie wasn't your fault," Marcus pleaded with Zoey as Annie watched from above.

"What do you mean 'it wasn't my fault'?!" Zoey exclaimed. "I blew her off when she said that she wanted to talk and then I found her dead body. How is it *not* my fault?"

Annie's heart grew heavy. What had she put her best friend through? Zoey blamed herself for her death, and Annie blamed herself for not telling her best friend about the brain tumor.

Now, it was too late.

Annie watched with tears streaming down her face as Zoey stormed off, away from Marcus. Annie followed her to her room and watched as Zoey cried into her pillow. Annie knew that she had to do something. Zoey needed to know the truth, or she would never find peace.

But how? How could Annie tell her the truth? Annie needed answers. So Annie went on a search for someone—or something—that could tell her how to show herself to Zoey.

Annie hated to leave Zoey alone, but she had to find a way to make things right. She headed to a local shop called *Mystic Lovers Shoppe*. It was the only one close by that sold paranormal items, such as incents, oils, potions, jewelry and even some books on ghosts and apparitions. She went inside the shop.

Even though she was a ghost, she was able to hold items such as books. That was another thing that she had learned to do in limbo, but she would place it onto a nearby table so that she didn't freak people out by seeing a book floating in the air. Although in a place like this, it wouldn't be so peculiar. While the shopkeeper was busy, Annie began her searching for answers. She found a book titled *Ghosts and Humans* and began to read it. As she was reading, she noticed that Zoey was outside. She hesitated, but walked into the shop. Zoey must be there for a gift for Julia. Annie knew deep down that Zoey could feel her presence, but Zoey was always the type that had an explanation for everything. Annie had hoped that she could find something to prove to Zoey that she wasn't to blame, and that she had been there with her all along.

Annie tried concentrating on finding answers, but kept watching Zoey to see if she could sense her presence there. Zoey kept looking over her shoulder toward Annie, but couldn't see her. Annie wanted to reach out to her and to tell her that everything was alright, but had no idea how she was going to do it.

Zoey perused the store and picked out some oils and incense, then a beautiful pair of dainty earrings with a charm shaped like an angel wing. She also picked out a necklace that matched it. Then, as Annie was reading, she finally found an answer. She was so excited that she dropped the book and froze when Zoey suddenly looked across the room in her direction.

According to the book, a ghost can show themselves to nonbelievers during the full moon if they gathered the light around them. Lucky for her, tonight was the full moon, but she had to learn how to absorb the surrounding light in order to project herself to Zoey before the night was over, or she would have to wait until the next full moon, which may be too late.

That should be easy, Annie thought to herself. When she looked up from the book, Zoey was gone. Annie wasn't sure when she had left, but she didn't have much time. She needed to show herself to Zoey and talk to her before the wedding ended, or she may never get a chance to get her and Marcus back together. Looking for a way to tell her, she went to Zoey's parents house and found Zoey and Julia getting ready for the wedding.

"Here, Julia," Zoey said, handing her sister the box that she got from the bookstore. "This is for you." Julia took the box from Zoey and gave her a smile.

Julia opened it and inside was a beautiful pair of earrings and a matching necklace. Tears welled up in her eyes as she gave Zoey a big hug. "Oh, Zoey!" Julia replied with a slight catch to her voice. "They're beautiful."

"I wanted to give you something special for such a special day." Zoey said, wiping her own tears away.

Annie stood by the window watching the emotion between the two sisters, but she also felt sadness coming from Zoey. She sensed that Zoey was unhappy, even though she seemed happy on the outside.

Annie went into the backyard where they were still setting up the decorations for the wedding. She watched as Marcus helped Zoey's father, Mr. Boone, set up all the chairs. She needed to practice showing herself, and what better person to try it on than Marcus? Annie smiled, waiting until she could get Marcus alone. It took Marcus and Mr. Boone about half an hour to get all the chairs set up.

"Marcus, could you pull my truck around here so that we can get the tables, please?" Mr. Boone asked Marcus, holding out his truck keys.

"Sure, Mr. Boone," Marcus replied, already headed toward the white truck that sat on the other side of the house.

"This is my chance," Annie said out loud to herself. "I have to appear to Marcus now before it's too late."

As Marcus walked towards the truck, he looked around. He knew that he was being watched, but had no idea by whom. Annie closed her eyes and in a big flash she was suddenly standing before Marcus, surrounded by light. His mouth dropped opened wide as he stared at his sister's ghost.

"Don't be afraid, Marcus," Annie said as she stood before Marcus. "I need to talk to you."

Marcus just stared at Annie, clearly in shock and suddenly couldn't find his voice.

"Zoey needs our help. She blames herself for my death."

"I know," Marcus finally said as he stared at his sister, glowing in bright light. "I've tried to tell her, but she won't listen."

"I know," Annie replied with a sweet smile. "I think she'll listen to me before she'll listen to you." Annie chuckled lightly as she watched her brother's face.

"But why now?" Marcus asked. "Why have you waited five years? How are you here now?"

"It's complicated," Annie replied. "I've been stuck in Limbo due to the unresolved issue concerning Zoey. I've tried to communicate with her, but nothing worked. I just now learned how to appear to people and wanted to test it on you."

Marcus smirked, chuckling lightly as he listened to Annie. "I have to do this tonight or I may not be able to do it again. The book I read said I can only appear to people during a full moon … and that ends tonight."

"Then we'd better hurry," Marcus quickly replied. "The wedding is set for dusk." Then, Marcus hopped into the truck and drove around to the other side of the house.

Annie sat beside him in the truck until they came to a stop. "I will always be with you," Annie said, smiled as she disappeared. Marcus looked over at the empty seat.

Annie watched as her brother unloaded the truck and set up the tables with Mr. Boone. Every now and then, Marcus looked over his shoulder and smiled, knowing that Annie was still there.

It was only about 20 minutes before the wedding and Annie was getting desperate. She needed to get Zoey alone so that she could talk to her, but how?

Annie smiled as Zoey, Julia, and their mother dressed for the wedding. "They all look so beautiful," Annie said to herself.

"Look at my two beautiful daughters," Mrs. Boone said, ginging each of them a hug. "Julia, that wedding dress suits you perfectly."

"Thanks, Mom," Julia replied with a sweet smile.

"And Zoey," Mrs. Boone said, placing her hands on Zoey's shoulders. "You look beautiful, as well. You look just like a sunflower."

"Oh, Mom," Zoey said, trying not to laugh. "Does it look that bad?"

"Oh no, honey," Mrs. Boone replied. "It's elegant. The yellow sundress and black shoes make you look so sweet. It reminds mc of whcn you were a kid and you and Annie …" She stopped right then when a frown came across Zoey's face. "Honey, I'm sorry." She pulled Zoey in for a hug.

"It's okay, Mom," Zoey said, looking away. "It's just been hard being here with Marcus and all, but I'm fine, Mom. Don't worry."

"Are you sure?" Mrs. Boone asked. "We haven't seen you since you … well … you know." She didn't want to bring up the past. Not now. Not before the wedding.

"I'm Fine, Mom. I promise," Zoey said, faking a smile for her mother's sake.

Annie wanted to cry, seeing how deeply her friend missed her and how sad she was about Marcus being there. She knew that Zoey wanted to be with Marcus, and Annie needed to make sure that it happened.

Annie would never see her own wedding day, but she was part of Julia's now and, hopefully, she would be a part of Zoey's one day, too, but she needed to act fast. "It's time." Mr. Boone said, standing in the doorway. "Are you ready?"

"Yes," Julia replied, giving a last smile at her mom and sister, then they headed out to the backyard.

Annie watched as Zoey walked up the aisle and waited for Julia and their father to join them. She looked so beautiful … both sisters did. Annie noticed the love that Marcus still had for Zoey when he glanced at her. Annie just had to make sure that they got back together.

During the ceremony, Marcus was focusing more on Zoey then the wedding itself. Annie stood behind the last row of chairs waiting for her queue to appear. Annie looked up at the sky, and the sun was starting to set. In about an hour, it would be dark. Annie knew that she had to act soon. She just hoped that it wasn't in the middle of the reception.

After the wedding ceremony, Julia and her new husband, Ron, led the way to the reception. Mrs. Boone had made an amazing buffet. Annie stood by the back table as she watched everyone enjoying themselves, that is, everyone except Zoey. And every time Marcus walked up to Zoey, she found an excuse to go a different direction.

"Zoey," Marcus said. "Can we talk?"

Zoey took a step back. "Um," she replied. "Not now." Then, she walked away again.

Annie reached out and touched Marcus' shoulder and he smiled. Just knowing that Marcus knew she was there made Annie feel better.

As the reception was winding down, Marcus walked over to Zoey. "Care to dance?" he asked as his face brimmed with pride.

"I don't know," Zoey replied, looking around, unsure what to do. "I'm not sure it's such a good idea."

"Please, Zoey … just one dance?" Marcus asked. Zoey was still unsure when she finally nodded, took Marcus' outstretched hand, and headed to the dance floor. "I'm glad I got to see you again, Zoey," Marcus said, holding Zoey tightly to him. "I've missed you."

"I missed you, too, Marcus," Zoey replied. "It's just been hard since Annie … well … you know." Zoey looked down at her feet. Annie stood behind Marcus as he and Zoey danced, knowing that she was running out of time. She had only 30 minutes left until dark.

"Zoey," Marcus said, placing his hand under her chin to raise her eyes to meet his. "Zoey, it wasn't your fault."

"But it was," Zoey started to say, but Marcus placed a finger on her lips to shush her.

"Marcus … I," Zoey began again, but Marcus leaned down and gently touched his lips to hers.

Annie got excited. *Maybe Zoey will believe now,* Annie thought to herself.

"Please," Zoey said, pulling away from Marcus. "Please don't."

"Why?" Marcus asked, searching her eyes. "Why won't you believe me?"

Zoey began to cry as she tried to pull away from Marcus.

"Zoey, no," Marcus said, trying to pull Zoey back to him.

Everything was falling apart. Annie knew that she had to do it now.

She closed her eyes and in a burst of light, she appeared. Zoey froze as she turned away from Marcus and stared at her best friend standing in a cloud of light.

"A … A … Annie?" Zoey managed to get out, trembling as she stared at Annie.

"Hello, Zoey," Annie said, smiling sweetly at her friend. "We need to talk."

Zoey wasn't sure what to say. Did Annie come back to haunt her for what she did or was she here for another reason? Zoey was so confused. "Talk about what?" Zoey asked, trembling.

"It wasn't your fault, Zoey," Annie replied, then added, "and you need to stop blaming yourself."

"But it is," Zoey said as tears rushed down her cheeks. "I pushed you away when you needed me. I should have been there for you."

"Now, Zoey," Annie said, stepping closer to Zoey. "There was nothing you could do to save me; no one could."

"If I was there, I could have tried!" Zoey replied as the tears flowed freely down her face. "And now it's too late."

"Listen to her, Zoey," Marcus said as he walked closer to stand beside Zoey. "There is more to the story than you know."

Zoey looked at Marcus, then at Annie.

"He's right," Annie replied. "I was dying. I wanted to tell you, but I didn't want you to worry. I wanted to tell you at the right time, but by then, it was too late." Zoey just stared at Annie, listening. "I had a brain tumor, Zoey. No one but my parents knew. Marcus didn't even know until it was my time to go."

Zoey looked over at Marcus. "Why didn't you tell me?" Zoey asked, her eyes filled with pain.

"I tried," Marcus replied. "I was going to tell you after graduation, but then you ran away. When you came back I tried, but you wouldn't listen."

Zoey looked up at Marcus. Her eyes red and puffy from crying. "I'm so sorry," Zoey said through her tears. "I thought you would blame me for what happened and that you would hate me."

"Oh, Zoey," Marcus said, wiping the tears from her eyes. "I could never hate you. I love you, Zoey."

Zoey looked into his eyes and knew it was true. "You … you do?" Zoey asked, a little shocked.

"Yes," Marcus replied. "I always have." Then, Marcus leaned down and kissed Zoey. Then, both Zoey and Marcus looked at Annie. Annie knew that she was able to pass over now, but she wanted to wait a few more minutes to say her goodbyes.

"Thank you," Annie said, giving them both a sweet smile.

"For what?" Zoey asked, confused.

"For releasing me," Annie said. "I've been stuck in Limbo for five years because I never told you the truth and because you blamed yourself. It took me this long to learn how to appear to you. I tried to leave notes, but they never worked."

"That was you?" Zoey asked, stepping closer to Annie. "You tried to contact me! You left those notes saying that it wasn't my fault! You tried to tell me, but I wouldn't listen."

"Yes," Annie replied, then added, "it was me. I was also to blame for telling Marcus that you were here. I used Julia's open minded view of the supernatural and called Marcus." Annie looked over at Julia, standing not far from Zoey, amazed. "I'm sorry about that."

"No problem," Julia replied with a laugh. "I knew that something weird was going on, but I wasn't sure what. Glad I could help."

Annie smiled, then looked back at Zoey. "I knew that I had to right the wrongs I was responsible for and to get you back to where you belong … with Marcus. You deserve to be happy and I'm happy if you're happy." Zoey smiled as tears of joy ran down her face. She reached out and touched Annie's arm, then gave her a big hug.

"I miss you so much," Zoey said through her tears, holding tightly to Annie.

"I know," Annie replied. "I've missed you, too, but always remember that I am with you … no matter what. I'll always be here to look over you and protect you from above."

Zoey slowly pulled away from Annie and smiled. "Thank you, Annie," Zoey replied. "Thank you for all that you have done."

Annie smiled at Zoey and then at Marcus. "Ah, Marcus," Annie said. "Please take special care of Zoey."

"I will," Marcus replied as he wrapped an arm around Zoey. "I'll always look after her."

"Good," Annie replied. "Well I'd better be going. Goodbye, dear brother." Annie reached out and gave Marcus a big hug. She missed her brother terribly, but she knew that he would be happy now.

A moment later, Annie stood in front of a big golden gate and watched as Marcus kissed Zoey. Then, Zoey put her arms around his neck and kissed him back. They looked up into the sky, knowing that Annie was watching. As Annie crossed over the threshold into Heaven, there was a twinkle in the sky. Annie was free. She was free from her restless wandering and could now have peace and joy. Annie never realized how hard it was being in limbo … until she saw the other side.

Toil and Trouble Too
A Dark Times Novella # 2
By: Susan Burdorf

Arnett Briggs sucked in her breath, making her face look like a fish that had just landed on the beach, gasping for air. That was how she felt, as if all the air inside of her had been sucked out and now there was nothing left for her to breathe. Around her, the world went on normally. People in her Economics 101 class at Baxter University were talking to each other, but she couldn't hear a sound. Arnett struggled to remain still, to identify the source of the blackness that was threatening to overwhelm her senses, but the need to breathe was so strong that it prevented her from finding the reason for her distress.

Then, it was gone so swiftly that even as she welcomed the air that rushed back into her lungs, she felt herself falling. Hitting the ground hard, Arnett groaned.

Great! she thought in frustration. *First day of class Freshman year and I'm already making a spectacle of myself. So much for staying under the radar.*

"Hey, sis. You okay?"

She looked up and her twin, Ashley, was at her side. She had rushed over almost immediately and helped Arnett back into her seat. Whispering intently, she asked, "Did you feel it? Is that what did this to you?"

"Did you feel it, too? Why didn't you …" Arnett left the thought hanging. Of course, nothing ever affected Ashley the way it did Arnett. While Arnett was proud of the fact that her detecting skills were stronger than her twin's, it was also frustrating because Arnett was usually the one who embarrassed herself when they came across a target.

Ashley grinned as she slapped her sister on the shoulder. "Hey! Sorry about that, everyone. Arnie just got too much of the Chef's Surprise at breakfast today."

As the rest of the class laughed, Arnett opened her book, trying not to get too red. Professor Martin stared at both of them with a measuring look before turning to answer a question from another student as the class resumed its normal activities.

Ashley returned to her seat after Arnett nodded to her that she was okay. A few minutes later the bell rang, signaling the end of class. Arnett stayed in her seat, rustling papers and rearranging her backpack, stalling for time to regain her equilibrium.

Ashley stopped by and said in a low voice that only her sister could hear, "We need to talk about this. I have a class, but I think I can get out of it. Are you okay for now? Meet me at the garden outside the library as quick as you can."

Arnett nodded. She wasn't sure what she could tell her sister at this point since she was not sure what had triggered her paranormal radar. The movement had been so quick that she couldn't even tell from what direction it had come. It was not there and then it was, but then disappeared again. It had never affected her that way before. Arnett wondered if Ashley had gotten a better grip on the signal than she had. She hoped so, otherwise she was pretty sure that they would be meeting up with the person who had caused that reaction in her. She did not want to meet them unprepared.

There must be some strong activity going on. Arnett rose from her seat just as the next class came in. She let a few students pass, moving when one tall boy almost stepped on her toes, and slowly walked down the stairs from where her seat was on the third tier. Her legs were unexpectedly wobbly and felt a little weak. When she reached the bottom she flipped her long brown hair out of the way and shifted the bag to her shoulder to balance the weight inside. Between her textbooks, notebooks, and laptop it was pretty heavy and always left her shoulders sore where the straps rested.

"Ms Briggs, if I may have a word with you?" Professor Martin looked at her with an expression that said he would not take no for an answer.

Stalling for time, to avoid the question that she thought he was going to ask, Arnett said, "I'm fine, Professor Martin. It was just something I ate, I think."

She shifted her eyes downward to her tall, brown boots. She noticed that one of the buckles was tarnished. She made a mental note to take care of that when she got back to the apartment after classes were over. Normally she wasn't one to care about her clothes, unlike her sister Ashley, who had monumental breakdowns if one hair on her head was out of place. Arnett couldn't care less how she looked, but she was very fond of these particular boots and always wanted them to look nice—a little quirk of hers that she had come to accept.

Although she and Ashley in appearance were identical twins, inside they were polar opposites. Arnett was neat and tidy as far as her space went, and Ashley could walk into a room and cause things to rearrange themselves like a tornado had hit the room. Arnett liked to cook and was precise and meticulous when she made anything, while Ashley was the kind who pinched and diced and threw things together that tasted like she had slaved over the stove for hours.

Then, there was their witch detecting abilities. For some reason Arnett had gotten the majority of the talent. Ashley also possessed of some ability in detecting the paranormal aura around the targets. She was more inclined to feel just a twinge in her core, unlike the debilitating reaction that Arnett usually incurred.

After all that had floated through her mind, Arnett noticed that Professor Martin had been patiently waiting for her attention to return to him.

Students filed past them, looking at the two curiously, but no one stopped to talk to them, either.

Professor Martin cleared his throat then addressed the class, "Please take your seats and open your books to Chapter 3. We will discuss the principles of the lesson when I return."

Gesturing first for Arnett to precede him into the hallway, he followed her out, closing the classroom door behind him. She waited for him to speak, leaning against the cool brick wall of the hallway.

Professor Martin seemed to be taking his time finding the words that he wanted. While she waited, Arnett took out her cell phone and made a point of checking the time. She looked up and met his twinkling blue eyes and deep chiseled features that were in stern contrast to the soft look that she saw in his eyes.

"I knew your mother," he said softly, taking Arnett by surprise. She had not realized that any of her instructors may also have known her mother, but guessed that she should have known since her mother had attended Baxter University in her youth, as well. That was one of the reasons that she and her sister had decided to come here; they hoped to find out something about their mother's past. Perhaps it was because they wanted to touch something that she had once touched and feel connected to her again. Since her death ten years ago when they were nine, they had learned very little about her or their father, who had disappeared at the same time. While they knew their mother had died, they did not have the same certainty about their father.

Both she and Ashley had been raised by their father's older sister, Aunt Cyndi, who had only met their mother briefly when her brother had married their mother. Not a close family, Cyndi had taken on the task of raising her small nieces, nevertheless, and raised them on her farm in the country outside the city that they had lived in for their first eight years. At first, it had been a traumatic adjustment for the three women, but in time they had learned to live together in peace. By the time of Cyndi's death last year, they had even grown to love their stern guardian.

Left on their own at the tender age of eighteen, they had decided to use their inheritance to attend the same college that their mother had attended in hope of finding out more about their family. Their Aunt Cyndi, their father's sister, had fed and clothed them, but was much older than her brother and not part of his life for many years. She had had no information for them about what his marriage, his wife, or his life had been like at all.

When clearing out some of Aunt Cyndi's things in the house before selling her farm and setting off on their new lives, they had found a set of books that had led them to the discovery that they had a talent for witch divining like their mother. In their mother's notes, they discovered that their mother had been a witch hunter for a secret society known only as "The Club." Soon, they had set out to learn all they could about the organization and its purpose. Just before attending Baxter University, they had run across and barely defeated a witch named Hespa. Before she died, she had told them that they were more powerful than their mother and less powerful than their father, and that the secrets of their purpose could only be found in the footsteps of their mother.

So here they were, following in their mother's footsteps, and so far all they had gotten were muddy boots. There was nothing of their mother here at Baxter University anymore, at least not that they had seen or felt … until now.

Professor Martin seemed to be deciding on something before he spoke again, bringing Arnett back to the present. "I would like to speak to you and your sister later this evening. Would that be possible? I believe I have something that you may need," he said, then turned from Arnett, but stopped

Love Bites

with his hand on the doorknob and looked over his shoulder at her. "I will see you both here at around four o'clock, then?"

"What ..." she replied, but before she could complete her sentence, he was gone. "Well, that was interesting," she muttered to herself, adjusting the bag on her shoulder once more. What could he possibly have that she might need?

She was so engrossed in her thoughts as she made her way down the halls to meet Ashley at the garden that she never saw the brick wall of a man that she ran into. He was tall and wearing tight leather clothes with zippers and snaps that bit into Arnett when she fell against him. Suddenly, arms tried to steady her. When she looked up, she saw that he was a gorgeous boy, with blond hair and green eyes with golden flecks in them, and a smile that could light up the darkest dungeon. He was looking directly at her as he held her, and she was only about a breath away from his lips. Arnett suddenly had a strong desire to kiss him, and she had never wanted to do that before with someone she had just met.

"Oh, sorry, didn't see you," she said, blushing. He wasn't letting her go, but she wasn't upset about it, which was odd because she hated to be touched.

Then, her witch senses tingled a little, but not a lot like earlier. This was odd because usually when her witch senses were engaged it was a full-blown effect, like she had felt earlier. There was no holding it back.

So, either this boy was not a warlock, or he was so far removed from any kind of warlock tendencies that her witch senses were only reacting to the *possibility* of him having any of the craft in his blood. That was interesting too, almost as interesting as he was.

Arnett stepped back when he released and nodded at her in apology. "Joss," he said, introducing himself as he extended his hand. His eyes were still giving her the once over.

Without realizing it, Arnett smoothed back her hair and met his glance with a curious one of her own. She had never seen him on campus before; she would have remembered him if she had. "New here?" she asked, not taking his hand. All thoughts of meeting her sister in the garden had left her mind.

"Yup, today is my first day. I had to take care of some … things … problems … at home before I start school," he responded. He seemed to want to talk to her as much as she wanted him.

"Oh, that's a shame. I hope that everything's okay now, though," she replied, trying to get him to talk about it. She wasn't sure why it mattered, other than that she wanted to keep him here, talking to her. She was sure that once the rest of the female population on campus got a load of this boy, a sexy combination of Johnny Depp as Captain Jack Sparrow and Orlando Bloom in *Lord of the Rings,* they would be swarming all over him and she would, as usual, be forgotten.

"It is now," he answered. He smiled at her and Arnett found herself responding with a smile of her own.

They stared at each other for nearly a minute before Arnett heard her name called from down the hall. Looking past her rescuer, she saw her sister waiting for her with an annoyed expression on her face, gesturing for Arnett to hurry.

"Gotta go?" he asked, looking down the hallway at Ashley. He looked back at Arnett with a sidelong glance that sent shivers down her spine. That kind of radar didn't need a paranormal trigger.

"Yeah, gotta go," Arnett said sadly, adjusting her bag on her shoulder as she brushed past him.

He reached out and touched her on the arm as she passed by. "See you later," he said, as his fingers running down her arm. Even through the cloth, she felt the heat from his body. Her witch senses still tingled, but wasn't strong, leaving her to wonder what he was.

As she hurried down the hall, Arnett looked over her shoulder and found that Joss wore an expression of interest as he watched her walk away. She waved and then grabbed Ashley by the arm and dragged her around the corner and out the door to the garden.

"So, who is *he*?" Ashley asked, giving her sister a lecherous grin that made Arnett roll her eyes.

"I am not sure," Arnett said carefully, realizing that that was true. Even though he had introduced himself, she wasn't sure who he really was.

"What do you mean?" Ashley asked.

"I ... I got a strange tingling when I met him," Arnett explained, confused by what it meant.

"Oh?" A wicked grin spread across Ashley's face as she teased, "And what kind of *'strange tingle'* did you get when you met him?"

"Not *that* kind of tingle," Arnett said, swatting her sister's arm. "It was more like a witch sense tingle, but not strong and unpleasant like they usually are."

"Oh," Ashley said, furrowing her brow as she considered her sister's words. "Was the tingle like when we met Dr Graham?" She was referring to the warlock that they had met just after coming into their powers, who had nearly killed them a few weeks ago, before they learned to control their abilities.

"No, nothing like that. It was more pleasant. Like I said, it wasn't threatening at all. It was more like ..." Arnett paused to consider what she wanted to say, then continued, "It was more like an introduction, I guess. Kind of like a handshake."

"A handshake? It looked like more than a handshake passed between the two of you from what I could see."

Arnett took the high road and chose to ignore her sister's baiting remarks. Instead, she decided to change the subject. "Oh, hey, Professor Martin wants the two of us to meet him in his class around four o'clock this afternoon. He said that he has something for us and …" Arnett paused to give her next words their full effect, "… he knew our mother. I think he knew her really well and wants to tell us stuff about her."

"Oh? And is that why he wants to meet us? Because he has stuff to tell us about Mother?" Ashley stopped fiddling with her hair as she looked at Arnett in confusion.

"No, I think the two things aren't related, but I definitely intend to ask him about Mother when we meet him. As a matter of fact, I'd bet that a lot of the professors here know about her. We should ask them all what they remember."

"Hummmm …" Ashley was nibbling on the end of her hair and Arnett knew this meant that she was concentrating on something that was puzzling her.

Arnett had a hard time keeping her thoughts from returning to Joss as she waited for Ashley to put her thoughts together. He was more than gorgeous, she finally decided, and definitely out of her league. She usually ended up with the leftovers: the nerds, geeks and really great guys who were misunderstood, but never a god like Joss. She returned her gaze to her sister's with a sigh.

"I think we need to talk about what happened to you today in Professor Martin's class. I think we have a problem and we need to identify whom your witch senses detected."

"I agree," said Arnett, "but I don't know how. It was the strongest reaction I've ever had. Even Dr Graham and the other witches witch senses combined had not been that strong. Either that, or I'm weaker than I thought after our experience with them."

"Not weak," Ashley admonished her sister, "depleted. Sensing them and taking on their evil, depletes you, I think it takes time for your talent to restore itself. Your sensing ability is like a glass filled with liquid that needs to be refilled once it's poured out. You are okay as far as that goes, and I don't think that you need to worry about it. It seems that you can replenish it fairly quickly, at least partially. You're just not back to full strength yet. I think that this was

Love Bites

just a case of a *really, really* strong presence … an evil presence … and we need to figure out who it is before something terrible happens. Something that strong is not here just to attend school; they are here to cause trouble."

"Agreed," said Arnett, biting her lip. That was her biggest vice, that and biting her nails, habits that she had from childhood and couldn't seem to break.

"So, who do you think it is?" Ashley asked.

"I don't think that it's someone in the class. I think that it's someone who passed by the classroom. I think I saw a shadow under the door when I first felt my witch sense engage, but I can't be sure that the shadow wasn't just someone randomly passing by the classroom. If it was someone in class, I would have felt it right away."

"Professor Martin?"

"Nope, it was definitely not him," Arnett said. "I didn't get anything from him when we talked outside of class."

"Then, we won't know who it is until your senses alert us again," Ashley said, disappointed. "That totally sucks."

"Why would you say that?"

"Because now that you reacted the way you did, you've probably alerted the witch to the fact that you can identify her," Ashley reasoned. "The only option the next time we meet is to attack."

"Crap! I never thought of that," Arnett said, biting a fingernail nervously. "If there's an attack, we won't know who it is until she or he strikes. You're right, that totally sucks."

Both sisters looked at each other with concern and then glanced around them. There was nothing in their vicinity but a few birds in the trees and some butterflies and bees buzzing about. Nothing more dangerous than a possible bee sting was in their future right now.

Arnett shivered, anyway, when the shadow of a crow passed high overhead. She looked up, watching as the crow circled them once, cawing loudly as it flew away. The two sisters linked arms and returned inside, missing the crow's return to the garden.

***

Perched on the branch of a tree near the entrance the girls had just entered, the crow watched them with its small dark eyes, its soft, *"Caw!"* the only sound in the suddenly still air of the garden before it dropped to the ground and transformed into the shape of a man in dark leather. Shaking his head, his hair floating around him like the wings of the crow that he once was, the man smiled at the backs of the retreating girls, but his smile never reached his eyes. The man blew into his hands and flexed them open then closed, as if the motion was unfamiliar.

A moment later a second crow landed on the ground next to him. The man glanced in its direction, pursing his lips into a thin line and gestured with a quick snap of his wrist. Suddenly, the second crow transformed into the bent shape of a woman. Her black leather pants and jacket creaked as she straightened. Glancing at the man, she also watched as the girls disappeared inside. Her lustrous hair, shining blue-black like the feathers she just shifted from, rippled down her back like a dark waterfall.

"The One, she is strong," said the woman without turning to look at the man.

"Yes, but the protection of the crow will keep her from sensing us anymore. It was a mistake to approach without knowing her capabilities," said the man.

"No matter," said the woman as she glanced at the man with a smirk. "They are young and untrained. We will have no trouble with them."

"What if they gain the notice of the Others before the ceremony?"

"They will not," she said with confidence.

Taking his arm, the two approached the doors and stepped inside. Looking neither left nor right, they quickly navigated the hallways until they came to a wall with no door. They touched a point on the wall and a door revealed itself to them. They stepped inside and then the door sealed itself back into a smooth wall.

***

After their classes, Ashley and Arnett agreed to meet at Professor Martin's office promptly at four o'clock. After Arnett's last class across campus, she ran across the square, hurrying to make the appointment on time. It felt good to feel the wind in her hair and tugging at her clothes. It had been a long time since she had been for a jog, though, and her legs were burning when she arrived at Clayton Hall. The weather had gotten chilly. It was definitely Fall and sliding into winter. The leaves were changing colors and running through them had created a crackling noise that was not unpleasant to her ears. Arnett loved this time of year with all the boisterous beauty that the colors of the season brought forth before the cold whiteness of winter blanketed everything in slumber.

When she got inside the building she almost ran into Joss again, who was on his way out.

Sidestepping the collision this time, Joss laughed and grabbed her arm to catch her mid-step as she ran through the door. His laugh caused a tingling in her that had nothing to do with her witch senses and made her smile widen involuntarily.

"Hey, we have to stop meeting like this," he said, his green eyes catching hers. She felt herself hesitating, although his hand on her arm was comforting instead of intrusive. Once again, she was surprised by her reaction to him. Her witch senses were definitely on alert, but on a cautionary level, not an alarm level. She felt a little light headed, but was not sure if that was from his close proximity to her or her reaction to his cologne, which she didn't remember smelling earlier.

Arnett wanted to come back with something equally witty to his cheesy greeting, but found herself tongue tied. She could not think of a single thing to say in response.

"Arnie, come on! We're late," Ashley said, who had come up to the two of them unnoticed by either. She grabbed Arnett by the arm and dragged her through the doorway without greeting Joss. Arnett looked over her shoulder as the door closed on Joss. He was watching them as they ran down the hallway away from him. When they reached the door to Professor Martin's lecture room, they found it empty.

"Did he tell you to meet him here?" asked Ashley, walking around the room, looking in closets, and up the tiered landings. Professor Martin was nowhere to be found.

"That's strange," Arnett muttered as she stood at the front desk with her eyes closed.

"What is?" Ashley asked returning to her sister's side. "Oh," she answered her own question as she stopped next to her sister.

"You feel it, too?" Arnett asked, looking at her sister.

"Not strong, whatever happened was a while ago. A half hour you think?" Ashley asked.

"Right after our class?"

"Not long after, that's for sure," Ashley agreed.

"He had a class after ours," Arnett said thoughtfully. "It feels like before, only weaker," Arnett said. She sniffed the air and there was a faint sulfuric odor, but it was so faint that it was almost unnoticeable. "Strange," Arnett repeated. "I'm not getting the usual reaction, but there was obviously some kind of event that happened here. Otherwise, I'm sure that Professor Martin would be here. He seemed rather insistent that we all meet."

Ashley gasped just as a voice spoke from behind them. Both girls spun around, taking defensive positions naturally. "Yeah, they were here," said a deep voice.

"Who?" asked Arnett turning to face Joss who had just entered the room. Somehow, she wasn't surprised to see him standing there. She relaxed her posture, but Ashley was not so convinced and remained at a distance in case Joss needed to be contained. Arnett shook her head, but Ashley still watched him with a distrustful expression.

"The ones you have been sensing so strongly, but that doesn't matter," Joss said. "What matters is that we have to get him back."

"Who are you?" asked Arnett. She didn't understand why this boy cared what happened to the Professor and how he knew about her witch senses.

"I'm a Sentinel, here to protect the witch finders," Joss replied, "but I'm supposed to stay in the background and only reveal myself in the direst of circumstances."

"A Sentinel?" Arnett asked, confused. She knew nothing of this protection offered to the witch finders. Heck, she had only just found out that she was someone who *needed* protection, let alone know that she had already been assigned a guardian.

"Well, you didn't do a very good job of staying hidden," Ashley said, laughing without mirth. She didn't seem to accept his presence in their lives.

Arnett, on the other hand, was pretty mad by it. Why hadn't he revealed himself sooner? Why did he only show himself now? And why, if he was only a Sentinel and not a witch or warlock, did he make her senses tingle? "Then why do I tingle when you are around?" she asked, taking pride in her forthrightness.

"Because I'm related to a warlock," said Joss. He appeared to be watching something out the window with a level of intensity that alarmed Arnett and captured her attention. "We have to go," he said, grabbing both girls by the arm and pulling them from the room.

"What?" Arnett asked, when suddenly the window behind them exploded and shards of glass pelted them before the door closed. Arnett caught a glimpse of black feathers and heard thumps and protesting '*Caws!*' against the door before Joss pulled it firmly closed. He sealed it shut with a blue fire that shot out of his fingertips.

Neat trick, thought Arnett, *I have to ask him how he did that.*

"That won't hold them for long. Follow me," Joss said, running down the hall with the girls close behind. As they rounded the corner of the building, three large crows broke the glass of the front door. After the crows flew through the glass, their feathers transformed into dark cloaks and figures with long dark hair.

"Hello, Joss. We meet again," said the tall man in front. He didn't appear to be happy to see Joss.

And by Joss' reaction Arnett assumed that he was not happy to see him, either. "Shit!" Joss said, skidding to a halt, reversing his forward motion. Grabbing the girls by the arms, he half-pulled and dragged them into an open classroom. "Hide! This is what I do," he yelled at the girls. Then, he pulled open a closet and forced both girls inside, despite their protests. "Don't argue with me. Just stay here and do NOT come out, no matter what you hear. Understand?" Before he closed the door he pulled Arnett close and kissed her hard on the lips. "For luck," he said with a smile before pushing her back inside and closing the door.

There was the sound of something crackling on the other side of the door, and Arnett was sure he had sealed them in with his blue fire. She grabbed her tingling mouth and smiled. "He kissed me," she whispered to Ashley.

"Yeah, I saw," Ashley said with a grimace. "We'll talk about that later. Right now, we need to figure out how we're going to help him. There is no way that he can fight those three and the others all by himself."

"He has that blue fire," Arnett said, but Ashley shushed her.

"I don't think his blue fire is a weapon or he would have stayed to fight them instead of running and finding us a hiding place."

Putting her ear to the door, Ashley tried to listen to what was being said on the other side.

"Ashley, what can you hear?" Arnett whispered, feeling the effects of the presence of the witches. It started as an incessant itching on her arms and then traveled up and down her body. She clenched her teeth and closed her eyes tightly, trying to concentrate on alleviating the feeling that her powers were detecting, the sensation of being bitten by a million fire ants. After a short time, the feeling went away.

Arnett sighed, relieved that the sensations had eased. "Ashley," she whispered, touching her sister on the shoulder. "Can you hear anything?"

"No," Ashley said in a hushed voice. "I think they've left the room."

"Should we leave the closet and see if we can help him?"

"I'm not sure that we want to get involved in this," Ashley said. "I have a feeling that this is between Joss and those ... creatures ... witches ... whatever they are. I'm a little worried about the way they changed from crows into humans, though. I've never seen that before. These witches aren't the normal kind that we are used to dealing with. And to top it all off, we know nothing about Joss, other than what he told us."

"What are you implying?" Arnett asked, touching her lips. The memory of his kiss was still warm in her thoughts. She refused to believe that he was evil, but she did tingle in his presence. Maybe ... maybe he was more than he appeared to be, but if he had a secret attachment to those crow things, then he could have easily helped them get captured. "Why did he hide us? Why did he kiss me, then?" Arnett asked.

Ashley to moaned in sympathy, hearing the pain in her sister's voice. "We don't know that he is one of them," Ashley said sympathetically. "Maybe he really is a Sentinel.

Maybe we need to wait and find out what Professor Martin has to tell us. Maybe it had something to do with Joss and those crow-man things."

"You're right as usual, sis," said Arnett. "I think we need to get out of here."

"Agreed," Ashley said.

Reaching for the door knob the sisters realized the door was still sealed.

"He used his blue fire to seal the door," Arnett said. "Do you think we can get out of here on our own?"

Both girls put their shoulders to the door, but to no avail. The door wouldn't budge.

"Okay, what now?"

Arnett looked at her sister and touched the door. It felt warm and there was a definite feeling of something magical in the woods. It sang against her fingers in a way that she had experienced only once before.

"Ashley, touch the door here."

Ashley touched where her sister had indicated and grunted. "This is old magic, the kind we encountered with mom's box."

"I thought so too," agreed Arnett, "but what does that mean?"

When the girls had been ten they had found a box at their Aunt's house that had belonged to their mother. At the first touch, it had sung to the sisters. The melody had wrapped around their minds with soothing waves of soft music and harmonies. It had frightened the girls at first, and their aunt's reaction had not alleviated this fear. She had grabbed the box from the girls and cradled it against her chest before sending them to their room. After that, the box had been put away.

The girls had protested that they had the right to keep it since it was their mother's, but nothing had changed their aunt's mind. They had not seen it again until after their aunt's death. The lawyer had given it to them with a note from their aunt instructing them to put it in a safe place until they needed it, which was sooner than any of them had suspected it would be. The box had saved their lives in their last encounter with the witches, and now here again was the imprint of that music and harmony in the door, in the very place where Joss had touched the wood with his blue fire.

"Is the blue fire some kind of connection to mom?" Arnett asked, thinking out loud.

"I don't know," Ashley answered. "But it would seem so."

"We need to get out of here." Arnett pushed harder against the door. "I think Joss can help us figure out the mystery about mom."

Both girls pushed again. Still, the door refused to budge. Arnett leaned against the door and kicked it in her frustration and the door slowly creaked open, to the shock of both girls.

Looking around the door, the girls found the room to be empty. The door no longer sang to Arnett and she wondered if the effect of the blue fire had a time limit. Perhaps that was why the door had finally opened.

"Now what?" Arnett whispered. Ashley had moved to the window and was looking outside. There was no movement on the campus. The sun was setting in the west, causing a golden light to fall over the slumbering trees. It was as if the campus were a ghost town.

"What has happened to everyone?" Arnett whispered.

Ashley shrugged her shoulders. The door behind them opened and Joss stepped in. He gestured for the girls to follow him, placing his finger to his lips, signaling them to be quiet.

Burning with questions, Arnett followed but when she tried to speak Joss gripped her arm and squeezed. His touch burned through her clothes and caused her to gasp at the intensity of her feelings for him. The tingling was rampant in every nerve ending in her body. In spite of her resolve to remain silent, Arnett moaned.

Joss dropped his hand immediately and looked at her with wide eyes, wearing a confused expression. Their glances broke only when Ashley bumped into a chair, causing it to scrape loudly across the floor.

Joss froze, then quickly stepped in front of the girls and glanced around the room. The air about them rippled. Suddenly, the crow people appeared. Arnett felt an intense pain in her head that nearly dropped her to her knees. Joss grabbed her with one hand and pointed at the first crow-man with the other. A smirk spread across the face of the figure in front of the group, putting the sisters and the Sentinel on alert.

Around them stood seven crow people, their faces expressionless, as if etched in stone. Joss and the girls watched as the seven spaced themselves around the room in a horseshoe shape, trapping the trio against the wall.

"Stalemate," said the leader. His voice was a cold breeze that chilled Arnett to the bone.

"Joss, give her up," spoke the woman to his left, her mouth barely moving over the words. "We only want the One. You and the Other are free to leave."

"Defy us," said the leader, narrowing his eyes as he spoke, "and you will die along with the Other and we will still have the One."

"Save yourselves," spoke the woman again. Her smile was a slash in her face that was not warm.

"Where is Professor Martin?" Arnett spoke, darting around Joss's protective arm to face the seven.

"Ah, yes, the Professor …" the man drew out the words as if savoring them, revealing a row of short, sharp teeth when he smiled. But he didn't answer her question. The woman standing next to him just smirked. They weren't ready to reveal their secrets … not yet.

Ashley joined her sister, then grasped her hand before facing the crow people. "We stand together," Ashley said, bravely raising her chin as she spoke.

Joss took Arnett's other hand. Confronting the seven as a united front, the trio sent their silent answer to the demands of the crows.

"Very well, then. Stand together, die together. It is of no matter to us," the leader said, then turned to the other six crow people. "We only need the One. Do what you wish with the Others."

Before Arnett was ready, Joss sent a blue flame outward that protected them from the darts that were directed toward them, tipped with poison, she was sure, and edged with the black feathers of the crows. Seconds later, the battle started.

Joss was amazing. Arnett watched as he sent blue flames toward the crows that flew toward them at breakneck speed. The first three flames struck down the crow people that had been in Professor Martin's classroom, turning to ash immediately. The remaining crow people split up: two turned back into crows and fled the room, presumably to get reinforcements, but the ones who remained were not afraid of Joss.

One of those was his nemesis. An evil grin spread across his face as he circled Joss. Joss kept one eye on him, hand extended, fingers spread as if to divide the blue fire between the three around them.

Ashley let out a small squeal of alarm when one of the crow people lunged at her. Laughing, the woman danced back. They were afraid of Joss, Arnett realized in shock. What did he have that they feared so much? The blue fire that had destroyed their companions? Somehow she knew it wasn't that. This leader did not seem afraid of anything, but it was obvious that he had come across Joss before … and had been the loser of that match.

"The Others will be here soon," the woman whispered to the leader. "We must leave before they arrive."

"Yes," he agreed, but he made no move to leave or change into the crow. He watched Joss even as Joss watched him. Without looking to his side he told his third companion to change and leave. The crow man did as he was told. His loud *caw* as he flew out of the building was the only sound other than the sizzle of the blue fire that leaped and danced at the ends of Joss' fingers.

"Now, Joss," hissed the crow man as he stood still in front of them. "What are we to do with you?"

Joss snorted, but did not lower his hand. Ashley and Arnett were getting more and more annoyed with Joss for acting like he had to protect them. They tried to move out from behind him to stand at his side as he faced their foes, but Joss maneuvered his body between him and their attackers, hissing at them under his breath. Both moved back behind him, glaring at the crow people.

"You need to give her to us," the crow man crooned to Joss, his voice soft and hypnotic. "You know you cannot protect them both."

"We only need the One. You and the Other can leave," said the leader.

"Now, Lechta, you and I both know that you can't have her, and even if you do take her, you can't let us live."

The crow man grunted, his chin sinking down into his chest as he puffed out the feathers of his cloak with his breath. Next to him, the woman looked around as if looking for something specific.

Arnett shivered. Who is the One? Is it her, or Ashley?

"You lost the other One, who is to say that you will not make the same mistake and lose this One too? Then, what will be your fate? They allowed you to live only because of her. If she is gone too, what will happen to you?"

Joss growled, but didn't answer. The growl was a deep, low rumble that sounded as if it had come from his toes and traveled throughout his body to erupt when it reached his head. His eyes never left the leader of the crow people.

"Oh come now. You know I have sent for reinforcements. When they arrive, I will have the One and then it will be done and you will be lost, as will all of humanity. You cannot stop it. You are only a single Sentinel. You are lucky that the Others even let you anywhere near her."

Joss still didn't answer, but Arnett did. "What are they talking about, Joss? What did you lose? Or is it not a 'what' but a 'who'?"

"Ah, the disgraced one has not told you his story, has he? Oh, this is rich!" The crow man laughed evilly, as the woman with him echoed the sound, harsh and mirthless. Arnett felt Ashley shiver next to her.

"Do we have time?" he pretended to check his wrist for a watch, and with that motion Joss dropped his eyes, but both Ashley and Arnett holding hands behind him did not. They saw what Lechta intended and focused their energy on him.

He never knew what hit him. Just as his companions returned with others of their kind, both Ashley and Arnett touched Joss' arms. With their combined power, they created a force field of such power that it crushed the crows against the walls and the minute the blue-fire force field touched them, they turned to ash. The blue dome continued to grow in the confined space until it covered every inch and there was nothing left of any of them but a fine black powder on the walls, floor, and ceiling. Only Lechta had escaped, singed where the blue fire had touched, just before he transformed into a crow and fled.

His caws were heard in the distance as he soared out of reach, and within minutes, he was just a black speck in the sky.

The two girls collapsed and the force field exploded with a slight pop that sounded anti-climatic in the aftermath of the battle that they had just waged.

"What happened?" Ashley asked after she had regained her breath.

Arnett just shook her head as if to clear it and both girls looked to Joss for an explanation. Except for a fine sheen of sweat on his upper lip, it didn't appear that the battle had sapped any of his energy.

"I'm sorry …" Joss' apology took both girls by surprise.

"Sorry? For what?" Arnett asked, getting to her feet with help from Ashley.

"For almost losing you," he whispered as he held her and gazed into her eyes. Arnett gently stroked his face, marveling at finding tears on his cheeks.

She licked the tears off her fingers. They were salty, as she expected, but they were also refreshing. She found that the more she licked his tears the stronger she felt.

"What are you?" she whispered back at him, stepping away before she gave into the impulse to kiss him.

He didn't answer. Instead, he pulled her close to his chest and lightly kissed the top of her head, breathing in the scent of her hair. He was rock hard, a brick wall, as she had thought when she first ran into him … literally. Something solid, something permanent. Was that what he was? Was that what a Sentinel was?

Ashley gasped, bringing Arnett out of whatever safe place her thoughts had gone to. Joss raised his lips from her hair and watched as Professor Martin and several other teachers filed silently into the room, careful not to step near the piles of black ash that had formerly been the crow people.

Still cradled in Joss' arms with her back against his rock-hard body, Arnett turned and waited for them to speak. Someone needed to explain all of this.

Ashley bit her lip, then went suddenly pale. She leaned against the wall behind them, closed her eyes, and slid to the floor with a soft thump. Arnett ran to her sister and cradled her head in her lap. She looked at the silent crowd with tears in her eyes and screamed. "What's going on? What *are* you people? What are *we*?" Then, she burst into tears as she rocked her frozen sister in her arms.

A few hours later when they were on campus, at the home of Professor Martin, Arnett and Ashley got the answers that they sought … sort of.

Holding glasses of Sherry in tiny crystal goblets, Arnett imagined she needed to hold up her pinky while she drank, but she didn't touch the blood-red liquid to her lips just yet. She wanted answers and not more riddles, but it appeared that riddles were all that was being offered tonight.

"So, let me see if I have this right," she said as she looked to Ashley for strength. "Ashley and I are part of a battle that has raged since the dawn of time? We are battling demons that take the shape of crows?"

"That's right," said Professor Martin. He swirled the liquid in his glass slowly, a tiny turbulence in an otherwise very turbulent world. "This battle has been fought by ones like you and your sister and the crows, who are the message bearers of the demons. They have been since the time before there was life on this planet."

"Joss and his kind are Sentinels. I believe he told you that. They are not supposed to reveal themselves to you or the demons. They keep the playing field level. You might say that they are the Gamekeepers, I suppose. But Joss … well … Joss has his own ideas on what a Sentinel is supposed to do. We will have a talk about this Joss."

His tone promised that Joss would not be too happy with the result of that conversation. But if Joss was at all concerned, he didn't show it. He merely raised one eyebrow and smiled, then raised his glass as if in toast to the scolding to come. Arnett noticed that he didn't drink anything. Now that she thought about it, she hadn't seen him eat anything, either. Was he real?

"Yet, somehow the balance was disturbed when your mother was lost here," Professor Martin's voice softened and Arnett could sense genuine regret in his tone.

"My mother was lost here?" Ashley asked. "But how is that possible, she had given birth to us before she died, and she wasn't in college anymore."

Both girls looked to Professor Martin for an answer, but he ignored her comment. Instead, he wandered to the window and looked out into the dark garden in the courtyard below. For several minutes the girls held their breath, waiting for his answer. Coming to a decision, he gestured for the girls to follow him outside.

They walked into the garden under a canopy of stars, traveling across the sky in a blur of meteor bursts of fire and flame and twinkling lights.

Arnett and Ashley held hands as they walked toward the center of the garden, feeling a pull that they couldn't explain. There was something in this garden, something alive. They could feel it, but it felt like it was under a shroud. It was like a crocus waiting to blossom from under winter's grip.

"Do you feel it?" asked Ashley. She gripped her sister's hand harder. Arnett knew what she meant. Something evil had happened here.

"We are keeping things at bay, but it is a constant struggle to maintain the balance. We are growing weaker," Professor Martin said as he gestured toward a bench for the girls to sit on. He and Joss remained standing. Both were looking behind the girls to the statue that was the centerpiece of the garden.

The girls turned slowly. Something about the posture of Professor Martin and Joss made them shiver. It was as if the two men were looking at a ghost. The ghost of someone revered.

Two ghosts, Arnett amended. She looked up to see a statue of two people twined together. The man held the woman with such tenderness and love in his face that it was as if his whole body were one with her. She, on the other hand was draped over his arms, her head tilted back as if waiting for a lover's kiss. Their faces were smooth in the way that only a statue can be, and a marbling of the stone that causing it to look as if blood ran down her body from her neck to the tips of her toes.

"Mother?" Ashley moaned. She grabbed her head and buried her face in Arnett's chest.

Then Arnett understood. This was her parents, encased forever in stone. "Who did this to them?" she screamed out at Joss and Professor Martin. Tears glistened in Joss' eyes. "Joss, was this your fault? Is this what Lechta was talking about? You did this to my parents?"

Ashley moaned again. "Make it stop! Make it stop! I can't take anymore!" She stood up and rushed back toward the house, moaning as she held her hands over her ears, shaking her head back and forth.

"Your sister ... what's her talent? Quick, tell me quick," Professor Martin asked. He grabbed Arnett by the shoulders and shook her in his excitement.

"I ... I ... don't know," Arnett stammered. She twisted out of his arms and rushed to Joss. He wrapped his arms around her and tilted her chin up to look at him. She could see the stars reflected in his eyes and she thought how he could have been her whole universe, but all of this was too hard to understand. She was not sure what they hoped to accomplish with these tales of unending wars, demons, and lovers lost in stone.

"Is she the One?" Professor Martin asked Joss. "We always assumed it was Arnett, but she doesn't have a Sentinel assigned to her."

Joss shrugged his shoulders pulling Arnett tightly to his chest.

"We have to find her; she could be the key. Tonight, tonight is the only window. The crows were sent to destroy them both because they didn't know which was the One. We need the Others. There is much to do and so little time."

Professor Martin raced back toward the door that Ashley had just entered moments before. His black robes billowed in the breeze behind him like the wings of the crows and Arnett shivered.

"These are my parents?" she asked, trying to confirm it within her mind.

Joss nodded without speaking. He stared intently into her eyes, lowered his face to hers, then gently brushed his lips across her cheek and the saltiness of her tears was on his lips when he kissed her.

Arnett closed her eyes, her arms wrapping around him as if of their own will. She felt herself melting into him, their bodies becoming one, her warmth a direct contrast to his coolness. When she slid her hands under his T-shirt, his skin was smooth like the surface of a river rock. She wondered if he were able, as a Sentinel, to have a relationship with a human like her. But then, was *she* even human? She didn't know what she was. Perhaps her parents had the right idea. Become stone because that was easier than feeling anything.

She moaned softly at the feelings Joss's hands were creating in her body, but stepped back. Lips burning, swollen from his loving kisses, she looked at him with a desire to know everything about him. "What are you?" she whispered, raising a hand to her lips as if trying to capture his kiss forever.

"I told you. I am a Sentinel," he answered, his eyes never leaving hers. His mouth was forming a wry smile as if her question was expected and already answered.

"And what, exactly, is a Sentinel?" Arnett asked, taking one small step back so that she could get the full picture of him.

"I am what you see … for now."

"For now? Are you even human? I mean, do you even have 'boy parts'?" Arnett hated herself for asking, but it was something that she needed to know if they were going to go further in this relationship.

"That …" he hesitated before answering, "… is something you will have to see to believe."

"Huh?" Arnett looked at him in confusion, but before she could ask another question her sister, Professor Martin, and several other teachers came into the courtyard.

They carried an odd assortment of brass receptacles, which they placed around the circle of stone that surrounded the stone lovers, spaced evenly apart. Each time a receptacle was placed on the ground, a chant was said. Arnett could not understand the language, but Joss spoke the chant under his breath each time they did. When all eight brass lamps were placed, they all stood together, holding hands and chanting.

The lamps flamed to life almost immediately once the chanting was done. Around them Arnett could feel an energy building that triggered her witch senses in an almost unbearable wave of power.

"Quickly, what are they saying next, Ashley?" asked Professor Martin.

"Ashley? What do you mean 'what are they saying?'" Arnett asked, taking two quick steps to her sister. The minute she touched Ashley's arms, she felt power surge in her head that nearly made her sick. It was so strong that it blinded her for a minute. Slowly, her vision started to return, but when she opened her eyes she could not see clearly.

A cloudy blue haze surrounded everything. Her sister's arm were the only solid thing in her vision. She could hear other voices, but could not make out the words. After a minute, things calmed down enough that she could make out a voice speaking gently to her.

"Let Ashley go, darling," said a voice she remembered from childhood.

"Momma?" she said, turning her head toward the sound of her mother's voice. It was strange that she could remember what her mother sounded like when she barely remembered what she looked like. "Momma?" she repeated, hating that her voice sounded like a little girls'. Suddenly, she was nine again, playing hide and seek with her mother on the day of her disappearance.

"It's okay, Arnett," Ashley said. "This is my time. I have to help Mom and Dad. You have to step away. If you don't, we will never get them back."

"Ashley?" Arnett said. "What are you talking about? We have to do this together! We do everything together!"

Arnett refused to let her sister go. She felt tugging and pulling on her body, but it all felt muted, like it was happening behind a curtain and she wasn't connected to it.

Didn't they understand? Ashley needed her! She had to help. Arnett moaned when they finally pulled her from her sister and she felt her body pop through the blue haze that surrounded them.

"Let me go! Let me go to her. I have to help, she can't do it alone. I have to help her," Arnett cried out, striking at Joss as he lifted her from the circle and set her on the bench across the circle of stone.

Ashley was standing with her eyes closed. Her hands were on the statue, touching the bare thigh of the woman. Her brow furrowed as she concentrated.

Arnett shot up off the bench, intending to join her sister at the statues, but was held to the bench by a thin blue flame wrapped around her ankle.

Reaching down Arnett snapped the flame and raced to Ashley just as the energy that she had felt building in the air around them circled the statues and her sister. The chanters swayed to the rhythm of their words. With their eyes closed, they never saw Arnett join her sister at the statues.

Arnett heard Joss cry out, but ignored him. Placing her hands on top of Ashley's, she acted as the conduit to channel the blue flames that raced down her arms and into Ashley's hands and then into the statues. For a moment, it was as if the world had stood still. No sound was heard other than the crackling of the energy as it flowed through the two sisters. In seconds it was over and both Ashley and Arnett crashed to the ground just before Joss reached them. The blue fire was snuffed out when they disconnected from the statues. They lay on the ground with no signs of life for almost a full minute before the chanters reacted.

Love Bites

Just as Joss put out his hand to touch Arnett's face, the statues began to crack and crumble. Giant pieces of stone flew off of them as if attached to strings, crashing to the ground around the stone circle. Joss threw up a blue dome that protected them as the stone continued to rain down around them. Arnett woke to Joss looking at her with such tenderness that she thought that she had died and that he was an angel.

Ashley stirred next to her. The two sisters groped in the grass to each other and joined hands, then smiled at each other. Joss smiled at Arnett, his eyes full of promise when she returned her gaze to his.

Outside the blue dome, they could see figures moving toward them as the stone stopped its downpour. For a second, there was silence and then Ashley said in a wry voice, "I think that bringing stone back to life beats witch finding any day. I am Queen of the Powers now, right?"

Arnett laughed. It sounded joyous to her ears.

They had a family again. Ashley had found her powers and Arnett had found love. She gazed at Joss as Ashley stood up and walked over to greet her parents.

Only one question remained unanswered for now, "So, about the boy parts you promised to show me?" Arnett said to Joss as she pulled him to his chest for one more kiss before the real world intruded.

A Shifter's Tale
A Moon Series Short Story
By: Becca Boucher

The clock on the wall seemed to tick slower the longer I watched it. Damn, I expected it to go backward any second now. I switched from scribbling on the edge of my test booklet, to putting my hat on backward over my unruly hair. I even tried mentally going through my last work out at the gym when that cute little blonde chick was checking me out. No luck. My eyes drifted back to the clock. I tried to avert them for just a few minutes, before I snuck another peek. Damn. The minute hand hadn't moved at all. I had been done with the freaking final exam for twenty minutes now, but according to the professor's rules, we couldn't leave until class was over. Ten more minutes and my undergrad days would be over. Two days until graduation and the whole summer would be mine. Sweet summer. Tomorrow, I'll turn twenty-one and the possibilities were endless. Grad school seemed worlds away.

Looking up I noticed that the minute hand had just hit two. Yes. Freedom. I jumped up and jogged to the front of the room, tossed my test on the professor's desk and turned for the door. I had almost made it out when his voice stopped me in my tracks.

"Mr. Matthews, I assume from the speed with which you finished this test that you aced it?"

I coughed and turned around. "Yes, Professor Higgins, all the way."

He looked at me over the rim of his glasses. "Good, because you still have two days until graduation. I would hate for you to have to start grad school late because you blew off my test, Mr. Matthews."

I looked at him intently and felt the fire in my chest spill out through my hands. *He doesn't mean anything by it, Cace, just relax.* The spells came more frequently these days. I didn't know what to make of them. I had never been a violent person. Taking a deep breath I closed my eyes and tried to relax. When I opened them, I noticed that Professor Higgins had lost some of the venom in his eyes. He stared at me intently, concern lining his weathered face.

"You may go, Mr. Mathews. Enjoy your summer."

I nodded to him, turned for the door, and jogged down the hallway. I hit the doors to the quad with both hands, pushing them open in a burst of sunlight and fresh air. Turning right, I started to jog across the grass and to the driveway that led to the main road. Our campus sat on the edge of a major highway going through the inner city, but because of the fences and hedges around it, you would never know it.

Hitting the sidewalk, I scanned down the hill and spotted Andrew's battered old Dodge waiting for me. Glancing in the back window, I saw him relaxing with his head leaned back and his old straw cowboy hat pulled low over his eyes. The bastard finished his exams yesterday. Slowing down I walked stealthy over to the back of the pickup and kicked the quarter panel ... hard. He sat bolt upright as I yanked the door opened and yelled, "Wake up, you pecker head!"

The look he gave me could have frozen a lake. "You bloke! What the hell did you do that for? And why the hell are you running for your life, mate? Jesus, man."

We had been best friends for four years and I had never tiered of his Australian accent. The cowboy hat maybe, but never his accent. I punched him on the arm.

"Higgins just started to try shit with me," I said, hopping into the passenger side of the truck. "The faster we are away from Holy Cross, the closer we are to Umass Med. New chapter in our life, man. But first, summer! I'm living this summer to the fullest."

Andrew slid the truck into drive and pulled away from the curb. "Med school for you, vet school for me. And don't you think for a minute that I'm going to let you drink yourself into oblivion this weekend … twenty-first birthday or not, you dumb bloke!"

I slapped him on the back of the head. "You're just pissed that we couldn't find any Fosters."

He gunned the truck and turned right onto Main Street. "Eff off, man. I don't even drink that crap. Where are we headed, anyway?"

Stopping at a red light, we looked at each other and spoke in unison, "The camp." I reached forward and turned up the radio until Garth Brooks was vibrating the speakers.

The camp was my grandfather's house, situated on two acres overlooking Browning Pond. The rustic log home was where I had spent most of my teenage years. My grandfather, Dr. Hyman Matthews, had built it himself as a getaway from the city. To me, it was salvation. After my parent's death, my sister and I lived here. Our grandparents looked in on us, but we were mostly alone. The last four years it had served as a secret getaway for Andrew and me. We never had parties here; we saved that for our rundown apartment off campus. It was even more bitter sweet now that Grandma was gone and Gramps was in a nursing home. Thank God everything was put in my name years earlier.

As we pulled into the drive, Andrew turned down the radio. "Remember mate, I have to go into Logan to pick up my sister Sunday morning. So, if you drink tomorrow night, you're on your own, bloke."

I looked at him. "Your sister?" He pulled up to the deck and shut the truck off.

"Damn, Cace! Do you listen to anything I say? I told you that my sister, Bina, was flying over for the summer. She's missing my graduation by a few hours. Damn bloody long flight and you said you were cool with it."

I shook my head to dislodge the fog that seemed to reside in it lately. I remembered something about the conversation, but it got lost in the jumble of studying for finals and running interference on my damn sister. Screw her theory of why I was getting so agitated!

"Oh, yeah," I said as the memories started resurfacing. "Yeah, it's cool. She can have Grandma and Gramps old room overlooking the lake. We can bunk downstairs."

Andrew took off his hat and ran his hand threw his dirty blonde hair. "Damn straight. Bina is a good girl and I aim to keep it that way. She's here to check out a couple of colleges and relax and to get away from all that shit back at the ranch."

Andrew had chosen to stay here on a work visa after college, and the faster he got Bina here, the better. Just convincing Bina to leave Australia was harder than it sounded, even with their abusive father waiting for her at home.

"You know she has a home here at the cabin for as long as she needs, Andy," I said. "Sharon will be more than willing to take her under her wing."

As if on cue, Sharon's black Dodge Dart pulled into the driveway. My sister was an original—stunningly original—and Andrew had a thing for her. Too bad she didn't return the feelings; they would have made a great couple. I got out of the truck and walked around to the tailgate to meet her and she threw herself in my arms.

"Damn, if this isn't good timing," she said. "So glad to have you guys home for the summer. Now you can take in all these groceries I bought for graduation. Do you know how many people to expect?"

Uh, oh. I never invited anyone for graduation. Something else that had slipped my overheated mind. "Umm … the three of us, plus Andy's sister, Bina."

Sharon slid down out of my arms and smacked me on the head. "What the hell, Cace? You didn't invite anyone? Where the heck is your head lately? There has to be some people you want to share this with."

I could see Sharon's lips moving, but I lost track of the words that were coming out of her mouth. The moment she hit me on the side of the head some kind of fire ignited in me. I felt my insides shaking, I could hear the beating of my heart in my ears, and the world seemed to shimmer around me. It felt if I was coming undone and, worse yet, I could feel the rage building up. I struggled to maintain composure and pull it all back in.

"Cace? Are you all right, hun? Andy get over here, something's wrong with Cace!"

By the time Andy made it to the back of the truck I was on the ground vomiting. Every muscle in my body was contracting.

"Cace! Mate, can you talk to me? Bloody hell, man!" Andy asked, panicked.

It was as if I was hearing Andy from outside my body. This was far worse than any other time I had one of these 'spells'. I slowly found the will to nod my head and try to push myself back up. Things were coming back into focus and the earth felt more stable.

"Sharon, can you help me get him to the house?" Andy asked, already aligning my arm around his neck, pulling me up.

A moment later, Sharon was on the other side of me. Each one of them were holding me up precariously by the arms. By the time we reached the back door I could feel my legs under me and my vision was back to normal.

"Cace, I told you last week that this was not good," Sharon said as we made it in the door. "Remember what Gramps said about family heritage? Maybe you should get this checked out."

I gave her a warning look and glanced toward Andy, who had now left my side to pull out one of the kitchen chairs. I shook my head at her and managed to mouth the words *not now*.

"Here Mate, sit down while we get you some water. Jesus, you ass, you had me near scared to death." Andrew seemed to notice the unspoken communication going on between Sharon and I. "You know what this is about, Sharon?"

She gave me a sad look. "Not really. The males of our family seem to have a medical condition that pops up around the age of twenty one. I just hope that this isn't connected." She gave me a look that could freeze water in July. "But Cace refuses to get checked out."

Andrew kicked the leg of my chair and sat down. "Bloody hell, man. You know better. It could be some kind of heart condition the way all the color left your face and your heart was racing. Fricken pre-med my ass, you dumb bloke."

I took a long drink from the glass of water that he handed me and mulled over the best way to approach this. What Sharon was talking about couldn't be found in any medical book. And I was in no mood to explain family lore to even my best friend at the moment. I refused to believe that I had the Mathews family gene. It should have died out with my dad.

"You can't hide from it any longer." Sharon's voice snapped me back from my thoughts.

I cleared my throat. "Well, there's nothing I can do about it now, with the weekend and all." I shrugged my shoulders and cleared my throat again.

Andrew looked between the two of us. "I really wish that someone would tell me what the hell is going on here. My best friend just keeled over and wretched for no reason, and now you're talking about some 'family condition'. Dumb ass Americans."

I reached over and clasped Andrew on the shoulder. "It's okay, man. Sharon has lost some of her marbles over there at her fancy new age shop." The toe of her boot kicked my shin under the table. "Ouch! What the hell, Sharon?"

She stood up from the table and looked down at me. "When you get up the nerve to face this, I'm sure Andy will be by your side. You know who you can go to. Gramps is still all there. Until then, keep denying it. Keep pushing it under the rug. Dad died trying to keep the secret and look where it got us." She turned and walked toward the door. "I have a car full of groceries that I need to bring in. You two better start inviting people."

Andrew stood up and followed Sharon to the door. "Wait up, Sharon. I'll help ya. Let this dumb bloke go get cleaned up." He stopped and looked at me. "Whatever this is, mate, it hurts that you don't trust me enough to let me in. You looked like you were at death's door. Nothing could make me think less of you. Just remember that."

Later that night I stood in the dark on the back deck overlooking the lake. The moon reflected bright off the water, the crickets chirped softly, and the gentle sounds of lapping water on the shore seemed to center me. In the quiet dark I could feel the presence of Sharon and Andrew in the house. I could feel their energy signatures and could tell where each one was, even though my back was to the wall of windows. Sensing their anxiety over me, I could feel almost tangible rays of energy radiating from them. This had been happening longer than the 'spells'. It was like I could see into the people closest to me and sense their emotions. Strangers? Not so much. I could see maybe a fleeting feeling of heat or a tinge of color, but with Sharon and Andrew, I could feel every emotion. It wasn't exactly mind reading, but it was close. Emotions were intimate. I felt Sharon's presence behind me before her hand softly touched my shoulder.

"Cace, you should go talk to him. If you hide from this anymore, ignore it, there's no telling when it will finally overtake you." Sharon sat down on the chair next to me and pulled her legs up to her chest.

I shook my head and continued looking out over the lake. "Is Andrew asleep?"

Sharon shook her head. "He's upstairs playing his guitar. Don't try to avoid me, Cace. I'm the only family you have left … me and that stubborn Aussie up there. I can help you. He can handle it."

Turning to face her, I shook a little from the stress that radiated from her in a cold blue aura. Luckily, she missed it.

"You think he can? We start talking to him about this and it sounds like we're psychos' going off the deep end. 'Hey Andrew, I come from an ancient line of Druids, interbred with Celts. We kind of have powers. I think I'm coming into mine. Want to see me shift?' That would go over awesome, Shaz."

She bristled at my use of her childhood nickname. "Give him some freaking credit, Cace. Andy knows that the world is not all black and white. He's always asking me for herbs and spells to help with something. He believes in me and you're his best friend."

I laughed a little. "He only puts up with your witch crap because he wants in your pants." Sharon stood up so fast that she knocked over the chair she had been sitting in.

"Nice, Cace. Witch crap? Yeah, right. You should have said that to Grams all the times she saved your ass with her knowledge," she said, her eyes flaring. "Way to insult your sister and your best friend in one shot. Maybe the change is frying your brain cells, you ass."

I grabbed her arm as she turned to walk away from me. "I'm sorry, Sharon. That was uncalled for." She pulled her arm free, but didn't walk away.

"You need to figure this out, Cace. If you don't go talk to Gramps, then I will. If you don't know how to handle the power, it'll destroy you. I know Dad should have been the one," she said, taking a breath. "Gramps prayed that it would skip you, but I don't think it did. You have to face it, Cace. One of these days it's not going to stop, and you need to know how to get back to yourself." Her boots clicked on the wood as she stormed back into the house.

The next morning dawned, sunny and warm. I woke in one of the chairs on the deck, stiff from being bent in an unnatural position all night. Why the hell did the damned fools leave me here? The inviting smell of coffee greeted me as I walked into the room. Sharon and Andrew sat talking in the breakfast nook. They grew quiet and looked up when I walked in the door.

"Did you sleep out there all night, Mate?" Andy asked, then took a sip of his coffee.

I shook my head and laughed. "Funny thing you should ask that, you ass. Neither one of you could have woke me up and brought me in the house?" Just then, I noticed that Andrew's fingers lightly rested on top of Sharon's, and they were sitting close enough that their legs were touching. I raised one eyebrow and Sharon blushed. Andrew's brown eyes danced with happiness and I clapped him on the shoulder as I walked by.

"So, all is forgiven then, mate?"

I chuckled as I grabbed a coffee mug from the counter. "I guess so. But if you screw with my sister, I'm likely to go all animal on you."

Sharon cleared her throat. "Speaking of going all animal, are you going to try to go in and talk to Gramps this morning?"

Love Bites

I looked over at them and Andrew suddenly became interested in the contents of his coffee mug. Shit. She told him. My senses were going through the roof and I could see the anxiety rippling off Andrew. *Take a deep breath, Cace, deep breath.* "She told you, Andy?" Andrew looked up and my eyes met his. They were impossible to read.

"Ya, Mate, and to tell you the truth, I'm having a hard time wrapping my head around it. The tribal people back home had stories of shifters, as you call them. They believed in a reptilian race that governed from underground. I always dismissed them as fairy tales." He stopped and ran his hand through his dirty blonde hair, a habit I knew he had when he was nervous. If you didn't hear him talk, Andrew could be mistaken for a surfer boy, not the Aussie ranchers' son that he was. I looked at him and he continued. "But Sharon paints a compelling argument and what would you both have to gain from spinning a tale like that? I'm just going to roll with it for now, mate. But one thing worries me: if you aren't embracing this and running from it, then are those closest to you in danger? I have to worry about the safety of Sharon and Bina. You need to talk to your Grandfather, and you bloody well better."

I looked at the two of them, the only family I had. What would happen if I lost it and hurt them? What would happen if I shifted on some random back road and got killed? Or worse yet, exposed our family's secret. If I left Sharon the way our parents did, in the dead of night by my own hand, could she recover from another loss? I was unaware of how long I stood with the coffee pot in my hand.

"What are you thinking, Cace?" The sound of Sharon's voice snapped me from my reverie. I shook my head, trying to control my breathing.

"I'm just … trying to… will I still be human, Sharon?" I asked, desperate. "Will I lose myself in all of this?"

She looked at me with pain in her eyes. "That's why you need to talk to Gramps. He's the only one who can answer the questions."

Andrew stood and walked toward me. "As long as I'm breathing, I won't let you lose yourself." He looked at me and pulled me into a tight hug. Suddenly, he pulled back. "By the way, happy birthday, you dumb bloke."

I chuckled and wiped some moisture from my eyes. "Shit! I forgot it was my birthday. Aren't you guys supposed to be serving me or something?"

Sharon threw her napkin at me and laughed. "Just you wait till tonight. You'll know that you have the best sister and best friend this side of the Atlantic."

I looked between the two of them and shook my head. "You two getting married already? Geezz, the brother is always the last to know."

Andrew shot me a dirty look. "Watch it, Cace. She just agreed to go out with me. I'm going to show this Shelia how an Aussie boy courts a girl. Honey, we are going to have the best day ever. Better get yourself together."

I looked at Sharon and burst out laughing at the look on her face. "You heard him, Shaz. Better get yourself together."

Two hours later I sat in front of my Grandfather's nursing home, staring through the windshield of my battered old Ford. I had to do this; I had to face my legacy. And what a legacy it was! I had spent my whole adolescence preparing to follow in my Grandfather's footsteps as a doctor. I wanted to make life easier for Sharon after my parent's death. I never took into account the shifter gene. Gramps told me that it skipped a generation, yet here I sat, bracing to face a future that included uncertainty. I sighed the longest, loudest sigh of my life and forced myself from the car.

As I entered the building, I braced myself for the onslaught of emotions that was sure to hit. In fact, it was the feeling of other people's emotions that was most unsettling to me. Hopefully Gramps could shed some light on that, as well.

As I walked down the hall to my Grandfather's room and exchanged pleasantries with the staff, I could feel all the different emotions the place held. I suddenly was bombarded with an intense feeling of sadness, fear, longing and depression. It wasn't like reading people's minds; it was more like just being in tuned with them. Outside my Grandfather's door, a young nursing aide was trying to get a resistant elderly patient back to her room. Red waves of anxiety were radiating off the patient, but her face gave it away for anyone who took the time to notice. The aide, on the other hand, was too frazzled to care. I had a choice: block them out and get the hell into my Gramp's room, or use my power to ease the woman's anxiety. *Oh, what the hell.*

"Excuse me, but I think she's trying to tell you something," I interrupted. "Is something worrying you, miss?" The aide gave me a dirty look, but the elderly woman's face brightened at my use of the term 'miss'.

"My son ... he told me to wait here and he would see me soon," the patient said with a dazed look on her face. "So, I really can't leave this chair. How will he find me?"

The aide started talking fast. "Come on, Gladys, let's go. I have ten other people to get ready for dinner and I don't want to have to try and explain this again!"

I looked in Gladys' eyes past the red waves of anxiety to the subtle plains of confusion. I didn't know how I did it, but I sent out calming rays of light and a smile lit up her face.

"Gladys, it's okay," the aide said. "Go on and get ready for dinner. I know your son and he knows where to find you, wherever you are in the home." I gave her arm a reassuring pat and she smiled at me as she started walking away. The aide's sneer made me smile, which I'm sure pissed her off even more.

"You don't know Gladys' son," I said to the aide, "but it's nice to see that my bedside manner rubbed off on you. What harm does it do to calm her down?"

She stormed away in a huff.

I walked into the room and my grandfather was lying on his bed, frail and weak. I sat down on the chair next to his bed.

"You heard that, huh?" I asked.

Gramps shook his head. "I'm paralyzed not deaf Cace."

I reached out and touched his cheek where I knew he would feel me. "How have you been Gramps?"

He chuckled, his brown eyes a reflection of my own. "Can't complain. Being on staff previously does have its advantages. But I know you're here for a reason, not a friendly catching up visit. You didn't go and mess up your finals, did you?"

I ran my hand through my unruly brown hair and rubbed them down my face. "No, sir. My finals went well and I'll graduate as planned tomorrow morning. Sharon has the video recorder all ready for you." I rested my head on the side of the bed.

His gravelly voice broke the silence. "Cace, you're twenty one today, son. I don't think this visit is by coincidence."

I raised my head and met his eyes, eyes I had looked into thousands of times, but had never seen. I could feel his fear as palpable as my own hanging like a curtain in the room. "Sharon thinks I'm going to shift. I've had some … spells. Shaking and anger out of nowhere. Dizziness, pain, vomiting, and the earth seems to move. It always feels as if I'm coming undone. The last one was the worst."

He used his right hand to move his left hand on top of mine. His right arm was spared the paralysis that marred the rest of his body from his stroke last year. As soon as his hand met mine I felt a calming warmth.

"When Cace? When was this last one?" Gramps asked.

I took a deep breath. "Yesterday afternoon. Sharon and Andy had to help me into the house."

A look of concern crossed his face. "Does Andy know?"

I nodded. "Sharon told him last night. It's safe, Gramps. I have a feeling that stubborn Aussie suspected all along."

He was quiet for a moment as his eyes focused on the window over my head. "I could have been wrong. I can feel it in you, warm like fire just beneath the surface. It's stronger than your Dad's. You can read people, can't you Cace?"

I nodded my head yes as he continued on.

"You can't fight the change when it comes, Cace. You have to learn to control it, to embrace this gift that we were given. You have to fight to keep yourself present in your shift."

Tears fell down my face of their own accord. "How, Gramps. It destroyed Mom and Dad in the end. How can I keep from losing myself?"

His fingers tightened on mine. "Pull up a chair, son. We have a lot to talk about."

***

I made it back to the cabin somewhere around eight in the evening. Lights were strung all around the deck and a small fire burned warm in the fire pit down by the water. A half dozen cars lined the drive, and the sound of music drifted in the fragrant night air. A smile lit my face when I saw Sharon and Andrew stroll down the driveway to meet me, hand in hand.

"Happy Birthday, Mate!" Andrew said, handing me a beer. "We got a couple of the guys here, some burgers on the grill, and we're going to rock your birthday into the morning."

Sharon let go of his hand and gave me a hug. "How did it go with Gramps?"

I took a long swig from my beer before I answered. "Okay. Our suspicions could be right, or they could be wrong."

She cocked her head. "Way to be cryptic."

I laughed. "We talked about a lot of stuff … trade secrets, so to speak. I just need time to wrap my head around things." I saw movement out of the corner of my eye. Someone was walking down the driveway, a very female someone. Andrew caught my glance.

"I got one more surprise for you, bro," Andrew said. As the girl made her way to him she reached out and wrapped her arms around his waist. "This is my sister, Bina. She came in early to surprise me and go to my graduation tomorrow. Sneaky little Shelia."

She laughed and held her hand out to me. "You must be Cace. I've been dying to meet you. I feel like we already know each other. Your sister has been amazing."

Even in the fading light I could see the red highlights in Bina's golden hair. Her accent was every bit as captivating as her brother's, but the little sing song spin she put on it melted me to the core. She was amazing, beauty and spunk all rolled into one, and when the breeze blew lightly off the lake it brought the smell of jasmine too me, coming from her skin. I couldn't take my eyes off of her. I held out my hand to her, praying that she would take it and never let it go.

"Bina, it's so great to finally meet you." As she took my hand, warmth radiated from deep inside me and pulsed through my hand to hers. I could tell that she felt it. Our eyes met, and her smile grew wide. It was as if time had stood still. All of the sudden, I became aware of Andrew clearing his throat.

"Hey mate, are you going to let go of my sister's hand long enough to go say hi to your other guests?" Sharon chuckled and wrapped her arm around Andrew's waist. He leaned in and kissed the top of her head.

I smiled at Bina and begrudgingly let go of her hand. "You two must have had a good day. Remember, that's *my* sister you have there, Andy."

Sharon shot me a dirty look. "I can take care of myself there killer."

Shaking my head I turned to Bina. "How was the flight?" She moved closer to me as we followed Sharon and Andrew down the driveway, brushing her arm against mine.

"Long. I won't be making that flight again anytime soon. The way my brother is acting, he has me here for good."

Andrew's voice carried back to us. "You bet your ass, sis. You're staying here."

I laughed at Andrew's back. "You know we always tell your brother he has Vulcan hearing."

Andrew gave me the finger behind his back.

Bina stopped to look at me. "Vulcan hearing?"

I slowed to a stop next to her. "Yah, like Spock from Star Trek." She doubled over with laughter. "What did I say that was so funny?" She stood up and looked in my eyes.

"You just don't seem like a Star Trek kind of guy. You're way too handsome for that," Bina said, looking into my eyes.

I looked back at her and decided then and there that I would do anything to hear that laugh for the rest of my life.

Sometime around midnight the rest of the guys left to get some sleep before graduation the next day. The four of us sat on the deck watching the fire die down and drinking the last of the beers. The last four hours had flown by for me in an amazing conversation with Bina. It was as if I had known her forever from all the times her brother talked about her, but hearing some of the same stories from her point of view, and how Andrew would get pissed when she told the truth about some of his escapades, just cemented my feelings for her. All those old poets were on to something when they wrote about love at first sight. The thought had crossed my mind that my powers may influence her feelings. Gramps and I had touched on that, and I was consciously trying to hold back anytime I felt myself reading her. But now with her sitting on my lap, looking at Sharon and Andrew content in their own little world, I was starting to let my guard down.

"You know as twenty-first birthdays go, that one was kind of disappointing," Bina said, snapping me from my reverie.

I twisted her to face me. "How so?"

She placed her hand behind my neck and started playing with my hair. "Well, I always thought you American guys partied until you were drunk on your asses. These guys were pretty quiet. I don't know, I might have to find my own group of friends to hang with this summer. You guys are kind of lame."

My face fell. I, for one, held back just because Bina was here. I wanted to make a good impression on her. I didn't want her thinking that I was some lush. I really liked this girl. "Bina, it's not about getting drunk. I mean, I'm pretty well buzzed right now, we have graduation in the morning, and I'm trying to be a responsible adult. Hey, you aren't even old enough to drink anyway, are you? What are you? Twenty?"

I heard Andrew laughing his ass off behind me. "You dumb bloke! She's taking the piss out of ya."

Bina lost it, laughing so hard that she almost fell off my lap.

"What the hell do you mean?" I asked, not getting the joke.

Andrew started to laugh harder, and Sharon couldn't contain her giggles after watching the two of them. "She's teasing you, Cace, and your there stammering over your words."

Bina leaned close and kissed my cheek. "Actually, Cace, I'm impressed. I had a wonderful night. Sitting and talking, relaxing, just being normal. I found it refreshing. You guys aren't trying to be something you're not." Then, her eyes suddenly grew serious. "I feel safe here."

I rested my forehead against hers. Looking into her eyes, I tilted my head and softly brushed my lips against hers. Maybe this would be my best summer ever. "Even though I just met you, I would do anything to keep you safe." I leaned back to gage her reaction and see if it was all right. When I did she tightened her grip on my neck and pulled me toward her. This time our lips parted, and she deepened the kiss. That's when I felt it, something was wrong. *Oh, dear god, not now!*

I gently, or as gently as I could, helped Bina off my lap and rested my head on my knees. The world was spinning and my stomach was churning. I felt hot, and I was shaking uncontrollably. A distant part of my mind remembered my talk with Gramps, and I knew this was it. Dear God, why did it have to be now? It was like hearing things from the other end of a tunnel.

Suddenly, Bina's voice made its way to my ears. "Cace! Dear God and bloody hell! Andrew get over here! Cace, oh my God, Cace!"

Her screams broke my heart and I tried to reach my hand out to her, but I vomited on the deck and felt the bones in my arm contort.

Andrew's voice joined the commotion. "Shit. Oh, bloody hell. Sharon, what can we do for him?"

I felt Sharon's hand on my head, and heard her whispers in some vacant part of my mind. Old Highland chants of my Grandmother's spilling from her mouth. Then, Bina's screams grew louder and faded as Andrew dragged her away from me. My world changed in a burst of light and pain. Bones broke and reformed into wings, my skin peeled away replaced by jet black and incandescent purple feathers. In a burst of wind, I was suddenly soaring above the deck. Taking in the images below me like a surreal movie, I watched as my best friend, sister, and the new love of my life, started to fade from my conscious human mind.

God knows how long I soared among the clouds in my raven form. Everything I did was from instinct. I felt free, but there seemed to be a small part of my mind that held onto human concepts and emotion. I could sense smells and feelings as I had when I was human. I remembered that I didn't belong totally to the sky. Sometime after daybreak I perched on one of the pines close to the cabin. My head cocked to one side and under my wing. I was tired; I needed rest. My instincts alerted me to voices, and I watched two figures come out of the cabin and look toward the sky. I felt like I knew them, they triggered something in me. The two seemed to be searching for something, then they held hands and headed back into the house. I opened my beak and let out a squawk before I flew from the branch and circled back over the lake.

I woke up to the bright mid afternoon sun. Rolling over in my human form, I flinched when a branch poked me in the back. Why the hell was I sleeping on the ground, and why was I naked? I sat up and shook my head. My neck felt stiff. In fact, my whole body ached and my chest was covered with scratches and blood. Where the hell was I? Looking around I realized that I was on the beach in some kind of camp. Looking out over the water, I could see houses on the other side. Slowly, the realization dawned on me. I was on the other side of Browning Pond, on the Boy Scout reservation. "Shit!" Standing up fast I got dizzy and dropped back down to one knee.

"Think, Cace, think. I need to find clothes and get the bloody hell out of here." I laughed in spite of myself as I sounded like Andrew, but really it was no laughing matter. If someone found me now, I would be arrested and flagged as some kind of creep. It would ruin my whole career. "But how the hell did I get here?" Did I drink that much last night? Slowly, the realization set in that I must have shifted. "Son of a bitch." Slamming my hand against the ground only served to piss me off more. The events of the night before were

Love Bites

starting to come back to me. And Bina was there; she saw the whole thing. Trying to calm my breathing and take in my immediate surroundings, I stood up and looked to my left. A boat house. What day was it? Saturday? "Damn it, graduation must be over." I made my way over to the boat house, praying that the door was unlocked.

The door slipped open easily and I squeezed inside. It was dark, but I managed to make out a pile of backpacks over by an upside down row boat. I said a silent prayer that clothing was in one of them. I lucked out. The second bag I opened held a pair of swim trunks and a T-shirt. And even more amazing was that they fit me. Holding my breath, I put the clothes on and peeked out the door. The shore was still empty, but I could hear voices in the distance. I looked down at the T-shirt and realized it said life guard. If I had to, I could probably pass as one of the staff.

I tried to figure out what to do as I stepping back into the shadows of the boat house. Being on the opposite side of the lake from my house, I knew that if I walked out of the camp and to the main road, it would be at least an hour walk back into town. But if I took one of the row boats and went across the lake, I could hit the woods and make it to the cabin in a lot less time. Okay, that's what I had to do. I opened the door and made sure that the beach was still empty. Dragging one of the row boats down to the water, I held my breath that no campers would see me. It must be lunch time. I pushed the boat into the water and jumped in. Tilting precariously back and forth, I reached my arms across and grabbed a paddle in each hand and started to row.

By the time I reached the middle of the lake I allowed myself to relax. No one had seen me, and the last time I looked back, the campers were just starting to make their way to the shore. From their perspective, I probably just looked like a guy out fishing.

The whole time I was rowing across the pond and then walking down Browning Pond Road, I refused to allow myself to think about the night before. I didn't want to face the thought of where the scratches and blood had come from, and what animal I had become. I focused instead on Bina. The way her face felt in my hands, the way her lips tasted when we kissed. The way her eyes stayed focused on mine whenever we were talking. Those captivating green eyes, that contrasted so beautifully with her auburn hair. Then, the unwelcome memories forced their way into my consciousness: the way she screamed my name when I writhed in pain on the deck, and the fear in those eyes when I turned in front of her.

"No!" I screamed at the top of my lungs. "No, damn it. It wasn't supposed to happen that way!" Picking up a rock, I threw it at the back of a passing car, not caring that they were innocent bystanders to my pain. "Why would she want me now?" I stood in the middle of the road and threw my head back, screaming to the heavens and letting the tears fall like rain. "I don't want these cursed powers."

I pushed my way into my house and fell onto the kitchen floor. I didn't know what I wanted more, a drink or a shower. My eyes focused on the clock over the kitchen sink, three in the afternoon. "Damn it!" Graduation had been over for a couple of hours, everyone should be to the house soon.

Grabbing a bottle of water from the fridge, I downed it while walking down the hallway to the bathroom. I stripped the borrowed clothes from my body, exposing the blood and scratches again. "What the hell did you get into, Cace?" Looking in the mirror reveled just how bad that I looked. My hair was matted and plastered on my head at odd angles. I had bruises and scratches on most of my body, and my face was filthy and covered in mud. Various spots on my back even had remnants of feathers stuck to it. Standing under the hot water in the shower, I let my mind try and focus on the night before. Curiosity was taking over and I wanted to know what kind of animal I had changed into. From talking with

Gramps I knew that embracing all this and learning to control it was going to be the key.

I remembered flying above everything, feeling like I was one with the wind. Then, I remembered sitting in the trees. My eyes snapped open. A raven. I had shifted into a raven. That would explain the feathers. It could also explain why I had scratches all over my body. If I had started to shift back to my human form while I was still in a tree, then coming down must not have been graceful. The water was starting to get cold when I heard voices in the hall. Stepping out of the shower I wrapped a towel around myself and leaned against the sink. What was Bina going to say? Did she even stick around after I shifted? For all I know, I might have scared her so badly that she hopped on the next plane back to Australia. A knock on the bathroom door made me jump a mile.

"Cace, is that you in there?" It was Andrew.

"Yah, it's me." The silence seemed to go on forever. Then he spoke.

"Are you you, man?" Andy stammered. "I mean, you came back to us? The girls are outside and they're kind of nervous."

Leaning my head against the back of the closed door, I took in several deep breaths. The death grip I had on my towel had turned my already scratched up knuckles white. My voice was barley a whisper. "They're scared of me." Pulling the door open I met Andrew's concerned eyes. "I'm me. Beat up and lucky I'm not in jail, but I'm me." Before I knew what was happening, Andrew had me in a bear hug. Damn, the Aussie was strong!

"Shit, man! I only have a towel on. Do you mind?"

He stepped back and ran his hand through his hair. I noticed his cowboy hat was missing. "Sorry, mate. It's just that last night was so damned surreal. The girls are nerved up. I mean Sharon took it better, but she's playing it up for Bina. We're not sure how much to tell her. You missed graduation. We had no clue if you were still out there, mate."

One thing that stood out in my overcrowded mind was that Bina stayed. She saw me change and she stayed.

"Bina Stayed? Thank God! I was so afraid that she took off after that." I slid down the wall and sat on the floor, *she stayed*.

Andrew chuckled and backed down the hall. "Yah, mate. She's here, but maybe you should put some clothes on, you bloke. Sitting there with your towel falling off and your guys to the world is not how I want you to greet my baby sister. I'll go outside and tell them it's okay, but put some damned clothes on!"

He shook his head as he walked down the hall, his cowboy boots clicking on the wood planks.

"Hey, Andy?"

Stopping, he stood with his back to me. "Yah, bro?"

I closed my eyes when I spoke, fighting off a headache. "Thank you for coming back, for believing in me." I opened my eyes to see him nod, then he walked the rest of the way down the hall.

The four of us stood in the kitchen and the tension was as thick as fog around us. Sharon stood next to me holding my hand, which I was grateful for. It took all the energy I had left not to break down. We waited for someone to speak. To break the spell that hung over us, to face the events of the night before.

Clearing my throat I broke the silence. My voice sounded loud in the tense stillness. "You guys are the only family I have. Thank you for staying. What you saw must have been terrifying. Bina, I especially want you to know that it doesn't change anything. I'm still the same guy I was last night. Beat up and battered from falling out of a tree, but still the same guy." My attempt at humor hung in the air like smoke. Hanging my head I took a deep breath and fought to continue. Half hoping that someone else would start talking. "I don't remember much of the time I was in my … umm … raven form, but I do know that I was in there. I saw you guys and I felt who you were. I flew over this house and I sensed your pain. Sensing feelings is something else that I can do, too. I feel emotions like waves of energy. It's not mind reading or anything. I just can tell what you're feeling. I know I'm rambling and all, but this is who I am. I tried to fight it, but fighting it only makes it worse. Fighting it killed my … our … parents, and I learned that I just need to embrace it."

Looking up I saw tears cascading down Sharon's tired face. She hadn't slept at all. I could sense it, but then it didn't take my powers to see that. Pulling her to me, I wrapped her in my embrace. "I'm sorry, Sharon. I should have listened to you." Suddenly Andrew's large warm hand was on my back as he kissed the top of Sharon's head.

"It's okay, bro. I'm not going anywhere," Andrew said. "We'll help you get through this. I never would have believed it if I hadn't seen it with my own bloody eyes."

A small voice spoke up from behind Andrew. I broke the embrace I had Sharon in and focused on Bina as she spoke. "So, you're a shifter." Her voice trembled. She twirled her shoulder length hair nervously around her finger. "Like werewolves and wisps of fog. The Aborigines called them snake walkers, spirit takers. You're not supposed to exist outside of nightmares and fairytales."

Andrew reached out to her. "Bina, I …"

She took a step back. "No, let me finish, Andrew. Cace turned into a bird in front of me … a bird of nightmares and ancient curses. This beautiful man I met last night and had heard great things of, is not who he seems to be. How do I know you guys didn't drug me and I had some freaky drug induced dream? That you're all playing me for a fool? Even my own brother? I didn't fly halfway around the world to be treated like a game … to be the butt of your half-baked jokes. These things don't exist outside of Hollywood movies." She turned and stormed to the back door, knocking a stack of cups off the breakfast bar.

Andrew took off after her. "Bina, wait. Bina, please ..." he turned and gave us an apologetic look before he followed her out to the deck.

I stood to follow them and Sharon grabbed me by the arm. "Let them go. Andrew will talk to her. She didn't take it very well, and the fact that we were calm about it just floored her."

The words *she stayed* echoed through my mind with less promise than they held a half hour before.

"You two were calm?" I asked.

Sharon sat down heavily at the table. "As calm as we could be. We knew it was coming, but I just hoped that it would happen after graduation. I think I prepared Andy enough that he was a little less freaked out, but Bina? She hasn't had time to get to know you, let alone adjust to the idea. I never thought it was going to happen that quickly."

My eyes watched the two of them as Bina paced and Andrew followed her. I could tell that he was trying to calm her down. She stormed off the deck and he ran after her.

Closing my eyes, I imagined my heat and my feelings for Bina leaving my body and wrapping around her. Envisioning warming colors and pushing them out to her I let my powers flow freely for the first time, comforting her the best way that I could right now. It was draining, as if I was giving part of myself to her. I gripped the counter and braced myself. Throwing my senses out as far as I could, concentrating, imagining all the peace I ever held in my heart, all the honesty, was soaring into her.

"Cace? Cace what are you doing? You look like you're in a trance," Sharon said, stunned.

Sharon snapped her fingers in front of my face and slowly things started to come into focus. I broke the tentative connection I had with Bina and looked at Sharon. "I guess I need to work on my poker face."

She raised an eyebrow at me. "What the hell are you talking about?" she asked, gripping my shoulders. "Are you going to shift again?"

I shook my head, chuckling. "No. That's another power I have. I thought I could for years now, but Gramps confirmed it. Even Dad didn't have it. I can sense and influence feelings. Everything you feel, your energy signature, I feel it, too. It's not like I can read your mind, but more like a sense of emotion. I was trying to send calming feelings out to Bina."

"You can control people's emotions?" Sharon's face went pale as ripples of fear trickled off her.

"No, nothing like that. It's more like I can influence them a little, try to defuse the situation. But more so, it helps me tap into you when I'm in my animal form. I can still feel who you are and your energy. It's extremely helpful in that sense."

Relief showed on Sharon's face.

"So, I was just sending some of my 'honesty' vibes out to Bina. It couldn't hurt," I said, matter of fact.

She rested her head on my shoulder. My sister had always smelled of the same vanilla body lotion for years. Today, especially, I found it comforting. She raised her head and looked directly in my eyes.

"You really like her, don't you?" she asked.

I nodded.

"Was it scary when you shifted, Case?" Sharon asked, then her voice lowered. "Did it hurt?"

Looking out the window, I watched as Bina and Andrew walked back toward the house. "A little, but once the change happened, it felt freeing. It was as if I was detached from my human self and still there at the same time, if that makes sense. Some of it is coming back to me in bits and pieces. I have to learn to control it."

Suddenly, I felt the unfairness of it all. I slapped my hand down on the counter, making Sharon jump. "Shit,

Sharon. I never wanted this. And last night had been amazing with Bina. I knew in an instance what every poet had ever meant about love at first sight; she was all that I had been waiting for. And then in that same instance, I was ripped from my body … from her … and then I knew why Dad did it … why he left us by his own hand. The weight of it all was just too much."

She watched me as I tried to wipe the tears from my eyes before she saw them. She turned me toward her and took my hands. "Cace, you're not Dad. If anyone can control this, you can. Gramps never let it take him over, either. He and Grammy were happy for years. They held it all together, and they raised us. You have the power to overcome this. I feel it in your hands. You're stronger than Dad ever was."

At that moment, Andrew walked back in the house. "I feel naked without my hat, mates. Sharon, where the hell did I leave my hat?" He ran his hands through his hair again.

"In my room, hon, I'll go get it," Sharon said, then gave me a quick hug before she walked out of the kitchen.

I raised my eyebrow at Andrew and smacked him on the head. "In her room, huh? You two were pretty cozy last night while I was out in the trees it seems."

Andrew cleared his throat. "Well, Sharon was pretty worried about you, and Bina fell asleep on the couch, so I just thought that … wait a minute, you bloke. I don't have to explain anything to you."

For the first time since I shifted back, I smiled. "It's okay, bro. I'm so glad you were here for her." I glanced out toward the deck to see Bina sitting in one of the chairs with her long legs pulled up under her. "I guess I messed that up big time."

Andrew was quiet for what felt like an eternity. "She'll be okay. I convinced her to stay until tomorrow to figure things out. It was actually kind of weird. She got quiet out there, like something came over her, and she just nodded and walked back to the deck."

I bit the inside of my mouth so hard that I could taste blood. Andrew didn't need to know the exact extent of my powers. Looking at him, I told him what had been nagging at me since I had made my way back to the house. "Was it that bad to watch? I really like her, Andy. I wish I could turn back time and stop it all."

He placed his hand on my shoulder. "It was positively frightening, bro. I was a little more prepared, but I had to question whether I was tripping, too. Bina's been privy to our Dad's alcoholic rages more than I have. To her, the world is black and white; there's no room for fantasy. You're something that shouldn't exist."

Sharon came back into the kitchen and placed Andrew's well-worn cowboy hat on his head and you could almost feel him relax.

"I knew there was a reason you're the Shelia for me." He spun her around and gave her a kiss.

I shook my head. "You guys really are hitting it off. I told you three years ago, Shaz. See? All that time you've lost …"

She blushed bright red as she punched me in the gut. "Better late than never, mate."

Her attempt at the Australian accent brought me into full-fledged hysterics.

Bina came back in the house and gave us a weak smile as she walked toward the stairs. "I think I'm going to go lay down, Andrew. Thank you for the hospitality, Sharon." I watched her as she crossed the room without so much as a glance in my direction. Sharon placed her hand on my arm. "I'll go talk to her, Cace."

Moonlight danced off the water and filtered down between the trees. Staring out over the lake, I could almost feel the desire to shift palpable in the night air, like a living, breathing creature next to me. The desire to fly surprised me. I longed to feel the wind as it pushed me on unseen currents. Could I soar as high as the moon? Be able to touch it? I closed my eyes and took in all the sounds and smells around me, tapping into my extra sense of perception … and I could block it, too. Standing there I felt on the verge of shifting, but I pulled my animal side back into my body, pushed it down and centered myself. Control was easier than I had imagined. Mastering the emotion also mastered the change. Could my Dad have felt the same thing? Before it all drove him mad.

"Are there more of you?" Bina's voice broke my concentration and brought my attention to the death grip I had on the deck railing. I turned to face her, flexing my fingers to get some feeling back into them.

"I thought you would never talk to me again," I said.

She hung her head. Her silky hair covered her face and she shivered in the spring night. When she brought her eyes back up to meet mine, I saw moisture reflected in them by the moonlight.

"That's still up for debate, but you didn't answer my question," she said, taking a deep breath. "Does America have shifter's running around her shores at night? Or are you a lone enigma?"

It was my turn to avert my eyes. "I don't know about America being over populated with shifters, but, yes, there are more. My Father and Grandfather were shifters. We are part of the North American Shifters. Our lines can be traced back to the Druids and their early settlements in America."

Bina crossed over the deck and stood to my left, about two feet away from me. She gripped the rail and looked out over the lake. She was quiet for a moment, so I just waited, relieved by the closeness of her presence.

"So, you knew it would happen. You knew that you were a shifter?" Her voice startled me in its sadness.

I looked over at her and studied her profile, even from this angle her beauty was captivating. I turned my eyes back to the lake. "Yes. But we thought it skipped me. My Grandfather stopped shifting in his fifties, and my Dad … he … umm … killed himself and took my mom with him. The pressure of the whole thing was too much for him. I thought that if I ignored it and made it past my twenty-first birthday without shifting, then I would be home free, but I was wrong."

Bina inched closer, finally allowing herself to look at me. There was sadness in her eyes, but none of the pity that I had expected to see … the pity that had always belittled me when people heard about the circumstances of my parent's death.

"That must have been hard for you, Cace. To lose both of your parents that way. We lost our Mum in a car accident when I was five. I barely remember her, but my father took it out on us every day. He still does."

I nodded my head. "Andrew told me how tough it is for you. He doesn't want you to go back, you know." I snuck a glance at her from the corner of my eye and added, "and neither do I." She shook her head and looked down into the water. "Bina, don't let last night color your opinion of us … of me. You can stay here and not have to see me, if that's what you choose. But I would hate to see you go back to that situation."

She nodded her head, closing her eyes as a single tear traced down her face. "It's not that simple," she said. "Andrew hasn't seen how our father has changed … how the drinking and hard work has aged him. I know Andrew remembers the fear and the pain, but he chooses to forget the good times, as well. It's not just last night that will factor into my decision." She looked at me and our eyes met. "Cace, you scared the shit out of me last night. What am I supposed to think? People just don't change into birds in front of your eyes. And those two dumb blokes in there didn't think that I could handle the truth." She chuckled. "You should have seen them stuttering and stammering over their words, trying to drag me in the house. And the more I thought of it, the more I thought that you fools were trying to take the piss out of me."

I looked at her with a raised eyebrow. "I'm starting to like that saying."

It was her turn to chuckle. "So, you do remember some things from last night?"

Growing quiet, I looked directly into her eyes. "I remember it all." My eyes searched hers for any emotion … any sign as to what would come next. Her eyes held mine for a long moment before she looked back over the lake.

"What's it like to fly?" she quietly asked.

Tentatively moving toward her, I closed the last few inches between us and took her hand into mine, but instead of pulling away as I expected, she laced her fingers with mine.

"It's freeing. My mind was closed to any conscious thought and all I could think of was what I could see and feel: the wind as it gently lapped over me, the smell of the night air, the tug of the slight changes in pressure. But the weirdest thing is that I never consciously felt it all until I changed back. It's more like an instinctual action than a conscious thought."

She nodded. "I think the world would run smoother if more of us acted on instinct than conscious thought. Humans tend to over think things, to build problems where there are none." She looked at me and smiled. "You calmed my nerves before, didn't you?"

If the night wasn't so dark, she would have seen the blush on my cheeks, but I felt the heat. "Yes. I'm sorry."

"Don't be. You gave me the time I needed to calm down and to think, but I still need more time. You startled me last night, Cace, but you don't scare me."

I leaned in closer to her, smelling the jasmine scent of her perfume mixed with the cool spring air. "As much as I would like to continue this conversation, I'm dead tired Bina. I don't think I slept at all last night. Unless you count when I woke up naked on the beach." She cocked her eyebrow at me. "Don't ask. It's really better if you don't know that part." Her laugh sounded like music, and her hand flew to her mouth to cover it. "Don't worry about waking your brother and my sister. They're fast sleep."

She looked at me quizzically. "How do you know that?"

Gesturing with my head toward the house, I choose my words carefully. "Their energy signatures, their auras, are both calm and relaxed. I'm not getting fuzzy static and blending colors. That's how I know." It probably wan't the best explanation, but it was the only way I knew how to say it.

She nodded as a look of contemplation came over her face, but she let it drop. Instead, she leaned onto me and placing her lips ever so gently on my cheek before she let go of my hand and turned toward the house. "Goodnight, Cace."

Sunlight filtered into the room through the large glass slider, waking me from my restless sleep. It took me a minute to remember why I was sleeping on the couch, and then the realization hit me that Bina had stayed. A huge smile lit up my face. Struggling to sit up from the tangle of blankets, I squinted to make out the time from the clock on the mantle. Seven in the morning. I thought for sure I would have slept longer.

I staggered across the open space from the living room to the kitchen, feeling like I had just ran a triathlon. Every muscle in my body protested against the movement. Every step felt like an iron bar was tied to my feet. The events of yesterday must have been harder on my body than I had first realized. Whether it was the actual act of shifting or what I went through when I was a raven, time would tell. Gramps told me that it would take time, but I felt ahead of the curve with being able to control the shift last night. During the night, I had started calling my alter ego The Raven … hardly original.

Starting a pot of coffee and taking some Advil took more concentration then it ever had before. The first time I tried to take the cover off the bottle of pain medicine, I launched it across the room. The second time the whole container crumpled in my hands and all the pills fell to the floor. It seemed that strength was something that I needed to add to my list of new powers. Halfway across the floor on my hands and knees chasing the last of the spilled pills, I noticed Andrew's feet on the other side of the kitchen table.

"Mate, it sounds like you're doing demolition work down here. What the hell is up with all the banging?" Andrew asked.

I rocked back on my heels to look up at him, and noticed indents in the floor where I had been knelling. "Shit, man. I guess this strength thing is coming along with the shifting, but at the same time I feel like I can't get back up."

He reached down and offered me his hand.

"Thanks." I gripped his hand and started to rise to my feet when I noticed a look of agony on Andrew's face. I quickly let go. "Did I hurt you?"

He flexed his hand open and closed a few times and shook his head. "No, not too bad … nothing worse than getting caught in a cattle rope. What the hell, man? You have to control that before you end up hurting the girls."

I ran my hands through my hair as I sank into one of the kitchen chairs. Andrew continued making the coffee where I had left off. He even placed a glass of orange juice and three Advil on the table in front of me, but we were silent, each one of us wondering where this was going to take us. He was the first to break the silence.

"I heard that you talked to Bina last night. How did things go?" Andrew asked, sitting down across from me with a cup of coffee.

It took me a second to answer as I was concentrating on putting the orange juice glass down without breaking it into a million pieces. "Better than I thought it would. She seemed to take things pretty well. I thought for sure that she would hate me."

Andrew stared at me with one eyebrow raised. "Really, man? She said that she was shocked, but not scared. Don't get me wrong, it's going to take time for her to come to terms with it, but I think she will."

We looked at each other intently for a while. "It's going to take a while for me to come to terms with it. Everyone thinks that shifters only exist in literature or horror movies. How am I going to have a normal life, Andy? Look, I couldn't even make coffee this morning without tearing up the kitchen."

At that moment, Sharon walked. "What are we talking about, boys? Whoa, what the hell happened to the floor?"

Andrew put down his coffee to envelope Sharon in a massive hug. "Your brother seems to have come into some superhuman powers ... one more advantage of being a shifter."

She looked at me and concern filled her eyes. "Did Gramps say anything about that?"

I shook my head. "No, but he said that he could feel that my powers were greater than his." I stood up carefully. "Look, I need to get some fresh air. I need time to think." Sharon started to protest, but Andrew grabbed her arm.

"Take all the time you need, mate," Andrew said.

Turning toward the back door, I felt the rush of energy that normally made me sick. It was the kind of energy that put you into flight or fight mode, and this time it was flight mode. I felt the shift coming and it was welcomed.

This time, I kept some of my conscious thought. I was able to control where I flew, and I felt every breath of air and jab of the cold rain that began to fall. The view of the lake from the sky was magical. I soared down and touched a wing tip to the water and caught an insect in my beak, all the while trying to figure out the emotions that tormented the human side of my brain. Sticking close to the cabin and the other houses on my street, I landed in trees and observed the comings and goings on a whole new level. It was easy to see how this power could be used for both good and evil.

Embracing the animal side of my existence was freeing. I decided that no matter what animal I could be, I always wanted to be The Raven. He was dark and mysterious, poets wrote about him, and he was a sign from ancient druid times. He was me and I was him. Opening my beak, I proclaimed to the world my acceptance with a series of musical calls. Bringing other birds to my side, we flew until the day grew dark.

Did my father fight acceptance? Is that what made him lose touch with himself? I vowed never to hurt those around me as he did. At that moment, I vowed to find a way to love Bina and to keep my family safe.

***

Sometime after dusk, I touched down in the tress behind my cabin. Fluttering to the ground, I let my wings fold in, and shook as pain contorted my bones. One by one, my limbs changed back to their human form. Soon, I was whole again. I looked down at my body and was surprised and elated to see that I had no new scars or scratches. My skin was intact … along with my sanity. I looked around for something to cover me as I made my way to the house and was startled by a soft voice.

"Cace? I have a blanket for you if you need one. It's quite chilly tonight." Her voice echoed through my ears. Music, mixed with the scent of jasmine … Bina. "Cace? I hope it's you out there. I've been watching for you."

Stepping out from behind a tree, I found my voice. "Bina, it's me. I just … I'm naked." It sounded like an unnecessary explanation even to my own ears.

"I know, silly," Bina replied. "We saw your clothes on the drive earlier. That's why I have been watching for you."

Swallowing hard, I took another step toward the sound of her voice. "Do you want to toss me the blanket? How should we work this?" The night air was starting to chill me. Parts of my body had goose bumps, and other parts were running for cover. Her voice floated on the wind.

"No, silly, I can just wrap you up," she said, surprising me.

Jumping, I realized she was right in front of me. Suddenly, the blanket slid down over my body. She gave it a tug, pulling me closer to her. She was quiet as our eyes met; my deep blue ones transfixed by her emerald green ones. A piece of hair blew softly across her face, and my body stiffened in response. My hands ached to tuck it back behind her ear, but they were trapped under the blanket. My need to touch her was almost palpable in the air.

"Thank you … for watching for me." My voice sounded small and unsure.

She nodded, and looked toward the sky. "How was it up there? To fly?" She loosened her hold on the blanket as she spoke and I was able to free my hands. Taking the blanket from her, I tucked the end in around my chest, and reached out to tuck her hair behind her ear. She shivered at my touch.

"It was freeing … surreal. This time, I was able to keep a part of my human consciousness and the feeling was totally different." I looked back toward the sky with a sense of longing, but the longing that I felt for Bina was even stronger. I took her hand and wrapped my fingers with hers. "I'm so happy you watched for me. I think I can manage these two worlds … to make them coexist. I can make this work."

She smiled so big that it lit up her entire face. Her fingers tightened around mine and she brought our entwined hands to her lips. "You can … and I will help you. I will share everything I know to make this easier for you."

Taking my hand from hers, I tightened the grip I held on the blanket. My voice was merely a whisper as I spoke. "What do you mean 'share everything you know'?"

Bina looked at me with a knowing smile and took a step back. She started to peel her shirt over her head, revealing the lacy bra that she wore underneath.

"Wait a minute, Bina, what are you doing?" She held her finger to her lips and continued to undress. When she had her pants off, and was standing before me in just her bra and panties, she looked at me with a shy smile.

"I've never shifted into a bird, but my favorite animal is the coyote," she said, then continued, "I can run for miles. Shifting helps me with all the heartache that my father has caused. I can run across the desert, climb mountains and go wherever I want." With that she dropped to all fours and turned into the most beautiful coyote that I had ever seen. Silver fur tinted blue by the bright moon that now was full in the sky. She looked at me, her eyes still the same brilliant Bina green that I had come to know. She padded on soft paws around me, then sat and held out one to me. I chuckled and shook it. She leaned in and lapped my face. Then, just as quickly, she was standing back before me … the beautiful woman that she was. Her bra and panties where a shredded afterthought lying at her feet.

I held open the blanket for her to come to me, and she ran into my arms. "Oh, my God, Cace. You don't know how freeing that was to show you. For all these years, I held it in and ran from my true self. I thought that coming to the states would let me escape it, and then seeing you … well … I panicked for a while."

Holding her in my arms, skin to skin, was more than I could take. I silenced her by pressing my mouth to hers. I ran my hands through her hair, amazed at every tingle that I felt where our bodies meshed together. It was as if I had never touched her before. Every sensation was magnified. Sliding to the ground I broke the kiss.

Love Bites

"Bina, does Andrew know? I mean how … thank you for telling me," I stammered.

She chuckled. "He knows. In our family, shifting is a female trait. My mother and I shared aborigine blood. Why do you think he accepted you so easily? He always knew that there was something of a kindred spirit in you." She knelt down between my knees and pressed her lips to mine. I fell back to the ground, pulling her on top of me. "There is so much I have to tell you, Cace. You can do this. I can show you how to control the shift … how to call on your animal instincts. I have legions of aboriginal training to draw from."

Running my hands down her back, I cupped her cheeks in my hands, so soft, so warm. Placing kisses on her neck and trailing down to her collar bone, I broke contact long enough to speak. "Later, Bina. There is plenty of time later, but for now let me love you." We tangled up in each other's arms. I kissed every part of her body that I could reach. I wanted to tease her as long as I could; It felt like my first time all over again. Every sensation was heightened, and her strength matched mine. I didn't have to worry about hurting her. The blanket was forgotten as we rolled around in the grass. When I entered her, she threw her head back and closed her eyes, only opening them so that we could watch each other's climax.

We made our way back to the house after the night had grown fully dark. I was still wrapped in the blanket, so Bina ran ahead to make sure that the path to my room was clear. Luckily the house was empty, with both Sharon's Dart and Andrew's truck missing from the yard. We ran giggling like teenagers up the stairs to the loft, throwing ourselves onto my bed to pick up where we left off. Bina had been staying in my room, so my sheets already held her captivating scent of jasmine. Later, as she fell asleep next to me, I vowed to never let her down, to never let her lose the light that I saw in her eyes tonight when I found out that we shared the same secret. I finally felt at home.

"When were you going to tell me that your sister is a shifter?" I asked.

From the way Andrew jumped when he heard my voice, I knew that I had taken him by surprise. It was early and the sun had barley risen enough to fill the kitchen with light. A faint mist rose from the lake, visible through the sliders. He turned with a wicked glint in his eyes.

"When were you going to tell me that you slept with her?" he asked. I chuckled as he raised his coffee mug to me. "Touché, mate."

I crossed the room, grabbed a mug off the counter and poured myself a cup. "Okay, we are even. But for the record, you don't have a leg to stand on because you're sleeping with *my* sister too. Touché, mate."

Andrew threw his head back and laughed. He rose to his feet and pulled the backdoor open, then pointed to the deck. "Want to have our coffee outside so we don't wake the girls?"

I followed him outside and pulled over two chairs. We both sat facing the lake, silent for a moment as we drank our coffee.

"I didn't know how to break it to ya, Cace," Andrew said. "When you first had that spell in the driveway, I had my suspicions. Then when you bugged out right in front of us … well … I thought you would be pissed to know that I knew all along that supernatural stuff existed."

I raised an eyebrow to him. "That supernatural stuff … yeah … it's a hell of a lot more than stuff. Why did Bina freak, then? You guys sure were convincing."

Andrew averted his eyes for a moment, staring out over the lake and draining the last of his coffee. "That had more to do with me than you, Cace. She figured that it was something that I had orchestrated to get her to out herself, to get her away from our dead beat Dad and make her vulnerable in front of my mates. And, for the record, Sharon doesn't know. Can we keep it that way?"

Love Bites

I laughed. "I'll try, but Sharon has a way of finding things out. You can't keep much from that girl. She knew that I was going to shift long before I did. I wouldn't be a bit surprised if she knew right now about Bina." I reached over and slapped Andrew on the arm.

"Bina doesn't talk much about it, the shifting. Not to me and never to my Dad. So, I don't know much about it. My Mum always said that it was a special gift to run with the animals. Does it hurt, Cace? I can't bear to think of Bina being in pain."

I wrestled with telling him. In my limited experience, it had hurt for a time, but not in the way that he would experience pain. "I can't speak for Bina, but the few times that I have shifted, it wasn't pleasant, but it wasn't anything that I couldn't handle, either. You'll have to take that up with Bina. Maybe with me being a shifter, things will be easier for her. Should I let on that we talked?" I figured that it was better to ask now rather than to mess things up with my big mouth.

Andrew stood up against the railing and looked at me. "Do you love her, mate? I mean, I know it's kind of soon, but I can already see it in your eyes. Do you love her, or is it just the idea of being in love with her? I can't have my sister hurt any more than she already has been."

Looking down at my coffee mug I contemplated the question. Crap. A couple of days ago, my answer might have been different. But after last night, after feeling the connection I felt, I was sure of it. "I'm in love with her. Not the idea of love, not the idea of another shifter, I am in love with your sister, Andrew, the total package. For the first time in a long time, I felt like I was finally home last night, if that makes sense."

Andrew walked over and pulled me into a tight bear hug. "That makes total sense to me, mate, total sense."

We were interrupted by Sharon, who chose that minuet to walk out onto the deck, dressed totally like a freak in hot pink pajama pants and one of Andrew's hideous rugby T-shirts. "I hate to interrupt this bro love fest, but has anyone seen Bina?"

I searched for days, flying out over the lake, flying as far as I would allow myself to test my fledgling powers. I even searched on the ground, concentrating all my power and shifting into a wolf. Alright, it was a Husky, but it was close enough. Nothing. Not a trace of Bina was to be found. Time spent in my human form was spent walking around like a nut case. I couldn't focus, and I couldn't eat. I wouldn't rest until we had heard from her.

All of her luggage was gone and her rental car was returned. Andrew called friends over in Australia, but she hadn't told anyone that she was coming home early. He had contemplated calling his Dad, but had decided that maybe it would be easier to grab a flight home. We told Sharon about Bina being a shifter, and about the night that we spent together before she disappeared. Sharon was at a loss.

I wondered why didn't she at least call. We had plans. She was going to teach me.

After a week with no leads, no news from her, and no sign of foul play that the police could find, Andrew had booked a flight. His gut feeling was that she had gone home. She was probably scared of being attached, regretted exposing herself, and just at a loss for what to do.

We were sitting in the great room watching Andrew pack the rest of his bag. Sharon was fighting tears. As much as she worried about Bina, she didn't want Andrew to go off alone. I couldn't help but think that it was my fault. That it was something that I had done, something about me that had turned her away. How could that night have been anything but perfect?

Just as Andrew was pulling the zipper across on his well-worn duffle bag, his cell phone rang. We all turned and looked at the screen where it sat on the coffee table, as Bina's name flashed across it.

Sharon jumped up and tossed the phone to Andrew. "Well, shit honey," Sharon said. "Aren't you going to answer it?"

He caught it and looked between the two of us. Slowly, he pressed the button to accept. "Bina? Where the hell are you? I'm … we are worried sick." He turned his back to us and started to walk toward the kitchen. Sharon sat down next to me and took my hand. I'm sure it was trembling even more than I felt it inside. My Bina. Why hadn't she called me?

He was quiet on his end. The conversation was marked by random words and grunts. There could have been more, but I had lost all sense of where I was, focusing hard on not shifting. Instead, I tried to funnel all my love for Bina through that phone connection. Sharon gripped my hand tighter. Then, Andrew was walking back toward us.

"She's in Arizona with a mate of hers. She wants to go to school there. I guess her and this girl decided to move in together," he said, looking at me with pity in his eyes.

"But why? Why didn't she have the common decency to trust me, to tell me, to let me …" My voice trailed off as ripples of energy cascaded across my body.

"Cace, man, she said that she wasn't ready for a relationship or a commitment. She said that she just showed herself to you to let you know you weren't alone. Shit, man! I'm more than pissed at her. I told her that she was wrong … that you love her … that you have feelings for her and she didn't want to hear any of it." He turned to Sharon then and fell into her arms. "I mean it, baby. I didn't know. I would have never let her hurt Cace."

The two of them stood there staring at me with pity on their faces and I just couldn't take it anymore. I gave in to the energy and shifted faster than I had before. I twisted and turned in agony. Every shifting bone and turning of my skin was a piercing, painful reminder of how I had lost Bina. I flew from the house, higher than the tree tops and sailed across the sky to the west, taking in everything below me as if it were child's play things. If I had to fly to Arizona, I would.

Two Years Later

"Well, Mr. Matthews, we normally don't let students pickup their scholarship late after disappearing for years, but at the request of your late Grandfather, whom I had upmost respect for, we are making an exception. I have to admit, you bare a striking resemblance to him."

I looked out the window of Dean Wilson's office across the vast campus of the University of Massachusetts Worcester and the Medical Center knowing that this was where I belonged. Two years of chasing after Bina across deserts and cities had hardened me. I knew that love would never be mine. Finally, I decided to devote myself to my medical career. "Thank you, Dean Wilson. I won't disappoint you or the board with this decision. I take my choices very seriously."

The Dean looked at me with sad and knowing eyes. "Where were you, son? I have to admit, we were saddened when you didn't show for your Grandfather's funeral. He always spoke highly of you."

Looking down at my feet, I sucked in a breath before I answered the Dean. "I had some personal business that took me out of the country. I couldn't make it back in time. Trust me, I kick myself every day for it."

"It was strange, Mr. Matthews. That day, the day we buried your Grandfather, a Raven sat atop the casket and refused to be scared off. A beautiful raven, like nothing I had ever seen. I still think of it to this day. Your sister seemed very protective of it even. And she had a beautiful voice. She sang in Gaelic that day. It was very sad and heartbreaking.

Well, anyway, I look forward to following your career for many years to come. Good luck, son."

I shook the Dean's hand and slowly made my way from his office. My eyes were trained on the ground through the maze like halls of the medical center. I looked up as I hit the parking garage and saw the old Charger that I had inherited from my Grandfather. Sharon and Andrew stood beside it, their eyes locked on mine.

"Is it all set?" Sharon asked. When I nodded, she took me in her arms. "Gramps would be so proud."

Andrew reached over, grabbed my arm and pulled me to him. "Thank God, mate. Do you have her out of your system yet?" Sharon reached over and smacked him on the back of the head.

I chuckled. "It's okay, Sharon. Yeah, I'm good. The raven is home to roost."

As we climbed into the Charger I patted my right back pocket and the key that was in it. Yes, the raven truly was home to roost.

Love to Death
By: Monica Blanton

My job is not easy. People mistake me for being this evil creature that looms and waits for an opportunity to take a soul that is often thought to be non-deserving of it. It doesn't work that way. I have rules to go by and it's my job to make sure that it's done. I don't mean to be cruel and I don't like doing it, but life has a cycle. There has to be balance. If it is not carried out, there would be chaos. There is a time and place for every life to end in order to make room for the new souls to come into the world. This is where my dilemma lies as of late. I am Azrael, the angel of death, the Grim Reaper. My job? Transporting souls to where they are supposed to go. So,what am I supposed to do if I fall in love with one of these souls? The Grim Reaper is not supposed to fall in love! Most think that I am heartless, without a soul or feelings, but they are wrong! I do feel, and because of my mistakes as a human long ago, I took on my job with dignity and no complaints, dealing with my own guilt and demons daily. I accepted it, but how am I supposed to deal with this situation?

***

3 days earlier...

"New assignments just came in. Here is your list, Azrael." I was handed a parchment of names. It also listed times, dates, locations, and causes of death. Once I carry out an assignment, we will appear where the soul is destined to spend their eternity. I nod my head and vanish, teleporting myself to the first stop on the list: a farm in Kansas, where an elderly man with a heart condition resides. It was a nice, quiet place where he and his wife had retired. He was already lying in his bed and in and out of consciousness when I appeared at his bedside. His wife was sitting in a chair on the other side of the bed, holding his hand with tears in her eyes.

"Please, don't cry for me, Serena. I will always be with you," said the old man, then his spirit was suddenly standing beside me. His wife had the feeling that he had moved on, bowed her head and rested it on his hand and sobbed.

"John Myer?" I asked him.

"Yes, sir."

"I am here to take you where you need to go."

"Yeah, I kinda figured that." He turned to look at me with a curious expression. "Say, what do you look like under that heavy robe?"

There have been a few souls to ask me this question because everyone expects the same answer. I just wear the big robe because I like it. I pulled back my hood and awaited the surprise I usually got.

"Huh! Well, I be darned! I wasn't expectin' that!" Most did not. The rumors and stories going around portray me as a skeletal figure, gruesome and evil looking, but I still look like myself from many years ago: light brown hair, green hazel eyes, and strong features. That's not to say that I can't make myself look like that. It's more of a parlor trick, a glamor. I like to use it when I pick up the bad ones! Watching their faces is priceless and I can change my voice to make them pee themselves. Maybe that's where the stories came from.

"It's time to go, John," I said.

He nodded and turned to his wife and said, "Goodbye, my sweet Serena. I love you … always." She couldn't hear him, but it made the souls feel better to say their goodbyes.

When he was ready, we teleported, appearing before the gates of Heaven. John sighed in relief. He looked at me and smiled. "Ya know, I always tried doing right in hope that this is where I would go to. Serena would be happy to know."

"I'm sure she already does," I replied.

He smiled and nodded, then walked up to the gate. John turned and waved one last time and walked on to his destination. Once he was inside and the gates were closed, I vanished and teleported myself to the next stop on my list.

The next two made it to the same place as John, but the third wasn't as lucky.

As I came to the last soul on my list, I appeared at a nice community college in Maryland. A young woman by the name of Kaylee Dillon was to be hit by a bus. It wasn't supposed to happen until nightfall, so I decided to cloak myself, making myself invisible to get a lead on her. I appeared in her dorm room where she was stretched out on her bed, talking on her phone and doing her homework.

Normally, I can go into a job with a clear mind. The first couple of times were tough, but I had to learn how to cope with it. I have to do my job, so getting cold feet is not an option. Over time, I was able to become numb and just do what I had to, but when I laid eyes on Kaylee, my heart stopped.

Never had I seen a young woman so beautiful. Sure, there have been pretty ones before that I've taken, but I've always been able to keep myself detached ... until now. Kaylee had wheat colored blonde hair that fell straight to just below her shoulders, brown eyes, and a smile to die for ... again. I couldn't move; I could only stand there and listen to her voice as she spoke of an upcoming party that someone on campus was having, unaware that she would never attend.

"Yeah, he asked me, but I don't know. I've never been into the whole jock thing. They're always way too into themselves than I could ever be."

She's funny, too, I thought with a smile.

"I don't know," Kaylee said. "I'll have to think about it some more. I still have a ton of work to do, anyway. Okay, I'll talk to you later." Kaylee hung up the phone and stared at it for a few minutes, as if she were waiting for it to give her the answers to her questions about going. Then, she just sighed and tossed it to the foot of the bed and rolled onto her back, rubbing her eyes in defeat. She stared at the ceiling for a while before falling asleep.

Still hypnotized by her, I couldn't bring myself to leave, so I stayed and watched while she napped. She tossed and turned, obviously not sleeping well. All of a sudden, Kaylee sat straight up with a gasp, as if waking from a nightmare. So badly I wanted to reach out and touch her face, to ask her what she had dreamed about and to let her know that everything was okay. She swung her legs over the side of the bed and put her feet on the floor. She looked around, panicked, until she realized where she was. Kaylee sighed, closed her eyes, and dropped her head in her hands, letting her wheat blonde hair fall over her shoulders. Then, she sat up again and looked at the clock. It read 6 o'clock.

"Crap!" Kaylee exclaimed and ran to the bathroom. She was ready in under ten minutes and headed out the door with her books in hand, already late for class. I followed, shadowing her every move, still mesmerized by her. I watched Kaylee while she was in her class, listening intently to the teacher give a speech. After her class, Kaylee headed out the front door and back to her dorm.

Forgetting the whole reason why I was even here and what time it was, I looked up and panicked. She was about to step out in front of a bus that was coming down the road. Without thinking, I lost concentration on making myself invisible, and yelled out, "Stop!"

She jumped back just as the bus passed her by and turned to look at me, startled.

I ran up to her, thinking to myself how foolish I was being. What was wrong with me? "Are you alright?" I asked.

This was wrong, very wrong! I was throwing off the balance of things by keeping her from meeting her fate, but I just couldn't go through with it.

"Yes, I'm fine. Listen, thank you for saving my life."

All I could do was nod because I wasn't supposed to save her life.

"What is your name?" she asked.

I almost told her my real name, but thought better of it, not that she would know who I was, but 'Azrael' is not a name you hear very often. I was trying to think quick so that she wouldn't think I was a crazy person and the first name that popped into my head was John. He had been a nice man. I could use his name. "It's John. And, you are?" I already knew her name. I couldn't let her know I knew her name, but I also wanted to hear her say it.

"Kaylee," she answered with a smile, but her expression suddenly changed, confused. "Are you a student here? I don't think I've seen you around here before."

Again, I had to think quick. "No, I was just visiting a friend. He told me about some party this weekend and to stop by and let him know if I was coming, but I'm not sure. I don't do well with crowds." Using my eavesdropping from earlier to my advantage, I was able to make her not so suspicious of me.

Kaylee nodded. "Oh, yes, the big party. Yeah, I don't know if I'm going either. Big crowds are just not my thing."

"I know what you mean," I answered.

Kaylee looked at me for a few minutes, and then asked, "I'm sorry, but I have to ask: what's with the cloak?"

I forgot to alter my appearance before showing myself to her. I looked down at myself, trying to think of a good explanation. Then, I remembered hearing about a game a while back that people liked to play in character and dress up, which sounded ridiculous to me, considering the real origin of the concept. "Oh, my friend and I were playing Dungeons and Dragons. Have you ever played?"

Love Bites

"No, I've heard of it though. Nerds in my high school used to get into it," she said.

Great, now she thinks that I'm socially impaired with a fantasy fixation!

"I'm sorry! That was rude of me," she corrected. "I didn't mean it the way that it came out. I just meant, typically, that's who you find playing the game, but you don't fit the profile."

"What profile seems more suitable for me?" I asked.

"I'm not sure. You just don't look like the Dungeons and Dragons type," she said, smiling, then added, "Listen, I have to run. I have early classes in the morning. It was nice to meet you, John. Thanks, again, for saving my life."

"You're very welcome. It was also a pleasure to meet you, too, Kaylee."

I turned and started to walk away, when she yelled, "Wait!"

I turned back around as she ran up to me. She looked a bit nervous, but asked, "I was wondering, would you like to hang out sometime? I know the guy is usually the one to ask the girl out, but since you saved my life, I wanted to know if I could treat you to a cup of coffee?"

This wasn't allowed, but I couldn't bring myself to say no. "How does tomorrow sound? I can meet you at the campus coffee shop."

"Sure," she replied. "I have an early class, so around eleven?"

"I'll be there," I replied, wondering what I was doing.

Once she was gone, I made myself invisible once again and went for a walk. It wasn't long before I felt the call: the pull from the other side where the assignments come from. I closed my eyes, dreading the trip, and teleported back. As soon as I appeared, a deep voice echoed in the void where I stood. "Do you realize what you have done? You are throwing off the order!" No visible being presented itself. I have never dealt with this kind of situation before, so, my guess was that this being was the one in charge, so to speak.

"I know, sir," I replied. "I'm very sorry. I'll fix everything and it won't happen again. You have my word."

"You're right it won't happen again! How did it happen this time? You know the rules!"

"Yes, sir."

There was a pause of silence, then a sigh. "Azrael, I realize that you are lonely and I also realize that this is your first mistake in the many years you have been doing this. I'll give you one chance to make this right or you will have to be sent to your original destination. Is that understood?"

"Yes, sir." The air suddenly went silent and the void felt empty; he was gone. How was I going to fix this? What was I supposed to do? Kill her? Wait for the opportunity to present itself again? Since her end was not met today, would fate come back soon to claim it's prize? The thought of her going away made me feel sick.

***

I arrived early at the little campus coffee shop. As I sat in a booth waiting for her, I thought about what I should say to her. More importantly, what I was going to have to do.

Kaylee walked in and spotted me right away. She crossed the room and sat down across from me. "Hey. Sorry I'm late," she said. Noticing the look on my face, she asked, "What's wrong? You look like someone just died."

I looked up at her and tried to smile. "It's okay. I haven't been waiting long. I just have a lot on my mind."

"Anything you want to talk about?" she asked, settling in.

"No, not really," I said, then decided to change the subject. "Instead, I'd like to know more about you. What are you going to school for? Are you from here? Do you have family close by?"

"Well, I'm going to school to be a counselor," she

replied. "It's something like a therapist, but without the license to administer medicine. I'd like helping people if I can. I grew up here. I was adopted, so it was only my adopted parents and me until about two years ago. My adopted father passed away and I started school shortly after. I wanted to go to college here so that I could stay close by, in case my mother needs me."

It was obvious it still hurt, but I knew that she was a strong girl. "I'm sorry for your loss," I said.

"Well, like the cliché says, at least he is in a better place," she answered with a shrug.

After an hour of sharing information about our lives—of course mine was mostly made up or half truths to hide my identity—we seem to hit it off. I made her laugh a few times, which was a good sign. Then, I remembered why I was supposed to be here, but I couldn't bring myself to do it.

"What's wrong?" Kaylee asked, noticing my sudden shift in mood.

I didn't answer at first, then shook my head and replied, "I'm sorry. I have to go." I stood up abruptly and started for the door.

"Wait! John!" I knew that she was coming after me. It was wrong to just leave that way, but it would hurt worse to just keep pretending. I kept walking, through the door and out to the sidewalk. "John! Please, wait!" she yelled after me again as I crossed the road, then there was a crashing sound followed by screams of passersby.

I turned in horror and saw that it was Kaylee who was struck by a car, just as she was meant to be. "No!" I yelled, running to her side. She was lying on the road, broken and in a pool of her own blood. Several onlookers had already started gathering around. I knelt down beside her and gently raised her head to rest it on my thigh. She coughed and weakly said my name again. "I'm here. I'm so sorry, Kaylee," I whispered, as tears coursed down my cheeks.

"You know … it's funny … I … had a dream … of this

happening ... didn't think ... it really ... would ..." she forced out with another cough.

"Shh ... just relax. Everything will be okay." I tried reassuring her as well as reassuring myself.

She took another jagged breath and then she was gone. Just like that. For the first time in my existence, I cradled her close to me and cried harder than I ever thought was possible. Once I was able to snap myself back to reality, I realized that I had to let her go. Not just emotionally, but physically. She would show up at any minute now, waiting to be crossed over. I gently laid her back down and stood, wiping my tears away.

I stepped out of the crowd that had gathered with a few eyes watching me, but I didn't care. I walked to the nearest tree and stepped behind it so that I could cloak myself and become invisible to everyone else. I had a job to do. Once I had stepped out from behind the tree and looked back at the scene in front of me, I saw her standing beside her body, looking down at herself with a mixture of emotions: horror, shock, confusion. The scenarios within which you don't see it coming is the most unsettling. They have to cross over with no answers as to why it happened. Instead of walking up to her, I just appeared next to her.

"Kaylee ..." When I said her name, she slowly turned to look at me with tears in her eyes.

"Wha ... how? Why? I ..." she said, shocked.

"I know this is going to be hard for you to understand, but this is really happening to you," I said, making no move to touch her. "I can see you because I am the one that is supposed to take you to where you need to go next."

"Like the reaper?"

"Not like, I *am* the Reaper."

"Oh," she answered with a nod, having trouble wrapping her mind around everything.

"Kaylee, on the night I met you and saved you from getting hit by the bus, I was supposed to let it happen because it was your time. I was there to take you then. The problem was that I couldn't bring myself to do it. I fell for you the first time I saw you." She just stared at me in disbelief. It was probably too much to understand at once, but I had to let her know and I wasn't sure of how much time we had left.

She closed her eyes, cleared her throat and said, "So, I was supposed to die last night when we met?"

"Yes."

"But you saved me because you fell in love with me?"

"Yes."

"I don't understand," Kaylee said, trying to put the pieces together. "How did you fall in love with me when that was the first time we met?"

Uh, oh. I guess I had to tell her the rest. "I came here early so that I could track down your whereabouts. When I found you, you were in your room talking on your cell phone to someone about a party and doing your homework. I know it sounds crazy, but I had never seen anyone so beautiful before. As I watched you sleep, you were dreaming, but I didn't know what you were dreaming about. I also watched you in class and I couldn't take my eyes off of you." At first, I thought she was going to start running away from me—anyone in their right mind probably would—but she looked at me for a minute, then looked away, thinking.

"You know, you're lucky that I am a hopeless romantic. Otherwise, I would have to kick your butt, you psycho stalker!" Kaylee said. She looked up at me and smiled. All I could do was smile back. Then, she reached up on her tip-toes and kissed me. As embarrassing as it is, I had never been kissed before. It was my turn to blush, and I never would have guessed that a girl could make the Grim Reaper blush. She put her hand in mine and asked, "So, where do we go now?"

"Well, the way this works is we teleport and we appear at the gate that you are destined to pass through," I said, already missing her.

"You mean like Heaven or Hell?"

"Yes."

"That's comforting. Well, lead the way, boogy man," she teased.

I laughed out loud at her joke, although I was far from the boogy man.

"By the way, I'm guessing that your real name isn't John, is it?" she asked. "I also thought that the Grim Reaper was supposed to look different …"

"I will explain on the way," I said as we teleported to the next plane.

***

I was expecting to show up at the gates of Heaven, but we appeared in the same hollow abyss that I showed up in before when I didn't carry out my job the way that I was supposed to.

Kaylee said, "Well, I knew I wasn't the greatest child in the world, but I didn't think I would be sent to Hell."

"The Gates of Hell look nothing like this," I explained. She was joking, but I was a bit confused myself.

"Kaylee Dillon, correct?" the same voice as before boomed.

"Yes?" she replied, looking at me unsure. I held her hand and waited to see what was going to be said.

"As you are aware, Azrael failed to carry out your sentence that first time around. The balance is slightly off, but not so disrupted that it can't be fixed. I can see the unusual bond that has formed between the two of you in this short amount of time. My question to you is: would you like to go on home where your soul will be forever at piece or would you like to have a job to work by Azraels' side for the rest of eternity? The choice is yours. This is a one time deal that no one else has ever been nor will ever be offered. You are the exception, my dear, so choose carefully." I couldn't believe what I was hearing! Kaylee turned and looked directly into my eyes, as if searching my soul.

"I think I have chosen my path, sir. I have never felt that I truly belonged, but something about Azrael made me feel more connected in the short time that I have known him. Maybe this is what I was meant to do. So, yes, I will stand by his side for eternity," she answered with a brave smile.

"So shall it be. Welcome, my dear. Azrael deserves your company."

"Thank you, sir," I said. When he was gone, we appeared on the plane where I belong, but it was not just my home anymore, it is now her home, too … our home together.

***

Since that day, we have completed a few assignments separate—once Kaylee got the hang of things—but we mainly work together. The more time we spent together, the closer we became.

Out current assignment is trapping a real bad soul. The best part about these kinds of assignments now is that she makes my job more fun. I hid in the shadows while she waited on a park bench in the dead of night where this maniac chose most of his victims. What the guy didn't know is that while he was on the hunt, the last deal he made went wrong and someone was now after him.

Kaylee made herself visible only to him. As he crept up with his eye on her, someone else came up behind him and shot him. She waited calmly until his soul rose from his body. Then, he looked down at himself then back at her, shocked. "What's going on here?" the creep demanded.

"Oh, nothing special …" she said as she rose from her seat and slowly walked toward him in her black cloak. "It's just your time, is all. I would like for you to meet my husband, the Grim Reaper." Then, she gestured behind him.

That was my que. I stepped out of the shadows and appeared right behind him in my skeletal form that everyone knows so well. The man slowly turned toward me and shrieked like a little girl once he got a full view of me.

I can honestly say that things will never be boring again with Kaylee by my side. What can I say? I love her to death.

Acknowledgements

A special thank you to the authors who are featured in this anthology! You are truly wonderful!

Elaine White

Kim Stevens

Theresa Oliver

Dana Piazzi

Stephanie Parke

Vanessa Hancock

Ashlea Burns

Susan Burdorf

Becca Boucher

Monica Blanton

Look for books from these authors!
Many have books with
Write More Publications!

www.ingramcontent.com/pod-product-compliance
Lightning Source LLC
Chambersburg PA
CBHW030112180626
46812CB00002B/380